King of the World

Winner of the
Editors' Book Award

KING OF THE WORLD

a novel by
Merrill Joan Gerber

Pushcart Press
Wainscott, New York

© 1989 Merrill Joan Gerber
ISBN 0-916366-60-X
LC:89–62667

Winner of the eighth annual Editors' Book Award

Sponsoring editors for the Editors' Book Award are Simon Michael Bessie, James Charlton, Peter Davison, Jonathan Galassi, David Godine, Daniel Halpern, James Laughlin, Seymour Lawrence, Starling Lawrence, Robie Macauley, Joyce Carol Oates, Nan A. Talese, Faith Sale, Ted Solotaroff, Pat Strachan, Thomas Wallace. Nominating editor for this novel: Cynthia Ozick.

While this book is based on actual
events, it is a work of fiction
and no reference is intended to
real persons, places or circumstances.

—*The Publisher*

King of the World

PART ONE

IN THE LIGHT OF COMING DARKNESS, on a beach just south of Ensenada, Michael commanded Ginny to bow her head while he crowned her with a broken starfish and christened her *Queen of the World*.

The starfish was flat and prickly and had only three rays. Ginny held it to her head, laughing. Michael extracted his pale feet with a sucking sound from the quicksand of the undertow and swooped his hands into the water. Stepping forward, he draped strands of seaweed over the bare bones of her shoulders, swirling the greenish-black threads in a spiral around each of her tightened nipples.

With the red sun sizzling into the sea behind him, Michael looked to Ginny like an electrified man, other-worldly and glowing, each red-gold hair on his legs alive with light, the fibres of his beard curling out beyond the edges of his face like a net enticing her toward him. She could hardly pull her eyes away from the pendulum of his long dark cock, which swung slightly, tugged by some heavy force toward the center of the earth. Whisper, her Doberman puppy, skidded from side to side in the sand, cutting the air with his powerful yips, shimmying the dome of his black rump in bursts of happiness.

Michael, I adore you!

Yesterday she had been working the graveyard shift at her new job as ward clerk in Mt. Olympus hospital in LA and today she was standing on a warm, wide beach in Mexico, naked in the sunset, nearly beside herself with a wild, scary joy. Michael had saved her again from her dullness, from her hopeless, small mind, from her frightened, useless way of thinking.

Michael, you always know what I need!

How unreal and hideous—that cold metal desk spread with *stat* blood test requisitions and glass slides thick with secretions. A near-fatal mistake she'd made, taking that job! What a monumen-

1

tal mistake—to have moved back home to live with her mother, who, since her father's death, had become a shrieking harpy.

Even her sister Paula had warned her, "Once Mom gets you in her clutches, you'll never get away. I'm not trying to be heartless, but I don't think you'll be able to stand living with her. No one in her right mind could, not now. And besides, be realistic, Ginny—what can you really do for her, anyway?" This was her legitimate way out: impeccable advice from Paula, her older, reliable sister, the one who had had the good sense to marry a psychologist, the model mother who was raising her two little girls to be amiable, well-adjusted kids—an accomplishment, in Ginny's view, on par with teaching them to fly.

But what about doing the "right thing"? Shouldn't she stay and help her mother, a grizzled widow at fifty-eight, left without much money and a garageful of old junk to get rid of? It wasn't easy to go through a dead man's personal effects: torn socks and out-of-style baggy pants and tie clips from her father's dresser drawers which would have to be packed up for the Salvation Army to take away. Surely she owed it, at least to her father, to stay and help out. This was what she had told Michael on the phone just after the funeral, when he called her from San Francisco, begging her to come back to him. She didn't tell him how bad it really was at home—how her mother kicked at furniture and screamed at her in the tone she had used when Ginny was a teenager and hadn't hung up her dresses or put her shoes in the shoe rack. Her mother cursed her for being a fool and moving to San Francisco to take useless art classes and for getting tied up with a bunch of spaced-out hippies. She was careful to keep from Michael her mother's monotone warning: "If you don't marry Jewish you'll be sorry all your life. I can't tell you a reason except that it's just not the same, you'll see. It's not the same and what else can I say?"

Jewish boys. They'd made her want to vomit in high school. *Big noses, little hoses,* Michael had said for a joke. But Michael was free of the worst flaws of Jewish boys—their bad skin, their eyeglasses, their fanatic interests in boring things, their scorn for hiking in the woods and climbing mountains. No Jewish boy would ever teach her the joys of fishing, as Michael promised to do for her. No Jewish boy, looking at her with his mother's mean, ticking

2

Jewish eyes, would ever gaze lovingly, as Michael did, on her deformed figure.

So there she'd been just last night, at her metal desk, on the very floor of the hospital where her father had died two weeks ago. She'd been sitting listlessly on a hard chair, wearing her new thick—soled white shoes and white nylon smock, listening to a "Code Blue" come over the loudspeaker in the blue hours just before dawn, when the elevator doors sprang back miraculously like a curtain parting on a stage, and Michael leaped forth, looking like the risen sun in yellow cotton pants and an embroidered red-flowered shirt.

At that very instant she had been holding in her mind the image of her father's dying eyes as they'd stared into her face the night she arrived in LA. With her mother close behind her, she had tiptoed fearfully into his hospital room. "Oh Daddy," she cried out, seeing his ravaged body. She felt he was sucking her into the hollow of his skull as he gave her one long hopeless look and then deliberately turned his back. Just like that. One scornful, baffled, giving-up look, and then he gave her his skeleton back, the ridges of his vertebrae, curving out of his fallen-open hospital gown, coming toward her like a deadly snake, his hip bones looking like ones on men in concentration camps. She had never been shown his back in all the years of her childhood; astonishing that she had never seen it. At once she saw that his spine, like hers, was crooked. So *he* had given her her bad gene! That was why he had hidden himself all those years and now was ashamed to speak a word to her, could offer her only his wasted haunches and hollow loins. Two days later he called for water and died.

The night the "Code Blue" rang down the empty hall, Michael was supposed to have been fast asleep in the headquarters of the Sexual Freedom League where they had lived together, four hundred miles to the north in San Francisco. Ginny shivered to imagine what he was doing there without her—in that house with so many pretty, perfectly formed girls who slept with anyone. She knew Michael's appetites—sex and drugs—the appetites of their generation. But he had made a great concession to her, she realized, leaving that easy cradle of satisfaction and speeding like a rocket to LA, to fetch her, to save her. He burst out of the elevator like a miracle and smothered her gasping mouth in the tangle of his beard and swept her off to Mexico in his pickup truck, with Whisper, her puppy, curled in a warm black swirl in her lap.

"I can't be doing this," she begged him as they were passing a cemetery on the outskirts of Tijuana. "I have to stay in LA and keep my new job and take care of my mother." Michael's inspired reply was to lean over and pull off one of Ginny's heavy white nurse's shoes and fling it out the window. She watched it arc like a flaring meteor before it came to rest among the crooked tombstones.

She wanted to worship him because look at her now—a girl who had never worn a bathing suit in public—here she was naked in the sun, her twisted back bare under the pink sky, and no whirlwind voice was swooping down to sweep her away, crying, *Ugly! Ugly! Out of sight with you!*

All that first afternoon on the empty beach she had lain on Michael's woven Indian rug, fully exposed in the sun's light, letting him drip crystals of sand down the length of her crooked spine, listening to him tell her that it sparkled like a winding mountain road at night while long lines of cars traversed it, their headlights gleaming like diamonds.

Michael—my poet angel!

She was dull as a gray puddle of water. He had in him all the imagination and bravery she wished she could find in herself. He chased her into the water, he splashed her, making her shriek and laugh. The seaweed tickled her back, releasing cold drops that ran into the crease between her buttocks. She had never lived a happier day than this one and could hardly believe her good fortune: that he wanted her this much.

That he had christened her *Queen of the World!*

Late the next morning, as they lay dozing on the inflated rubber mattress in the bed of his pickup, Michael said, "Be fair. I blew up the mattress—now it's your turn."

4

"What are you talking about, what do you want me to blow up?" Then she reddened because he was laughing, smiling with the knowing power he had over her, immense with the power he had. She had never known a man who could talk dirty and be wholesome at the same time. Even as he leered, then lunged his beard into the hollow of her neck while her vagina clutched in a spasm of involuntary desire, he laughed also. With obvious relish, he took in her shock and thrill, approving her response, applauding the sudden flaring excitement he had caused in her. It was impossible to feel shame in Michael's presence; he knew her human needs and encouraged them. There was no shame, no forgiveness involved. Michael believed that if something sexy and dirty and juicy-wild came to Ginny's mind, it belonged there and was right. Whatever was human was right. His mind was different from everyone else's—sometimes his wild blue eyes rolled in his head, vibrating with an intensity that alarmed her. But her vague tingle of doubt was nothing to the excitement she felt in his presence. He understood far more than she did. Men were supposed to know more—at least some women thought they did. But he really did. Michael was beyond her.

Far down the beach near a cluster of rental trailers, a skinny donkey, even bonier than Ginny, with a child on its back, dragged itself slowly over the sand, its head hanging. The donkey was led by a Mexican in a sombrero. "Rides for the gringos," Michael said. "Donkey shit on the sand, so be careful."

Lying beside her in the bed of the pickup truck, he kissed her quickly in the curve of both of her armpits and whispered "Thank you." His penis hung soft and sweetly satisfied by her attentions. He yawned, stretched his arms to the sky, pulled on his jeans and jumped down from the truck bed.

"Big doings today, I have big plans for us. But first let's eat—not the stuff I brought down in the truck, but *real stuff*." He pointed down the beach to a figure of a man with a basket on his arm, not far from the donkey. The night before they had bought their dinner from a vendor carrying burritos and hot chiles. "Let's see if we can find one with fresh shrimp and limes this morning," Michael said. He smacked his lips.

"We should be careful about dysentery," Ginny said. "In the hospital . . . "

"Hey," Michael warned her. "Don't rain on my parade," and he was right of course, so she shut up at once.

She knew her father had turned away from her in the hospital because she'd been living in sin with Michael up in San Francisco and her father was disappointed in her. She was ashamed of herself, seeing it her father's way, but seeing it her way she knew there was no other choice for her. A girl didn't talk to a father like hers about the secrets of sex; even if he were *not* dying she couldn't have laid it all out for him. The best defense she could have mustered was that she was lonely. But you don't tell a father about the empty sucking place in your body, the pulsing, throbbing, waiting place. Nor do you confess to him your fears about your ugliness, which he has always pretended not to notice.

Could a man, a father, understand the miracle? *This miracle?* That when she was twenty years old, after a lifetime of no luck at all with men, *none,* Michael appeared like a balm from heaven and filled her. Michael appeared to her in her art class at San Francisco State and hovered there beside her easel where she was painting a picture she'd titled "Sad Girl"—a portrait of a girl sitting on a bench at the end of a pier, staring out to sea. She had no talent in art. Michael had stood close behind her, where he could clearly see her crooked back, even hidden and layered over as it was with a turtleneck and a blouse and a sweater. He watched her paint for fifteen solid minutes and then he leaned over and kissed her. He kissed her on the curve of her jawbone, just under her ear, and she knew right then that the longing was over, it was over for good, and that to have even a taste of the sensations he would offer her would be worth all that it would cost her.

They ate breakfast sitting crosslegged on the beach in the shade of someone's old Airstream trailer, rolling their warm tortillas into tight cylinders, dripping butter in little yellow tears on the sand. A group of kids—all American—were beginning to line up for the donkey ride; a few surfers were carrying their boards down to the water's edge. Ginny looked up at the sound of a loud explosion to see a circle of men lighting firecrackers and tossing them forward toward the sea. One of them turned his head and caught her eye. Weighing at least two hundred pounds, looking like a shaggy black bear, he suddenly swiveled around on his thick legs and came lumbering toward them over the sand. Ginny touched Michael's knee, where the blue denim was worn smooth as baby flannel, and Michael raised his eyes into the glare of the sun coming off the man's white undershirt.

"Good looking girl you have here," the man said, coming right up to them, touching Ginny's bare toes with the tip of his heavy sandal. She was wearing a T-shirt of Michael's; she realized the man couldn't see her back. She withdrew her foot. The man was dark-skinned, black bearded. Black wiry hairs curled from his wrestler's chest along the edges of his undershirt.

"Thank you," Michael said after a second's silence. He bent over his tortilla, opening his legs further so the grease would have a clear fall to the sand.

"Your wife?"

"To be," Michael answered. Ginny glanced at Michael, recognizing that this was a marriage proposal. Her heart began to pound.

"I'd like to fuck her," the man said. He motioned to a pickup with a camper shell about twenty feet up the beach. "We can do it there. I would say no more than a half hour. I could give you thirty bucks."

"Thirty bucks," Michael repeated.

"I'm a sailor," the man said. "From Barbados. I have a nice house there; if you and your wife ever come over, I would put you up free, as long as you want."

"Barbados," Michael said. "Nice weather there."

"A free vacation, anytime," the man said.

He waited. Ginny stared at his huge feet.

Michael nudged her with his shoulder. "Well?"

"Well what?"

"Do you want to?"

She flung her head toward him so fast that her hair whipped her face.

"I'll give you a few minutes to talk it over," the sailor said, backing off. He walked toward the surf, stopping to shake his foot and curse because he had stepped in donkey shit.

Ginny stared at Michael's eyes, which were cold, alien, frozen blue.

"We might get to Barbados some day," he reminded her.

"What?"

"Fifteen, twenty minutes," Michael said. "At the most."

"Are you serious?"

"It's up to you," Michael said. "It's no big deal one way or the other."

"I thought you want to marry me."

"I do. But I don't own you, you know. We live in a fucking new world—men don't own women anymore."

"Thanks, Michael." She stood up and threw the rest of her breakfast, paper plate and all, down at his feet. The sailor had turned around and was watching them. She felt her lower lip drop in disgust. Then she began to run toward Michael's pickup truck, a long red box far down the beach. She glanced over her shoulder to see if Michael was following her; she saw him talking to the sailor, the two of them blurred together, heads almost touching.

She wasn't going to make a thing of it—she had to forget it as fast as possible or it would ruin everything. It was probably something she didn't understand, wasn't used to, something between men, something ordinary, unmomentous. Maybe it had to do with Michael's theory about sex being as natural as eating and drinking. Besides, Michael had given her a choice, had respected her feelings, had let her be the final judge in the matter. This was probably nothing to get excited about, nothing to ruin their vacation for. So why was she crying?

These were new times for women, better than the old. She had to grow up and not expect men to be gallant princes on white horses. For her own good she had to wipe out those outdated rules her mother had planted in her. Michael was going to be her husband soon. In her mother's book, husband-material was a man who didn't screw around, who was stable, who made a good living, who was kind and caring. Michael didn't even show up on a list like that. Sometimes he had a job, but mostly he free-loaded. Often he was kind and caring, but sometimes he was mean as a monkey. Maybe if she went back north with him, she could convince him to get some job-training, think about getting a real job. They could look for a place of their own far from San Francisco. She was ready to get out of there, move out of that scummy house. Michael was ready, too. They had to move on sometime.

The important thing to remember was that he had told the sailor she was going to be his wife, the very offer she wanted most in her life—the offer that settled everything for her and cleared up where she was going tomorrow, next year, forever. Why shouldn't she choose to be part of Michael, his excitement, his energy, his imagination? To have Michael was to be able to leave behind her hysterical mother, her dead father, her ravaged back, her lost opportunities. To have him was to take on his brilliant colors and lose her invisibility. This might be her only opportunity to lead a life different from the one laid out for her.

She leaped into the cab of the pickup truck, where Whisper lay asleep on the seat, and sat herself behind the wheel, holding onto it while the earth spun and the horizon tilted. After a long wait she saw Michael ambling along the sand, bending now and then to pick up a shell and toss it, with a violent jerk of his arm, into the sea.

"This is fun," Ginny said cautiously.

"I told you it would be fun," Michael agreed. "Fun is being with me." He pulled on the starter cord of the outboard motor a third time, but it didn't catch. Whisper's paws pattered nervously for balance on the curved wooden bottom of the rowboat. His toenails made a clattery sound and Michael said, "Keep him still, will you!" Sweat was running down Michael's face and a clear drop quivered on the tip of his straight, handsome nose.

"I guess we can't expect a perfect outboard if we only paid that old guy five dollars for the afternoon," Ginny said.

"Yes, we *can* expect a perfect outboard!" Michael said. "I told you this will be a perfect vacation, and it better goddamn well be!"

"Well, yes," Ginny said. She knew he was upset about something else—the mushrooms. It hadn't rained, so the magic mushrooms hadn't come up in Huatla, where he wanted to take her. He was angry, he had told her, that the Rain Gods were against him.

She was quiet till he finally started the motor and the rowboat was chugging bumpily out of the shallow water and into the waves. Ginny hoped he would cheer up. After the offer from the sailor, Michael had spent a long time smoking a joint and rattling things around in his tackle box. They hadn't spoken to one another. For a while, even though the sun was hot, Ginny slept on the air mattress in the back of the pickup.

Now she hoped they could clear the air between them, make this the perfect vacation again. If anything was perfect here, it was definitely the air. Ginny breathed deeply, closing her eyes. She sat on the middle seat, with Michael behind her, and Whisper jiggling tensely at her feet. Far away on the horizon she saw a steamship with two smokestacks gliding peacefully out to sea. If she kept her balance, didn't react the wrong way, everything would continue to open up before her. She had to remember that two weeks ago she had been choking on grief and loneliness, that just two days ago she had still been shrinking to nothing, all avenues of escape cut off.

She counted how far she had come from that day in the hospital room when her father had shown her the snake of his spine and her mother had whispered to her that he turned his back only because he was dying and that he didn't look good and wanted to hide from them the open sores on his lip and eyelid. Her mother actually believed her father was ashamed of looking bad. It was her pride in life that she had married a very hand-some man. The man was dying and the woman didn't understand a thing. Her mother only thought about how people looked and never about how they felt.

God—how Ginny had wanted to fly out of that room with the leaking bent straws on the table, and the kidney-shaped tray her father vomited into from the nitrogen mustard they had tried on him as a last resort.

Why was it that, where her mother was concerned, every-thing came down to looks? Ginny knew she had always been worthless in her mother's view. At fourteen, she'd had bronchitis, a cough that hung on forever, and finally her mother had taken her to the doctor, followed her right into the examining room and waited till Ginny was forced to show herself naked. The doctor had lifted up her shirt to listen to her breathing, and he had called out to her mother, "My God! Look at this! Your daughter is a cripple! Don't you people know?" Then he had apologized for calling her a cripple, but the astonishment of his discovery was still in his eyes.

Ginny had known for years her backbone was not growing straight, but she didn't think there was anything anyone could do about it. The last thing she wanted was to confide this fact to her mother and then have her mother start peering at her naked body and making comments about it. Even when Ginny was fully dressed, her mother did plenty of that, her little Jewish eyes tak-ing in every last thing—hair, makeup, breasts, legs, and she had plenty to say about them: too long, too little, too flat, too mosquito-bitten.

Once the secret was out, about her backbone going crazily to the side, she was in for it. Every three months they had to appear at the hospital where four young doctors would make her strip to the waist and then stand around drawing red dots on her spine. They'd circle around her as if she were some kind of freak, star-ing at her nipples which were shriveled with cold, making nota-tions on their charts. Ginny's mother would have a long free look, too, and then would do all that stuff in her mind that Ginny hated, making judgements, comparing her to other girls, to cous-ins or neighbors' daughters who were prettier, or luckier, or had bigger bosoms or rounder hips. It was nightmare time, all right.

11

She had to have thirty x-rays at each session, from every angle, turn this way, turn that way, on a hard cold black table, with the men touching her naked back and chest, putting tape all over her, and saying *Hold your breath, now breathe, Hold your breath, now breathe* till she wished she could just stop breathing and have it all over with forever.

The threat hung over her: if her spine grew in one certain direction too far she'd have to have an operation and stay in a hospital in a cast for a year; if that didn't work, there would be another operation and a second year in the hospital. She might as well kill herself.

She remembered the day they were to find out if the bone had stopped growing in time. Her mother was white as a sheet. Ginny half hoped her spine had sprouted barbed-wire spikes in every direction and would break through her skin and stab all of them. Finally her mother would realize she was ruined for life and there was no need to scrutinize her any longer. She'd be imprisoned in a thick white plaster cast up to her chin. Then it couldn't possibly matter in the slightest to her mother or to her or to Holy Jesus Himself what her body or her hair or her face or her legs looked like. She'd have a right to feel as sorry for herself as she often felt when she was walking around like a regular human being on two legs.

But luck was with her, if you could call it luck. The doctors announced that the bone stopped growing the wrong way just one zillionth of an inch in time, and she wasn't going to be a total cripple, just a minor cripple, and she could live with that, they said.

Her sentence was clear to her: for all the rest of her life she would never be able to wear any piece of clothing that was sheer or revealing, since she looked, up close, like the hunchback of Notre Dame. She could never put on the simplest of outfits—a T-shirt and shorts, for example, or a bathing suit. She would forever have to wear thick piles of layers, anything that would disguise the hump.

She was determined nobody would ever know. She would fool them all as long as she could keep her clothes on. And with her clothes always on she'd never run into that other problem, the one of having children, which the doctors warned her against.

12

She should probably never have them, they told her, because all those x-rays might have ruined her ovaries and she could possibly give birth to a mutation like the children who were born after Hiroshima, or she might have a child who could die of leukemia at age two. That didn't scare her as much as what she really believed: that if she had anything, she might have two-headed scaly lizards instead of kids.

Michael killed the motor. Then he leaned forward from the back of the rowboat and with one jerk of his powerful arms pulled Ginny's shirt over her head. She gasped, and covered her breasts with her hands.

"Give me back my shirt, Michael," she said.

"Later, if you're good."

"What do I have to do to be good?"

"Just listen to me and do what I say." He stuffed the T-shirt under his seat and said, "Put your head back in my lap."

She laughed.

"Laugh again. I love your laugh, it gives me hope," he said.

"Okay," she said. It was hard not to laugh when he played with her this way, gave her such complete and violent attention. She leaned back awkwardly till she felt the depression between his thighs under her head. "Why do you want me to do this?"

"So I can watch your tits get warm," he said. "I like to see them loosen up and get soft and big."

"They'll never be big, Michael." She knew he regarded her small breasts as a flaw in her. She found it odd that her back, with its hump and its curve, didn't bother him at all. Big breasts were what he missed in her.

Cushioned by his thighs, she closed her eyes and let the sea air wash over her face. They had come a long way out from shore. Now there was only the sound of an occasional gull flapping overhead and the lapping of the waves against the side of the boat. Far away, where the waves broke and flattened on the sand, a small plane carrying a banner droned along with a dull buzz.

Whisper scraped and rattled his claws on the floor of the boat. He was busy licking a piece of dried bait stuck to the floorboards. It was probably bad for him—she nudged him gently with her foot, unable to see him. She heard him scramble about and suddenly Ginny felt him lay his long snout in the V of her crotch.

"Hey," she said. She pushed him away, but his nose bounded into her again.

"Smart boy," Michael said. "Knows right where to go."

Ginny held her palm out, feeling her dog's wet nose soft and rubbery against it. Whisper pushed past her hand, pressing his nose hard into the crossseam of her bluejeans.

"Quit it, dumb dog," she said.

"Listen, Ginny, . . . why not let him?" Michael whispered.

"*No* Michael."

"Why not? It could be a trip."

"Let him find a girlfriend," she said. But her breathing was changing as Whisper kept butting his nose between her legs and Michael began tracing his fingertips in circles around her nipples. She gasped, not so much at the physical sensations she felt, but at the *idea! At the wildness of the idea! At the places Michael could lead her!* She never dreamed these places existed till she was right there with him, in them, at the very moment. That was when her mind finally opened, like the sea parting, and took it in, in astonishment.

Michael unbuttoned the fly of her jeans. "Lift up," he said into her ear, and then leaned forward as she raised her buttocks and he pushed the jeans down her hips. He kissed her on the forehead as he did so.

She kept her eyes closed, the sun burning black spots against her lids. She could sense him behind her, stepping out of his jeans. No one could see them. She was far from home. This was her chance to let it happen, to feel what she had never experienced.

"Slide off your pants the rest of the way," Michael instructed from behind her.

She raised her knees, one at a time, and slid off her jeans and panties. Whisper began at once to lick between her legs, his rough tongue not quite in the right place, but close enough.

"This is blowing my mind," Michael said. "I love it."

Ginny was concentrating, trying to give him what he wanted, what he needed. She surrendered to his instructions, she let the sun burn her face, let the seagulls watch her thrilling shame. She had never known two people could act this way together, could go so far. Michael helped the dog, she helped Michael, they went the distance again, together, in the salty hot wet heat, then fell on each other in collusion and exhaustion.

"Now I'm going to catch us a fish for dinner," Michael announced.

Ginny, her head still in Michael's lap, was staring, trance-like, into the blank blue sky, when he roused her by shaking his tackle box at her ear. They had already eaten some cheese and bread, which Michael had brought down along with some clothes for her in the truck from San Francisco. They'd drunk warm root beers. Ginny felt herself to be floating in a great, peaceful lethargy. She didn't want to move, to think. She was getting sunburned; she could feel her skin tightening around her like a cocoon. Her bare feet brushed Whisper's back; his black fur was as hot as a sheet of glowing coals. She sat up, dizzy.

"Pray for a big fish," Michael said. He placed the gray metal tackle box on his bare knees, its lid up, its edges battered and rusty. She could see the shadow of his penis hanging beneath it. "If only I can get this fucking stuff untangled . . . " He lifted a clot of wires and hooks and sinkers and flies into the air and let them fall with a clunk back into the box. Whisper leaped upright at the sound and began to bark.

"Shit," Michael growled. Ginny decided to put on her clothes, not easy in the confines of the boat. Michael was getting into a state she recognized; when he cursed and made angry noises she had to be very careful about what she said. Anything could set him off, especially if he was coming down off a high.

"Maybe we can catch a tuna," she said agreeably.

"Stupid bitch," he said. "There's no such fish as a tuna."

"Don't, Michael—" she cautioned him. "I didn't mean to annoy you. I was just talking."

"Then don't talk!" he said. "I need absolute quiet right now."

She turned away from the tangle of junk in his lap. The contents of the box was disgusting to her—the flies, whose colored, matted feathers were supposed to resemble tiny fish (they had mean sharp hooks hidden in them); the dull silvery leaded balls with rough seams on them (used to sink the flies beneath the glittering water into the dark silent places where the fish swam and swirled); red and white corks designed to float on the surface, and bob a signal when the fish was impaled upon the hook. She'd just as soon eat burritos for dinner, and pass up the ritual of Michael's catching their meal. She'd seen Michael fish before, fly-casting from the beach near Half Moon Bay, wearing rubber waders. She knew how angry he got if he didn't catch a fish, or if one of them got away from him.

Whisper began to bark at the waves. His jack-hammer yelp was piercing.

"He's getting restless, Michael," she said. "He wants to get out of here. He's hot. Maybe we should start back."

"Just shut him up. Just keep him the hell quiet. We'll go back when we're ready and not any sooner."

Ginny tried to soothe the dog. He pulled back from her hands, his ears flickering, his stumpy tail jerking in muscular contractions, his rump shaking. He barked in an increasing crescendo of panic, at the sky, at Michael, at nothing.

"Hey, holy *shit!*" Michael shouted. Ginny turned to see Michael hopping up, dropping the tackle box onto the seat, standing suddenly in the curved bottom of the boat, nearly toppling them over with the wild rocking vibration of his hopping. She grabbed the sides of the boat. Whisper fell on his back; his legs flailed the air.

"Holy fuck!" Michael screamed.

"What is it?"

He thrust his hand at her; she saw the hook stuck in the soft hill of his palm just under his thumb.

"Let me try to get it out," she said.

"You can't! No one can! They don't *come* out!"

She thought he might be beginning to cry. She felt his panic and fear; she wanted to bear it for him. She swung her legs across the seat to face him but he couldn't wait for her. Even as she reached her hands out to him he tore the hook from his palm and screamed. Blood flowed across his wrist and down his arm. She looked for something to wrap his hand in—her shirt was the only clean cloth. She lifted it over her head. As she reached for Michael's hand, he pulled away from her, bent down and lifted the tackle box into the air. With blood striping his arm to the elbow, he half-grunted, half-moaned, and heaved the box into the ocean.

"Don't!" she cried, but the box was already sinking into the sea, the red and white floaters bobbing out and flashing on the surface till the tangle of gear pulled them under.

Michael sank down on the wooden board and let his bleeding hand fall into his lap. He was still naked; blood flowed along his thigh and spotted his penis. She wished she could dress him, cover him, so that she could believe he wasn't made of such tender ominous flesh, so tearable, so weak, so clearly destructible.

Ginny began to wrap his hand, pressing hard against the laceration, and suddenly Whisper slithered under the seat and brought his head up between Michael's legs. He was still excited, shimmering, shaking, butting his head against Michael's exposed genitals.

"Fucking crazy dog!" Michael cried, trying to kick him away. Whisper began to bark hysterically, again, his eyes glittering, as he did when he thought someone was about to play with him. "You fucker!" Michael screamed, and wrenched his hand with the shirt hanging from it from Ginny's hold and lifted Whisper in one convulsive movement and threw him overboard.

Ginny screamed. Whisper sank and re-emerged, seeking her, turning upon her the most baffled, terrified expression she'd ever seen. His little black face went under again and came up, his eyes, streaming water, black holes of fear.

"Swim to me!" she begged him. "Please, baby, dog-paddle!" She leaned over and reached her arms out but he was too far away for her to grasp.

"My God, Michael! What should I do?"

Michael had sat down. His eyes were closed.

"God! Would you go after him? Please, Michael! You know I can't do it! I'd drown."

17

Whisper was paddling quite strongly now, but away from the boat, directly out to sea. At a certain instant he paused and turned slowly in a circle. Though he seemed to be trying to twist his head to locate Ginny's voice, he set out again, continuing to paddle away from her.

"This way! Come this way, come back to me," she pleaded. The sun was directly in front of them; a red vacuum sucking Whisper in.

"Start the motor, Michael," Ginny said, turning to him.

"I'm still bleeding," Michael whimpered. "I'm weak."

"But he's dying," Ginny answered. "Please."

"I'm dying," Michael said, staring at her face. Then he stood up very slowly, and, with his uninjured hand, he began to pull on the cord of the outboard. "I'm probably done for. Tetanus. Lockjaw."

"Pull the cord!"

He tugged listlessly. The string snapped back; the motor remained silent.

"Try again!"

Whisper was still paddling away, toward the open sea. He was very far away now, where the water turned from green to black. Michael had tears on his cheeks. Ginny moved him aside and sat him down, and then she pulled, with all her strength. There was a grating jerk, the snap, the silence. She pulled the starter over and over till her shoulder was wrenched and burning. The sun was going down quickly. She saw her dog go under and bob up. Then Whisper went under and the sea became blank.

"Oh please, oh please, oh no," she sobbed. "Come up again. Don't die. Don't die."

"Don't cry," Michael said, crying. He butted his head against her thighs, shaking with sobs, wiping his eyes on the wrapped bandage of the shirt.

"I don't believe this, do you?" Ginny asked him. Michael was crying like a child, his entire back shaking. His bare spine curved toward her like an offering.

She sank beside him on the splintery wooden seat and rubbed her fingers along the ridges of his vertebrae. "I didn't mean it," he sobbed, pressing his face into her lap. "Please, you have to believe me, I didn't mean it."

18

"I know," she said, staring out at the quiet, blackening water. She stroked his golden-red hair.

"Don't go away, don't leave me, Ginny," he begged. "Don't be mad, I didn't mean it, I need you so much. I can't live without you."

"I need you, too, Michael," she said quietly.

"We'll be happy together, the rest our lives," he said. "I promise you."

"I know we will," she told him. "I know it."

PART TWO

GINNY WAS WALKING ON WEST RICHMOND, past the old Granada Theater, when a man—huddled on the ground against the locked doors of the movie-house—called out to her. He said, "I have no—." She didn't catch the last word; was it *hope, home, hate?* He said something again. *Horny? Money?* She hurried on.

"Hey!" he called. "Come back, please. Listen to my concert, it's free. I have no harmonica so I pretend I have one, I make one up. But, believe me, I can hum like a harmonica. Exactly like one."

She glanced over her shoulder at him. He couldn't have been more than thirty-five, her age, but his eyes were those of an old man. "That's nice," she said, and she hesitated just a moment too long because there he was getting up from the pile of blankets and garbage he carried around with him; he was coming toward her.

She hurried into the bank next door, her face blazing. Once she was on the line moving up to the teller's window she glanced toward the street and saw him there with his face pressed against the glass, scanning the customers, trying to find her. She turned away. She thought, *That's Michael, that's Michael without me, that's Michael in a few years if I ever left him.*

She withdrew thirty dollars, cash, and put it in her purse. Then she pretended to be reading some brochure about a high interest account with a $10,000 deposit, which of course she would never have. "Double your money in ten years," it promised. She had been married to Michael for fifteen years, and they didn't have a dime. They couldn't double their money if they had none.

Eventually, when she had the courage to turn around, the man was no longer at the window, but she could still see in her mind those lost-dog eyes, and the kind of sweet-Jesus beard that made her heart melt.

When she came out of the bank, she saw the bearded-man standing at the street corner. A big van was rolling down the street—a giant moving van with a lion painted on its side. As it slowed down, the red light changed to green and it picked up speed and the bearded man ran out into the street after it, yelling and waving his arms, but the truck just kept traveling and roared away and disappeared.

The man looked over at Ginny and he nodded at her as if to say, *See? That's how it always is,* and he went back to sit in the corner by the theater-doors, huddled there as if it were winter, and snowing, and not southern California in the fall.

Jesus. What was she supposed to do? Now the owner or manager pushed open the doors and came out of the dark lobby. He was a creepy guy wearing a suit and a tie, and he said something curt to the man. The man said, "Yeah, I know all about it," and then he slowly picked up his junk: some kind of case with a strap, which he hooked over his shoulder, and an old sleeping bag with a torn blanket tied around it with rope. He came up right beside Ginny as he walked along the street and she heard herself say, almost as if someone else were talking, "Where are you going to go?"

"Nowhere," he said. "That's where I live—nowhere." He walked past her, straight down the street, his head bowed, and then he was gone.

What was she crying about? He was nothing to her. He was just another mess that life dished up, just a guy who got a raw deal like everyone else.

She probably should have let Michael go for good when the sailor from Barbados wanted to fuck her. But it was insane to be thinking this way. She hadn't left him years ago and she wasn't leaving him now. She had hung on while he tried a hundred jobs in a hundred places. She had clung to Michael while the world outside killed off thousands of healthy young men in Viet Nam, while assassins had opened the arteries of Bobby Kennedy and Martin Luther King, while Nixon cheated every trusting American. With Michael at her side, she had watched history tick by: Ford and Carter and now Reagan and still their luck hadn't changed; Michael was still trying to get it together. Since they'd met, children had grown up and gone to high school, and college, and law school, and still Michael was trying. God, how Michael tried.

But maybe, just maybe, things were looking up now. She was determined to be hopeful. She might be a mother soon, and a baby needed both a mother and a father. Michael couldn't understand why things never worked out, but maybe they were working out now. Michael always said the lucky break was coming. He knew it like he knew every spot on her body.

She wondered if the lucky break was destined for her, and she had missed it. If she had stayed in school she might have been the one to get the lucky break. She was the one who could keep a job, but she always had to let it go when Michael wanted to leave, try some other place, some other city. All those cities since San Francisco. Now she wanted to stay put, in this place where they had been for three years. Michael promised he wouldn't pull her up again, even with the shock of Irving's kicking him out; he promised he would settle down in case the baby came through. A baby needed a stable environment, they both knew that. And a baby would make them happy again. The joy of a baby. She dreamed about the day it would happen, imagined holding a baby's soft precious body against hers.

A baby was her last great hope.

BANG! WITH A SINGLE STROKE, Michael blew up the world. His head, thrust into the dark hooded recesses of the video game, trembled with ecstasy. This was as it should be. The cataclysm was destined, he was only expediting it, giving it his approval, his energy, his blessing. It had to be. The world was not working, any fool could see that. It was beyond help out there—the oceans full of shit and poison, the sky gray with smoke and soot farting out of motors and machines. Ginny's ovaries, shriveled by the violence of x-ray beams, could not spit out one single perfect egg to meet his heroic, soldierly sperms—there could be no future replicas of himself to set the world right, and he—with his unique adjustment to human existence—could never live long enough to do the job the way it had to be done.

It was something he had known since he was a small boy, that nothing could keep him long enough to do the task which needed to be done. Not food, not sex, not the goddamn flash of the sun on the sea, only Ginny, maybe, with her chugging laugh that blacked out his hammering worries and gave him occasional moments of light and relief—but he doubted even she could hold him. The void was just beyond her skinny shoulders and her vampire black hair, it always summoned him, kissing right at him like a dare, two fat sausages sizzling with juice like the juices in his cock which pumped it up like a hot air balloon and made him follow strange women in shopping malls.

The world deserved it. Look what it had done to him. He could have been an Eagle Scout. He could have been the boy in the picture in the newspaper, with his hair neatly parted and his Boy Scout tie knotted just right. He could have had the badge to pass on to his sons—the badge with its red, white and blue ribbon, and the little silver eagle dangling down—but he would have no sons because of Ginny's zapped ovaries. His mother had said it was because of pull. Eric's mother must have had some pull with the Boy Scouts. Eric Feldmutter's name lived like an after-image on the screen of Michael's brain. Pow! Pow! Blam! You are *incinerated* Eric Feldmutter, wearing my Eagle Scout badge, because your mother gave head to the head of the Boy Scouts.

Michael's mother had told him that's the way the world was—it screwed you. You deserved something and someone else got it. It had always worked for her that way. "Look at me," Agnes said on the phone last week, "at my age living in a trailer when I should be dancing the nights away! It's just lucky I have the insurance money put away for bad times. If only your father hadn't died young on me. If only your sister had listened to me and had got those silicone implants she would be a Hollywood star by now."

It would all have been different if they'd picked him to be the Eagle Scout. It would have been all easy after that. Success breeds success. The rich get rich and the good get screwed.

On the screen the mushroom rose, capped, expanded its red fog till it covered every living thing. Blammo! Kaboom! The lights at the end of the long black tunnel were flashing good news to him: YOU HAVE DESTROYED THE WORLD! Michael laughed. He needed some more tokens but he was out of money. He had spent the five dollars Ginny had given him with instructions to bring home milk and yogurt.

Fuck it. His wife shouldn't have to dole out money to him. He should be a millionaire, a *multi*-millionaire! Men far stupider and uglier and less deserving were millionaires. Men with weak little legs and flabby arm muscles were millionaires; men with hanging bellies and thin little useless cocks were millionaires. Men who didn't care if the sewer of the world drowned or choked or radiated everyone to death as long as they had their speed-boats and their sports cars and their tight-titted little lays, all of them assholes who didn't care if he, Michael, ever had a son, or if Ginny ever grew a better-made version of him in her womb, or if her breasts, her anemic shriveled witches' dugs finally glowed and bloomed and pressed into Michael's mouth like a volcano spurting nourishment and wildness into him. He could squeeze those tits and watch the drops fall on his body, on his magnificent strong chest and his straight-as-an-arrow, tall-as-a-redwood cock.

His cock was pumping now, twanging against the wooden box of Galactic Destruction. He could feel it begging to burst into phosphorescent stars; his come would wiggle and fade away like firework-fish on the black night of the screen.

He would go and see those girls now. He'd been saving them and now he would go and see them. One of them had even smiled at him one day. He had seen himself reflected in a car window crossing the street just after that, with his handsome red beard, and his sun glasses, and his beautiful beautiful body, and his feet like a God's feet in leather sandals. He couldn't see his feet, but he sensed them, moving like live white animals that could see without eyes. Those girls really wanted him, he knew. It was lucky that they did because he was a good person and he didn't want to have to hurt them.

THE GOLD ELEPHANTS CLICKED IN MICHAEL'S pocket. He imagined that they mated there, their needle-like tusks dueling in the dark place where his money should be. At night when he couldn't sleep they loomed twelve feet tall and locked together in mortal combat. They threatened him from the foot of the waterbed he and Ginny slept in, their footfalls on the wooden floor shuddering through him like the deepest crackles of the organ in his mother's church. King Of The Jungle. The elephant was king, not the sly, wily lion. You didn't accept who they *told* you was king, you made the *rightful* one king. Everything they told you was wrong, how to live, how to work, how to think. Well, fuck them all.

He had made the elephants when he couldn't look at one more bicuspid mold, when his back ached and the light coming from the crook-necked lamp was bad and the high green metal stool made his coccyx bone burn as if acid were eating away at it.

"Too slow," Irving Fuckface said. "You don't produce. You grind your teeth and you make me nervous. I've got two sets of bridges waiting to be made and you spin on your stool like some kind of whirling dervish and you do push-ups in the can and you make me nervous, Michael."

Jesus. He made those crowns like they were for God Himself. He was an artist, with his scrapers and drills and his sharp little silver probes. He was better than the dentists, those fat cats in white coats, those creeps who were on the phone to their brokers every minute, who worked with flesh, with blood, with all that doomed human matter, while he, Michael, worked with the purest of gold, the most brilliant, longest lasting mineral on earth.

"Are you stealing my gold?" Fuckface accused him. "What's going on here?"

"I'm making my wife a piece of jewelry."

"On *my* time? With *my* gold? Like hell you are!"

"I'm taking a late lunch today, I'm doing it on my own time. And it's not with your gold either."

"Then whose gold? Where would you get gold?"

"My mother's wedding ring."

He was pretty sure Fuckface had believed it, but then at the end of the day he got fired, without notice, no reason. After three years of breaking his ass for the bastard. Just that some changes had to be made. That's all.

That was the reason Michael had been driving lately to Irving's house at night and parking down the street in direct line of view of the front door. He liked to squint as if he were sighting down the barrel of a rifle. He had visions of taking a dental drill and drilling through Fuckface's eardrums, eyeballs, into his spine, and through the eye of his cock. Such an ugly little guy! So ugly he didn't deserve to walk in the same streets where trees grew and wind blew.

Michael had promised Ginny he'd go to a job interview tomorrow morning. In order for them to adopt the baby he had to be employed. She wanted the baby and he didn't much care one way or another. It was some kid's baby, some teenage kid who made a baby, made it with another teenage kid, both of them just screwing for fun, and out came a baby, while he, *he*, with all his beauty and poetry couldn't make beans. Ginny couldn't fool him with her speeches, it would never be *his* son, it would be a kid, and it would live with them, but it wouldn't do the two big things he needed: it wouldn't make Ginny's breasts big and dripping with juices, and it wouldn't carry on his special qualities which were given to him as a test. His mother said that Jesus gave you the burdens you could bear, and, if you were strong, He gave you the most. The more you suffered the more like Him you were. Suffering was a way of turning into God.

He didn't want to get started hearing his mother's voice. His mind wanted to go back to what it was caught on—breasts. It happened to him all the time; he'd think and think about a million things and then one idea would hit a snag and he'd come back to it, for hours and hours. It was like having a jagged edge on a tooth; you kept digging your tongue into it and around it. It hurt, or maybe it was just interesting, or maybe it felt mysterious and private, as if you were rubbing your cock through your pocket. That kind of secret body-thing. He could count on secret body-things to distract him. Hunger—he was always hungry, always imagining *chile rellenos* or *enchiladas*, something hot that would burn his tongue and make him writhe. And fucking—it came to his mind like a balm, soothing part of it and heating up part of it so that he became restless but also directed; he knew he had to come before he could get on with anything else. Sometimes he just went home and jacked off, and sometimes he went to a porno movie, and sometimes he just sat in his car and watched women in the street, big overweight women with shopping bags and huge thighs that he imagined slapped together with a wet sound as they walked, or little scarecrow women with bony shoulders and no tits.

If Ginny had had tits she would have been perfect, but if she had been perfect she wouldn't have taken him, he knew that. She had a bone problem and had had all those x-rays that ruined her. He had to be grateful she wasn't perfect and forgive her for it because he wasn't perfect either. His mother had said that it wasn't true that opposites attract, but more like similars attract. Ginny didn't agree that they were similar; she gave him long lists every night about what was wrong with the two of them being together, but he ignored the lists, what could he do about them?

All Ginny could think of now, anyway, was this baby, this teenager's baby, who was going to be born soon, and he had to be employed or they couldn't get him. He should have had a job, he *would* have had a job if Irving hadn't screwed him and now it was going to wreck his home life, too. Actually, the job from the newspaper ad didn't sound as bad as the job at Irving's—(his mother used to say that God worked in strange ways)—but if he got it he would be driving a catering truck, he would be his own boss, and he could eat all the leftover *burritos* he wanted. He had told Ginny there was one trouble: he would have to sit in this catering truck all day and it would be absolutely essential for him to have an operation to have his bladder stretched first, otherwise he could never hold his pee that long. Ginny had looked at him with her "You're crazy" look, and said, "Michael, all you have to do is stop at a gas station and use a rest room." She always had simple solutions. His were original and brilliant.

31

But the big wheeler-dealer guys always looked at him squint-eyed in those job interviews, like they were daring him to give the right answers. He always had advice for them, right off the bat, about how they could make their business better, do a quality job, be more efficient, give their workers better conditions, a nicer atmosphere. If there were two men talking to him they gave each other the "look"—and then he just knew, he shouldn't have wasted the gas.

Breasts. Tits. He knew there was one sweet idea in his brain there somewhere that didn't make him grind his teeth; he had to get back to that right away. Breasts: the color of big squeezable breasts. Pink with hot brown tips. Maybe with one brown mole, a kind of thrilling first sign of human rot. Do it now because tomorrow will be too late. Rubbery, full of fat and blood inside. You touch them and they destroy you. But you take the chance.

He was breathing fast now, and he drove the car to Banyon Road near the college where the girls lived. He had first seen them when he went to the college to type up his resume on the library typewriter. Ginny said he had to type up a resume if he wanted to get a job. But when he got there he couldn't think of what to type. He didn't want to mention Irving's dental lab and spread Fuckface's detested name any further, make him famous and known throughout the world. And what other jobs had he had? Cleaning typewriters, delivering mail for a while, trucking pickles to grocery stores. If only those art classes at San Francisco State had made him an artist of some kind. But all they had made him do was marry Ginny, he had found her in an art class, his work of art. He was shaping her into something perfect. And if they didn't get the baby, she was going to be pissed. Worse than pissed. She was going to kill him. So instead of doing his resume he went back to his car and read a paperback called "Wild Swedish Servants". That was when he first saw the girls After that he came back to visit their walls, their doors, their windows, all the time, whenever he needed perking up.

Now he parked on the street and watched their bedroom window. All the apartments were the same in that complex. A bedroom with a high window facing onto the street and a bath with a narrow clouded window. Then, opening to the courtyard, a living room and a kitchen

They secretly loved him. One of them, the dark, Spanish looking one with the long black braid, had smiled at him. The other one was pure California, blonde, nothing but a filled bikini. Not really intense enough for him, but she was clean and young and he didn't think she'd have any signs of rot on her yet. The first sign of rot he saw on himself and it would be over. He wasn't going to wait for Jesus to test him that way. The only thing that made it worth the struggle was his beauty, his muscular legs and his exquisite cock and his taste buds, open to chile peppers. The stuff that came into him from one lick of a chile pepper could almost electrocute him.

He didn't intend to do anything now. But he held the girls in his mind like a chalice, brimming, waiting to slake his thirst.

THIS WAS MORE LIKE IT. *This* was the kind of work Michael felt he was suited for. A silver limousine, with him in the driver's seat. The vibes were brilliant in this environment, a thousand times better than at that prison camp owned by Irving Fuckface; Michael had a wife who hugged and kissed him with gratitude now that they had a good chance to get the baby, he had a truckful of food behind him, which—if the end of the world came— he could just drive right home with, and he'd have a big advantage over everyone for survival.

He'd made out his order list with high hopes. Burritos, average order 15, he'd ordered 75! Glazed doughnuts, 3 dozen advised; he'd ordered 6 dozen. Cigarettes, 6 cartons advised, he'd ordered 10. Ham and cheese sandwiches, yogurts, orange juices, fruit pies, candy bars—he automatically doubled the order they suggested. He was going to make it big in this new job. He wasn't only going to go to the stations they'd mapped out for him, he was going to hit some other promising places, too. Maybe he'd surprise the boss with triple the ordinary sales. The guy who hired him had hardly grilled him; just asked a few questions, nodded a few times, looked at his driver's license, and then shook his hand heartily and sent him out with a million dollar investment, this silver truck with quilted sides, the coffee machine, the refrigerated case. His boss' name was Manny. Manny warned him that whatever he ordered he'd be responsible for; at the end of the day he had to buy whatever didn't get sold, but Michael said, "Don't worry, I'll sell it."

He was touched by Manny's trust in him. When the world trusted you, it made you want to work ten times harder, to prove you could do it. Oh, he could do it. This was a job he could live with. Driving in the fresh air, seeing the sights of the world go by, shooting down the streets in this silver rocket of a truck, all eyes on you, men in business suits wishing they were you, with all that freedom, all that food. It had been a mistake to go to dental tech school after all those crummy jobs. He only did it because Ginny thought he needed some training. She believed in a man's working his way up in the world, whereas he believed in the lucky break. If you waited long enough, the breaks found you, you just had to be ready and open for them, that was the secret. His mother used to say "Money is round. One day you have it, the next day I have it." One of these days he would have it, no question about it. The dental-tech job had just been a little set back in the life-plan. It had been back-breaking, and if you were slow, like he was, and you got paid by the piece, you ended up with nothing.

But this felt like a turning point. Ginny had been so kind this morning, so grateful. She had pulled down the covers and kissed a cross across his chest and down to his cock. He didn't even let her do the whole thing, he wanted to be on time, to have all his energy intact, but she whispered that she would do it when he came home if he wanted her to.

He didn't tell her this, but he was going to call a surgeon after he got off work and find out about having his bladder stretched. If he didn't have to stop to pee, he'd have more time to cover more sites. Right now he was on his way to his first assignment, a construction site on Figueroa, about two blocks away and he was due to get there at 8:30, but here it was only 8:15, and he was passing right by a high school. He pulled into the parking lot. A bunch of tough looking kids came rushing over to him.

"Hey, here's the Roach Coach! We thought you guys weren't coming back. Hey man, you got any good dope like the other guy had?"

Michael jumped out of the truck and flipped up the silver side of the van with a great swinging movement of his arm.

"Not today," he said. "Maybe tomorrow."

"Hey, guys, there's enough here for an army. Catch!" The biggest blackest kid threw a sandwich to another kid, and then grabbed a handful of them, and started tossing them to all his friends. Then a bunch of them ran up under the silver overhang and started plucking candy bars and cigarettes from the display shelf.

"Please, you guys!" Michael called. "Pay for one at a time, will you?"

"Pay? We thought you was the Red Cross," one of them yelled. They all laughed. Michael tried to lower the overhang, but their big stupid heads were in the way. They were grabbing gum and doughnuts and cans of juice and playing catch with them.

"Fuck off!" he yelled, and then he jumped into the van and started the motor, and drove the truck a few feet. The silver coffee maker crashed out of the van and smashed on the cement. He could see the steam rising as the black coffee slithered out on the concrete.

"Holy shit!" he screamed. "You fuckers!" He kept jerking the truck forward till he was clear of the kids, and then he took off out of the school yard with his overhang still up, and food falling out of the van in a trail of waxpaper sandwiches and yogurt cups. When he was about three blocks away, he stopped the van and got out to close the overhang. God knew how much he'd have to fork over for the coffee maker. But he still had plenty of food left, plenty of burritos. The kids hadn't gotten to them, they were in the warmer, hidden under the napkins and cups.

He had missed the first coffee time at the construction site he was assigned to, so he might as well not go there at all. He still had lots of opportunities to make up what sales he had missed there. It was just too bad people were so rotten, that's all. He couldn't understand it, why people wanted to be cruel just for the hell of it. He didn't have a bone in his body that worked that way, not a single one.

Okay. This was more like it. At this place there were decent guys, the hard-hats, hard working honest guys like he was. They were orderly, they came up to the van and bought their stuff and paid for it. He wondered why this site wasn't on his list, it was only four blocks away from the one he was supposed to have gone to first this morning, and there was a big crew here, maybe 50 guys building this skyscraper. A few of them cursed because he didn't have any coffee, but he said it was just a screw-up and it wouldn't happen again. In fact, he said, he would give them each freebee coffee tomorrow to make up for it. When some of them still looked angry, he said—"How about you each take a glazed doughnut, free, on the house?"

They liked that, all right. It was nothing, a few cents, and he was building up good will. He handed out maybe two dozen doughnuts, feeling great, feeling powerful and charitable.

"How about free cigarettes?" one guy asked him, and before he could even think he said, "Sure. Why not?"

That was a mistake, but it was too late to fix it. Before he knew it, the cigarettes were gone, and the guys were laughing, just like the jerks at the high school. He would have to have better control in the future, he would have to think things out more clearly before he made any more offers of presents.

Even so, he wasn't doing that badly. He had taken in quite a few bucks already. It would work out. He still had the whole day ahead of him. Lots of stops to cover, lots more money to make.

"What the hell are you doing here?" a voice yelled, and Michael looked up to see a twin of his van turning into the parking lot. A red-faced Mexican was leaning out the window, shaking his fist.

"What's it to you?" Michael said.

"This is my territory," the wetback said. "You get out of here. This is my place. Only I can sell here."

"Who said? Isn't this a free country? That's why you're here, buddy, because it's a free country, and don't you forget it."

"You're crazy, man, I don't know what you're talking about. This is my place, only I have rights here!"

"Fuck off," Michael said, "or I'll call immigration."

The hard-hats laughed, and Michael felt good about that. They were watching him and laughing, so he said, "Fuck off or I'll have you back making tortillas in Tijuana, you shit-faced taco."

Just then Michael caught a glimpse of himself in the silver side of his truck as he stood there, sliced by the quilted lines, distorted into little fragments of light and waviness. He felt a hundred feet tall. The wind was blowing, the air was clean and fresh, and he was finally going to make it. Success breeds success. He would come back here tomorrow with free coffee, and these guys would be his permanent customers for life.

Smash! Something knocked into the side of his head like a hammer. He reeled, turned, saw the wetback coming for him again, felt the blow this time on his nose, felt the blood burst out of him saw it fall on the cement, in rivulets.

"You come back here once more and you'll be dead meat," the wetback said.

A cheer went up from the hard-hats. Michael looked to see who they were cheering, and it wasn't him. They were slapping the little Mexican on the back, and laughing.

Motherfuckers, all of them. It was time for the world to end and start all over. There was no hope for anyone. It was too far gone, nothing could stop it now. His blood dripped from his nose and stained the pavement in clotted black clumps.

Oh God, Oh God, Michael thought. *Why me? Why now? Why are you doing this to me?*

By late afternoon, he thought he had his problems solved. He had spent the last hour waiting in front of a print shop while they made up a hand-lettered sign for him. Now all he had to do was attach it to the side of his truck, and go to the last scheduled stop on his list. He realized that today had cost him more than he would earn even in the first week, but at least he had it all together now.

He paid the sign-maker $50 and shook his hand. He considered asking to use the bathroom, but he decided against it. He wasn't going to leave his truck even for 60 seconds; someone could rip him off, he wouldn't take that chance, ever again. That's why he had the sign made.

When he got to the last stop, a factory where Mexican women sewed awnings and outdoor umbrellas, he displayed his sign proudly.

STOP THIEF!
YOU ARE TAKING FOOD FROM MY WIFE AND CHILDREN!
STEALING IS A SIN AND YOU WILL BE PUNISHED FOR IT!
PLEASE PAY ME FOR EVERYTHING YOU TAKE.
GOD BLESS YOU.

When the women came out with their kerchiefs on their heads and their hands in the pockets of their aprons looking for money, he watched proudly as they read his sign.

Then he felt them staring at him in a way that made him feel bad. They started to talk among themselves in Spanish, babbling and gesticulating. He felt he was in a foreign country. Then suddenly, they all turned around like soldiers obeying a command and went back into the factory, one by one, without buying a single stick of gum.

When he got back to headquarters, Manny was waiting at the loading dock to greet him.

"You crazy or something?" Manny said. "I got calls all day, with complaints. What's with you? Calling people thieves! Taking over the territory of other guys! What kind of fucking business is going on with you?" Manny threw up the overhang and saw that the coffeemaker was missing. "I don't believe this!" he said. "God must be punishing me for something I don't know about, to send you to mess up my business like this. You know what you owe me? You know how much that machine cost me?"

"I'll do better tomorrow," Michael said. "I have the picture now."

"Tomorrow my ass!" Manny said. "You're finished, buddy. And you owe me 500 bucks for my machine and for losing me my two best stations. If you don't pay me, I'll take you to court. I'll have your fucking head."

"Hey, don't take it so hard," Michael said. "Give me a break."

"I'm not in business to give some stupid jackass a break. I'm serious. This is the bottom line, Fisher! You bring me that money within two days or I'll have the police breaking down your door."

"I thought you were a nice guy," Michael said. "You seemed real decent this morning."

"Get the hell off my property," Manny said. "I don't want to see your stupid face around here ever again."

Grinding his teeth, Michael walked a few steps away and whirled to shout at Manny's back. "I'm taking my food anyway! It belongs to me, you said it did, and it's mine. If I have to pay you, I'm taking what's rightfully mine."

Manny went inside and slammed the door on Michael. After a minute Michael went over to the catering truck and unloaded everything that was his. He carried it by armfuls to his old Chevrolet parked out on the street. The wrappings of the burritos were stained with grease. The fake cheese on the ham sandwiches had turned a hard orange-yellow where it stuck out of the edges of the bread. The sugar on the glazed doughnuts was cracked and crazed, chipping off in little translucent crumbs.

Michael licked his fingers when the last bit of food was piled in his car. They were sweet to his tongue. He sucked on his fingers, one by one, over and over as if they were the tits of a woman, all the long way home.

GINNY WAS AWAKENED BY THE SCENT of bayberry incense. It opened her breathing passages as if a jar of Vicks Vaporub were being held under her nostrils. Orange candlelight flickered on the wall; as her vision came into focus she saw Michael blowing on the stick of incense that was rooted in the belly of the brass buddha on their nighttable. Then he held a round glass jar over the candle flame. She quivered, knowing what he was doing, what was coming: he was warming baby oil, swirling it round like brandy, watching it as if he were a pharmacist mixing a critical potion, judging its potency as it climbed in striated layers up the side of the jar.

Finally, he leaned over her and pulled up her nightgown. She closed her eyes and waited, her head turned to the side. Michael poured a stream of oil into his palm; next she would feel it smoothed upon her back. She inhaled, felt the waterbed surge beneath her as he pressed the oil in a circle of penetrating moves deep into her back. The bed rose and fell in soft lapping waves, filling the spaces beneath her breasts and in the triangle where her thighs came together. Michael could make the pain of the day disappear the moment he laid his hands upon her flesh. Her back always ached when she came home from the hospital after being on her feet all day, running up and down the halls with lab slips for *stat* blood tests, and extra sugars for the doctors' coffee. The waterbed was like a mother and Michael was like a father. Pressed between them, in the aura of their warmth and gentleness, Ginny rocked in a cradle—precious, beloved, safe from harm.

With her one fish-eye, she could see the candlelight illuminating the reddish-gold hairs on Michael's naked thighs. They glowed like filaments charged with current, almost blinking, one after the other, as sparks of candlelight rode through them. Michael's hands could make her whole; he drew them across her back, and her deformity disappeared. Her atrophied muscle grew

41

strong, her hump grew flat, the fish-bone of her back ejected the s-shaped snake which inhabited it and became an arrow, beautifully straight and strong and perfect.

When he did this for her, she forgot her anger, she forgot the lists on the kitchen table and the lists in her head and the lists in her heart of all the things he needed to do and had not done, could not do, or refused to do.

"Unnh," she grunted with pleasure. "Oh yes." His hand sectioned her buttocks in two, deftly, purposefully. He heaved the bed at the same time, making the wave under her grow more violent and dangerous. The water, spinning in its confining membrane, rode up the length of her body and crushed her breasts against her breastbone with elemental force. Like a magician, her husband heaved her into the sea with his hand a rudder between her thin buttocks; he guided her like a surfboard over the rise of the breakers and under their dark hooded tunnels. He upended her in the swirling foam and rode her, straddled her, his thighs nearly severed by the sharp points of her hipbones, his golden hairs drenched by surf and the slippery secretions of the fishy sea.

She drowned, she rose, she drowned again. He let her float to the surface and pushed her under. He thrashed, a bronze-skinned whale, against her tender skin, slapping and flapping the whole glistening swell of his body against hers. Gladly she gave herself to it, gladly she was submerged, covered, obliterated. She had no doubt that he had the strength and knowledge to save her, to save them both, to bring them to some victorious conclusion, a thing she could never do for herself in a million years.

When the waterbed was still, when finally he was sleeping deeply, trustingly, at her side, she extricated herself from his embrace. A tiny thread of saliva hung swinging from the edge of his lip to the tip of the pillow, a spider web spun out of his fragile human insides.

She was starving. The great athletic event had made her hungry for nourishment; her reserves were very slight. She had to eat ten times a day, in a hurry, almost desperately. She only needed a little at a time, but she needed it in a panic, as if she would fall to the floor, weak and helpless, if she didn't get food into herself almost the instant she realized that she needed some. She had been asleep last night when Michael had come home from his new job. He had refused to talk about it; what he wanted to do was massage her, heat the shimmering oil and pour it in rainbow streams upon her back by the light of the candle.

Now she opened the refrigerator door and a landslide engulfed her! Hard cold objects hit her feet and legs; they danced like hail upon the kitchen floor, they slid and scurried like a cageful of rats set loose.

She began to understand what she saw. Burritos, doughnuts, sandwiches, cups of yogurt, poured down upon her. There were so many, they were stacked, stuffed in the refrigerator like the underwear she packed into Michael's drawers when she could not get them to close. The top of a cup of strawberry yogurt popped off, spilling its pink cream upon her bare toes.

What did it mean? She knelt and swooped her finger into the cold gelatinous cream and sucked it off angrily. She wouldn't wake him and ask questions because she knew the answers had to be bad news. She'd know the answers soon enough in any case. She'd see him, face to face, on dry land in the morning. She'd eat her heart out soon enough, because the social worker was coming to talk to them, to see their house, to meet Michael, and to find if their home would be the best of all possible worlds in which to raise a tiny little baby.

"I've already made the baby a mobile," Ginny said to the social worker. "I made it out of margarine container tops and nylon fishing twine." She tried to sound relaxed and casual. The

social worker's name was Adele Ginsberg, so she was Jewish—
that was a good sign. While the woman was looking around the
kitchen, Ginny dug out her grandmother's menorah from the
back of the linen closet and stuck it on a dresser in the baby's
room. When Adele Ginsberg came in to check out the crib, she
peered at the Hebrew letters on the menorah with interest.

"I think it's from Israel," Ginny said.

"It's very beautiful."

"I should clean out the wax," Ginny said. "I will, before
next Channukah."

"Are you going to raise the baby in the Jewish religion?"

"Oh definitely."

"And your husband has no objection?"

"Oh no, he loves the idea of Jewish family life. Jews are
much closer than other families..They give their children so
much support. Michael wishes his family had been Jewish."

"So his family wasn't very close?"

Ginny felt an alarm go off in her head. "They were pretty
close," she said guardedly. ". . . but not as close as my family
was."

"Was?"

"Is!" She was beginning to sweat. She had sent Michael out
of the house this morning, with all his stinking burritos and stale
doughnuts. Just in case the social worker opened the refrigerator,
she didn't want all that junk pouring out around her feet. She
didn't want to have to explain it. "Just stay out till 7 tonight,"
Ginny had warned Michael. "She's coming at 4:30 because I said
you'd make a point of leaving work early in order to meet her,
but now I'm going to tell her that Irving gave you extra work,
and you didn't want to turn it down because we want to have as
much extra money as we can for when the baby comes." She
could tell Michael was surprised that she wanted to lie and let
the agency think he still had the job as a dental tech, but it was
the only thing to do. If she admitted that Michael had no job,
they wouldn't get the baby, it was that simple.

"Do your parents live nearby?" Adele Ginsberg asked. She
wasn't really listening, she was counting, it seemed to Ginny.
What was she counting? Square feet? Number of windows? How
many smudges of dirt there were on the walls? The woman

walked around the apartment with her eyes narrowed, as if something hard were going on in her head, even though she was smiling and stroking the soft leather flap of her shoulder purse.

"Only my mother lives nearby. My father died of cancer a few months before Michael and I got married. He was only 55."

"Oh, that's very sad," Adele Ginsberg said. "What a grief for your mother to bear."

"That's why the baby will make her very happy. If it's a boy, we're going to name it for my father."

"That will be wonderful," the social worker said, and Ginny took a deep breath. The bad moment was turning around now. It looked positive again. The woman's eyes were less narrow.

"You'll be giving up your job, of course," Adele Ginsberg said. "At least for the first six months; we expect that."

"Of course! I want to be home with the baby."

"You realize, Mrs. Fisher, that in a private adoption, the kind you are arranging through your gynecologist, we have fewer checks and balances, we have less of an opportunity to match up all the things that will make a successful adoption. We don't have the same depth of information about the natural parents, their medical histories, their physical characteristics, their genetic backgrounds."

"We'll love the baby no matter what. It doesn't matter to us what its background is."

"And there's always the danger that the natural parents will change their minds. They have six weeks before they sign the final papers. In agency-arranged adoptions, we have very few young parents who change their minds and back out at the last minute. We take great care to assure that that won't happen. In this case, you're taking a greater chance."

"I know," Ginny said, "but Dr. Arnold told me he's certain they won't change their minds. They're only kids themselves, and they don't want this baby at all. They have no way to take care of it, or support it. All they want is a good home for it, with parents who will love it."

"Everyone says that at first," Mrs. Ginsberg said. "I'm not suggesting you'll have trouble, but I want you to be aware of the possibilites."

"I'm very aware," Ginny said.

"I was hoping to meet your husband," Mrs. Ginsberg said, looking around as if Michael might be hiding behind the couch. "I thought we'd arranged that he'd be here; it is one of the conditions of this visit, you know, Mrs. Fisher."

"I'm really sorry," Ginny said, "but Michael had a chance to work this evening and earn some extra money, and we want to earn every extra penny we can . . . so the baby will have every comfort we can buy for him."

Ginny and the social worker exchanged brief insincere smiles. It was another bad moment.

"You say *him*, as if you're sure the baby will be a boy. Do you have some preference in this area?"

"Oh no, we would love anything we get. I just said him but I could just as easily have said her."

"Well, I do have to be going now, but I thank you very much for our nice visit."

"I thank *you*," Ginny said, holding out her hand. The woman seemed as if she had made up her mind about something; Ginny watched her taking one final look around.

"I'll be in touch with you very soon," Mrs Ginsberg said, taking Ginny's hand. "I'm really sorry your husband wasn't here."

"I am, too," Ginny said. "You would like him. He's real warm, and really good with children."

"No doubt. We just like to make sure."

"He'll be the best father in the world," Ginny promised. "I just know it."

"I may try to get by here again, in the hopes of meeting him," the social worker said.

"Will you call first?"

"Not necessarily, but don't you worry about it. We don't have to stand on formalities . . . do we?"

"I hope not," Ginny said. She watched the woman walk to her car, one foot in front of the other, gingerly, as if she were trying not to step in dog shit.

GINNY DRESSED HERSELF LIKE AUNT JEMIMA, with a kerchief wrapped around her head and a big white apron that Michael liked to wear when he was barbecuing. It was time for drama in her life; she recognized this and imagined that she was Cher or some other famous interesting woman being interviewed on the Johnny Carson show. "Right before I adopted my baby I disguised myself," she would say to the talk show host, "and I went to the clinic parking lot where I hid behind a doctor's fancy Mercedes. And then I waited there till the teenage couple who were my baby's natural parents came to see the doctor."

Ginny crouched down now in the clinic parking lot. She caught a glimpse of herself in the side view mirror of the Mercedes and she knew she looked ridiculous. Since the parents didn't know her from Adam, there was no reason for her to have disguised herself at all, but it was part of the drama. How many moments like this did an ordinary person have in her life? She counted her big moments: the day she got her first period; the day they told her she didn't have to have her back operation; the day she met Michael in the art class at San Francisco State; the day (which was the same day) she went to bed with him. Then there were some other big moments, her wedding, her father's deathbed.

But this was the biggest so far. She was so excited that her teeth were chattering. What did the young mother look like? If she saw her face, would she always remember it, always have it living in the back of her mind like a ghost that could never be laid to rest?

She had learned by accident that the natural parents would be coming to see Dr. Arnold this afternoon. After the social worker had left yesterday, she had begun to worry about the baby's heritage and background. She called Dr. Arnold's office and told the nurse that she wanted to find out if there was any

47

insanity in the baby's family. She had had her private worries about Michael for a long time, especially when his eyes would start flashing in their sockets and roll around, not really seeing anything. Sometimes his lips would move, and sometimes he would grind his teeth together till she couldn't stand the sound. She didn't know if that was insanity or nervousness or just a bad habit, but she knew it frightened her when she couldn't get his attention. He always denied he had been off in space somewhere in a place she couldn't get to. He said she was just imagining things. So, to put her mind at rest, she just wanted to be sure this baby didn't have any disturbed relatives in his background. Maybe she was lucky her ovaries were dead as dry fruit pits, then she would never have to worry about her bone problems being passed on to a baby, or about Michael's spinning eyeballs turning up one day in her baby's face.

The nurse had said, "Oh, no problem, the girl is coming in today, she's getting close to her time, you know, so we'll be sure to ask her to fill out a medical history."

"When is she coming?" Ginny asked, casually, almost not asking at all.

"She's coming around four. She wanted a late appointment so her husband could come along with her."

"Her *husband?*" Ginny asked. "I thought he was her boy-friend."

"Oh, they just got married yesterday; Dr. Arnold probably hasn't spoken to you since. Don't you think that's lovely? I mean, for the baby's sake?"

"But does that mean they're going to change their minds?"

"Oh no, I don't think so," the nurse said. "It was just to make it right, in the eyes of God. I think they're both very religious."

"Well, thank you for the news," Ginny said. "I appreciate it."

And now she crouched behind the Mercedes, living her moment of drama. If a person just lived long enough, something big came along to make up for the endless boring hours of nothingness everyone had to live through. Weeks would go by, even years, with nothing promised, nothing to look forward to. And then some idea would start up, like a miracle, like the time she decided to go to San Francisco, or the time she just let Michael talk her into sleeping with him, and the excitement would rage up like a forest fire, making her brain spin with noise and a thrilling kind of panic.

One day she had been on Dr. Arnold's examining table, having him feel for her ovaries, to see if they had disappeared, or had cysts on them, or whatever the problem was he was looking for, and he had said, "Some women go through hell to have a baby, and then this girl walks in, and she doesn't know what hit her, she wants to try out to be a cheerleader in her high school, and instead she's three months pregnant. I'm going to try to find someone to adopt her baby," he confided in Ginny. "I'm going to ask some of my infertile patients if any of them are interested in a private adoption. I'd like to help this teenager find a good home for her baby."

"I want the baby," Ginny had said, just like that, and then the wildness started up in her brain, and hadn't subsided since.

So it wasn't only that life did things to you and you had to wait for them to happen; sometimes you could make life *move*, you could step into something and *cause* it.

There they were! A blue pickup turned into the lot. When the girl got out, her belly looking big enough and tight enough to pop open and spew the baby across the parking lot into Ginny's arms, she looked to Ginny like Mary-Mother-of-Christ. She looked as if she had stepped out of a tent in Egypt somewhere. She wore a black scarf draped over her head, and a burlap maternity dress, sand-colored, long enough so that its hem scraped the blacktop of the parking lot. The boy helped her out, she was slow as a hundred-year old woman. They walked step-by-step, inch-by-inch, toward the door of the clinic.

Ginny waited two full minutes, and then came into the waiting room herself. If they noticed her at all, they would think she was there, like anyone else, for a Pap smear or a pregnancy test. The receptionist wasn't at the window, so there was no problem with that for the moment. Ginny picked up a Redbook magazine and opened to an article about sex during pregnancy.

The mother and father of her baby sat close together on the plastic couch, their faces turned toward each other, their noses touching as they whispered painful, frightened messages into each other's mouths. They were so beautiful and tragic they brought the beginning of tears to Ginny's eyes. Now that they were married to one another the picture had changed. They weren't just kids who had thoughtlessly screwed and got pregnant; they were in love, like Romeo and Juliet. He touched the girl's cheek, just under her eye. Was the girl crying? Ginny hoped not, because if she was crying, Ginny might have to reveal herself, promise them that she would adore their infant, worship it, guard it from harm day and night, give her life for it. Then, to Ginny's relief, the girl just leaned her head back against the wall and closed her eyes.

The scarf slipped off her head. Her hair was black, as pitch black as Ginny's. The boy had brown hair. He was wearing blue jeans and torn running shoes. He had muscular thighs, she could see his muscles powerful and curved under the denim. She felt a clutching spasm low in her belly, a blaze of desire. She could imagine the moment it happened, the leap of fire from the boy's cock to the girl's patient egg.

"Excuse me, do you have the time?"

The girl was speaking directly to her, her head still leaning back against the wall, her eyes half-open. Ginny's heart paused; her vision began to dim until she felt her heart start up again, irregularly, skipping, then pounding like a hammer.

"4:20," Ginny said. "Don't you have a watch?"

"I lost it," the girl said, giving Ginny a weak, sweet smile. "Usually I can find the time somewhere if I need to."

"Here, you can have mine, I don't need it." Ginny was on her feet, standing over the girl. Then she sat down on the couch beside her, already beginning to unbuckle her watch strap. "It's only a cheap digital," she said. "I have one in every color. My husband and I buy them at flea markets, they only cost a couple of dollars, so here—I can easily spare this."

The girl glanced at her husband. He shook his head at her.

"Don't be silly," Ginny said to her, not to him. "I really want you to have it." She took the girl's arm in her hand and started to fasten the watch in place on her wrist. The girl giggled slightly, but she let Ginny hold onto her arm. The arm was thin as a flute; she could feel the bone almost at the surface, just under the skin.

"Think of it as a present for the new baby."

The girl smiled apologetically. "We're not going to be able to keep the baby," she said, " . . . but I sure could use the watch."

The boy was frowning. His lips had an ugly pouting look. Ginny hoped her baby wouldn't ever look that way.

The girl winced suddenly. She put the flat of her hand high up on her belly. "He kicks very hard now," she said. "He's wanting to get out."

"Oh, could I please feel it?" Ginny asked. She was so sympathetic, a sister to all women. The girl could not really object. Other women in the waiting room looked on with benign approval. Ginny put her hand on the curve of the girl's belly, felt the thrilling movement beneath her palm. The assertive tiny life knocked against her, a greedy, tenacious signal. It took her breath away.

"It's a miracle," she said to the girl. "You're making a miracle."

IT SEEMED AS IF GOD'S EYES were looking out at Ginny from the depths of the blue blanket. What a peculiar thing to think. She didn't even believe in God; it was Michael who liked to talk about forces and spirits and the fact that people used 10% of their brain power and the rest of it was just waiting to be used to discover hidden mysteries. But who else could it be looking out of the baby's blue-black eyes? There was such intelligence in that stare, such knowledge and wisdom! The baby had only been in the world three days and yet he seemed to understand everything. He understood how badly Ginny wanted and needed him. He even understood how Michael felt, driving home now much too fast, his ego hurt because the baby was not his own true blood, did not have his red-gold hair, or his special configuration of heart and muscle and brain.

The baby in her arms continued to stare at Michael soberly, with compassion. His eyes were fixed on Michael's face; they never wavered, even as the steering wheel swung this way and that as Michael took corners too fast, spun in and out of turns as if he were trying to prove something . . . or kill them all.

Ginny adjusted the blanket, touched the baby's smooth cheek. The nurse had said if you even touched his cheek, he'd turn his mouth to the side to find the nipple and try to suck, but the baby just kept staring at Michael without blinking.

"He's watching you," Ginny said. "He loves you."

Michael punched his horn four times till an old man wearing a hat pulled his Lincoln over to the right lane. "When is that social worker coming again? You don't think she's going to be sitting on our doorstep when we get home, do you?"

"Oh, no—not today," Ginny said. "It's not like it was the agency's baby, this is different. Michael. They don't have the same responsibility, not if it's a private adoption. They just have to check it out briefly; just to make sure."

"I don't like the idea of her coming around."

"She just wanted to know if you had a job. That's reasonable, don't you think?"

"I don't think it's any of her business."

Ginny made a kissing noise with her lips to attract the baby's attention. He was staring so hard at Michael she was beginning to feel left out. "Adam, my darling little Adam," she thought. The baby felt like a warm roast beef in her arms. Solid and delicious.

"Besides, I *have* a job," Michael said. "Tonight at least."

"Tonight?"

"I met a guy in Griffy's a couple of days ago. He's giving a big party tonight in Beverly Hills and they need a bartender. He'll pay me fifty bucks and he guarantees some tips."

"Michael, tonight is our first night at home with the new baby."

"I thought you wanted me to have a job. We owe the hospital plenty now, did you forget?"

"But this isn't a *job*."

"It sounds like money to me."

"How can you even trust some guy you met in a pool hall? He could be a complete flake. Who's going to be at this party? How do you know it's legitimate?"

Michael laughed. It was an ugly sound, making fun of her, mocking her. "Fifty bucks will buy a case of Gerber's baby food," he said. "So lay off me, will you?"

Ginny sat back and closed her eyes. *Drop dead*, she thought, and then she was sorry to have thought it. *Who needs you?* she thought, and then felt a shiver of misery go through her. She reached over and touched Michael's hand on the steering wheel. "Please," she said. "Let's be happy. This is one of the happiest moments of our lives. Let's not mess it up."

"I'm happy," Michael said. "Don't I look happy?"

But the thought, *Who needs you?* stayed in her mind. Now that the baby was in her arms, Michael seemed dispensable. Maybe that's all women ever needed from men: babies. And Michael hadn't even given her this baby. Who *said* her eggs would have made bad babies? Maybe a bad baby would have been *his* fault. Maybe his sperm had bad tails and couldn't swim; maybe he had no sperm at all in that milky fountain that shot out of him so profusely when he was coming. Who could know about those secret things that went on deep inside people, in the dark bloody insides of their bodies?

This baby, so clean and fragrant in her arms now, wrapped in this soft lemon-scented blue blanket, had just a few days ago been covered in blood.

Ginny had seen a delivery on television showing everything; the woman grunting and moaning, her face going red with the strain of pushing. And after that it was all blue blankets and little booties, cute little rattles and blue ribbons. She looked down into her baby's endlessly deep, brilliantly shining eyes, and she tried to remember the blood and pain. It made him all the more precious, more valuable, more mysterious. It bound her to him by the secret ceremony of birth. Mother and son. Madonna and child. If Michael were in the right mood, she could have told him she was thinking that and he would be pleased, since he still had all that church junk left over in his head from when his mother used to take him to church.

He was still really a Christian believer deep in his heart, though he denied it. He thought Jesus or someone would save him someday. He said things like that and it made Ginny worried. He liked to have the buddha incense burner in their bedroom; he liked the buddha to watch them make love, with his happy smiling face and his pot belly. Michael liked to think *someone* was in charge of this crazy world.

"What shall we name the baby?" she asked Michael. "Do you have any ideas?"

"No."

"I was thinking something poetic. Like *Adam*. You know, the first man."

"You mean the first man to be screwed by a woman."

"That's not what I meant, Michael." Ginny knew what Michael thought of women—at least some women. She remembered a story Michael had told her about how his mother had torn up the drawings he had brought home from first grade to show her. She had been ironing when he came home from school, and she was furious about something—he never knew what. But she had grabbed his papers and crumpled them and then ripped them into shreds, and if that wasn't enough, she took her iron and grabbed Michael's little hand, and brought the iron down on it! She held his hand on the ironing board, and she pressed down on his knuckles with the burning wedge-shaped iron, and she branded him with her hate.

When Ginny looked for it she was able to make out the faint brown outline of the iron's tip on the back of Michael's hand. Maybe Michael held some grudges against women. Maybe he had reason to. But she had never done anything bad to him. She was good to him; she took his temper tantrums, his moods, his wild angers. She let him carry on and she cleaned up after him. She always loved him up and put him back on the track. But now, with the new baby, she hoped he'd calm down, and set a good example.

"I'd really like to call the baby Adam," she said. "It reminds me of a picture I once tried to paint in art class at school of the Garden of Eden, full of flowers and trees and green vines."

". . . and the serpent," Michael said. "I remember your serpent, with his glowing red eye."

"If I was painting that now," Ginny said, "I would leave out the serpent. He was the only ugly thing. I don't think I would need an ugly thing now. I think we're going to be happy from now on, Michael."

"Let's hope you can see into the future," Michael said. "Let's hope you're a fortune-teller."

IT WAS A RELIEF TO GET out of there and into the fresh air. A whole day locked in a house with a crying baby, and his head was tight as a drum. He had been having a beer and reading up on how to build a solar home when he heard a strange whine coming from the bedroom. He had actually looked up and said to Ginny, "It sounds like a cat got in the house."

"That's our baby," she said. "Did you forget?"

He denied it, of course, but he had forgotten, completely forgotten. Not that he really minded it; the baby was scary and thrilling in a way, with its flailing arms and its tongue like a red arrowhead, beating against its gums. When it screamed, it gave off a smell, a hot red smell, that made Michael uneasy. It wasn't the regular smell of pee or shit, or even of vomit which was all over the baby, but was something different, hot and alive, demanding, coming from its urgent demanding soul. *I need, I need*, it had yelled all afternoon. Well, I need, too, Michael had thought. I need a good meal. I need a good job. I need some attention, God damn it. He went into the bedroom where Ginny was diapering the baby, and he cupped her ass in his two hands and said, "Hey, I need your attention."

"I'm busy," she said.

"I need, I need," he said.

"Don't be a baby," she said.

"Why not? He's a baby. He gets what he needs."

"Get on line," Ginny said, with a laugh. "You'll be next."

But he wasn't next. She had to make up formula and boil it, and she had to sit by the baby's crib and stare at his sleeping face, and touch his curled fingers, and hold his tiny foot in the palm of her hand.

Well, she was certainly happy. At least she wasn't on his case about a job. Soon enough she would be. Mrs. Nosy-body-social-worker would be on his tail soon, and so would Manny from the catering truck place. And the hospital bill would be another big one. A baby pops out and the hospital charges two thousand bucks for catching it. Well, why worry? Being short of money for a while was never the end of the world. Nothing was the end of the world unless you killed yourself. No matter how many things went wrong, there was always a meal coming from somewhere and a bed to sleep in. If worst came to worst, there was Ginny's mother, or even his mother to go to. Both old women cried poor all the time, but both had money, he was sure of it. His father had had life insurance and the way his mother lived, in a little trailer in the middle of nowhere, it must have tripled in the bank. And Ginny's mother—she bought everything second hand, even day-old bread at the bakery, so her money had to be someplace; she wasn't anywhere near to being in the poorhouse, either.

Money. Everyone had money. Michael wasn't stupid or any more ignorant than the people with money. He was better and smarter in every way. One of these days he would have money. It was just a matter of time. His mother used to say *"Money is round, one day you have it, one day I have it."* Well, pretty soon it had to roll his way. It was time.

He thought of all the things he had done, all the jobs he had tried since San Francisco. A long time since those days. He wasn't a kid anymore, either. He and Ginny had come a long way together and now they were what her mother had threatened them they would be, old hippies.

God, it was so long since those San Francisco nights when he had felt that sense of ease and release. Drugs, that old druggy-town, those nights with rainbow colors and furry animals on glass. Sex that blew out the inside of your head. Trips, bummers, good ones, bad ones.

Ginny hadn't fit in with that at all. Uptight. Always holding herself away from it, from the drugs and the sex and the turning-on. She never held herself away from him, though. From that first night, when he had sauntered over to where she stood at her easel and kissed her, she had never held back from Michael, not for one minute. She just didn't give it away like the other girls who were loose, happy, easy. She said it was her Jewish glue; it held her together, it kept her from falling apart, it made her sane and stable—it would never let her slide and be a flake, it kept her whole.

Secretly, he believed that's what he loved best about her; she was a rock. Like Jesus, she was his rock. He was like dry clay himself, ready to crumble, crack apart, break open, but Ginny was all solid and she knew what she wanted and what she didn't want she stayed away from.

Michael was trying to find an address on the dark street. It was a canyon road up above Sunset, a winding street without street lights. He hated to get uptight looking for an address; he'd start sweating, and his heart would pick up and make him nervous, and by the time he got to where he was going, he was tired, and not at his best. He liked to be at his best when there would be women around; he liked to be easy, relaxed, funny. He was never very funny. The things he thought were funny fell flat. Ginny was funny, people always laughed at what she said, and he loved to hear her laugh, it gave him hope, but he never thought anything she ever said was funny. She said they weren't on the same frequency; she said maybe it was Jewish humor. Something he would never understand. Well, if she wanted Jewish she should have married a rabbi or something. Yet he really loved her laugh. It freed something up in him, let him have hope that one day he'd laugh like that, or make someone else laugh like that.

Maybe with the new baby around she'd laugh more. That would be something to look forward to, wouldn't it?

Michael saw the house he was looking for. It was pretty fancy, with a fountain in the front and lots of expensive cars parked on the curving street and in the long driveway. It ought to be okay; a party was a party. He'd pour two and drink one. That ought to make it worth his while. Ease up his worries, tone down his fears. Why not? Fifty bucks, and tips and all the booze he could drink. Why not?

He hardly recognized the guy he'd met at Griffy's. He looked like he was up for an Academy Award in his ruffly shirt and black bow tie.

"Hey buddy," he said to Michael, pumping his hand. "Come upstairs with me, I have a jacket you can barkeep in." Michael followed him up a carpeted staircase and into a plush bedroom. A woman sat at a dressing table, sniffing a perfume bottle. She was wearing something satin and clingy. Michael felt a throb starting in his private parts, a nice thought to come back to if the party got dull. It was time to go visit the girls on Banyon Road again; he was beginning to miss them—if he didn't go to see them for a few days they hammered on his mind, urging him to come back. Not that he ever really saw them, but he sat in his car and imagined them doing their little things in the apartment—studying, filing their nails, cooking up vegetables, taking hot powerful showers with a hand-held shower massage, aiming the spray here and there, down from above, up from below, right between . . .

"Thanks very much," Michael said, slipping his arms into the jacket. He looked pretty good in the mirror. The woman in satin thought so, too.

"Mmm," she said, "That's nice."

He wished those girls could see him now, in this wonderful bedroom, with soft lights, in a roomful of modern expensive furniture. The bed alone was as big as a dance floor. He commented on it. The guy who hired him confided that what he saw was two beds under one immense bedspread.

"One bed is for sleeping," he said with a low laugh, "the other is for you-know-what. That one's a waterbed."

"My wife and I have a waterbed," Michael said proudly. "We have a new baby, too."

"How new?" the woman asked.

"Brand new. Just home from the hospital today."

"Oh—and you left your wife tonight?"

"We could use the money," Michael said. "My wife doesn't mind." He knew at once they would give him more than fifty bucks now. He felt pretty damn good about the whole thing. He wondered how an ordinary man got a wife like that, a house like this, a party for all those friends pouring in downstairs. Where had he learned about that kind of thing? Had his mother and father taught him how to be rich and lucky? Had it come as the grace of God? He could never figure it. This guy was maybe even a little younger than Michael, maybe only thirty-three or so. And look at his empire!

"Help yourself to any food you want," the woman said sweetly as she passed by Michael in a perfumed breeze. "Make yourself at home. We'd like you to have fun here."

At 3 a.m. after the party Michael drove straight to Irving Fuckface's street and parked smack in his driveway. He felt brave, almost tough, and he wished Irving would look out the window and see his car there, and start shaking in his boots. A man like that shouldn't get away with his cruel actions; Michael had always gotten the work done, even if he was a little slow. At least he was thorough, careful. No one walking around with a tooth in his mouth made by Michael would ever feel that his bite was off-center or ever have to go back to the dentist and demand a remake. Michael wished he had been born a century or so back, when craftsmen had the respect of the world, when things were made with care and attention to detail. Everything was made like paper these days; his car was rusting out to nothing underneath. Rot and corruption in the human body, in the world, in human values.

The party had made him sad. He and Ginny had no friends who would ever invite them to a party. It was probably because of him, because of the way he turned people off. He didn't understand it; he'd talk to new friends with all the honesty in him, telling them what he thought, what he believed, giving them tips on how to live better themselves, and he never saw them again. Ginny said he just didn't know what the appropriate thing to do was. He didn't act in appropriate ways. What did she know! Did she have so many friends? She was on the phone with her sister Paula every day. Paula was her only real friend. Michael would have liked to call Taffy, his sister, if he knew where she was, but she was a flake. She went from one job to another, one man to another. Even on Christmas she didn't turn up to visit their mother in her trailer. Well, she had taken the brunt of it at home; maybe he shouldn't blame her. Agnes gave it to Taffy when they were kids twice as often as she gave it to him. She would lock Taffy in her room, and Taffy would climb out the window. Taffy had been hot to find boys and it worried Agnes. She used to hit Taffy with a hanger. She had a thing about clothes being hung up, and once, when Taffy had ironed a dress she wanted to wear, Agnes grabbed it from Taffy, all starched and smooth, and crumpled it to a ball in her fists, much as she had crumpled the papers Michael had brought home to show her from first grade.

Well, it looked like Fuckface wasn't going to come out tonight. . . . He was probably snoring his head off. Well, the time would come, Michael knew that. It was just a matter of when. He had all the time in the world. He would just wait it out.

He knew he ought to be getting home. He smelled like a brewery. Some drunk at the party had upended a bottle of scotch and it spilled all over Michael's shirt and pants. He hadn't had much to drink himself; maybe two drinks, that's all, because he was too busy pouring and watching the women dance. He wished Ginny could let go like that, shake her body like a free spirit. She had a beautiful body, she really did. If the world were a better place, she could walk around like he would like her to, with thin little halters and sundresses, and no one would be judging her. She had a beautiful spirit, she was good through and through, like an angel. She was kind to everyone; she loved animals, and would stop on a busy freeway to pick up a limping dog. She would give her life to take care of injured or crippled creatures. It was a pity what had happened to Whisper. He didn't want to think about that. He hadn't meant to throw him in the ocean. It had just worked out that way.

But she had married him anyway. That was the miracle, the true miracle of their love. Another girl might have decided not to go through with it after that, not after they had both watched the dog paddling around with his pathetic black snout pointing at them and then going under, coming up and then sinking down, watching them with those wild eyes. Michael had thought the dog would make it, just come paddling back to the side of the boat and they'd haul him in, but the moron animal just let the waves carry him the other way, out to sea, paddling like a wind-up toy. Michael had tried to start the outboard, but he couldn't get it to start and it just nearly broke his shoulder, pulling and pulling on the cord, and by then the dog just gave up and slid under the water, turned himself into a hamburger for a shark.

Michael started the car. He ought to get back to Ginny because he wanted to kiss her feet. He adored her. He was so grateful to her. She knew him. She knew how good he was deep inside, and he never meant those things to happen, none of them, not when he threw her dog overboard, or when he lost his jobs, or when he didn't make friends so they couldn't have a normal social life. She was his only love, his only hope. She kept him alive. He had to go home.

He remembered the baby was there, but that was okay. The baby would keep her busy and happy, and take some of the pressure off him if he had to go out on his excursions, his investigations, his jaunts. He could get away to watch the two girls on Banyon Road more often.

He would just drive by there now for a minute on his way home. It was so late, it didn't matter, Ginny would be asleep anyway. Just one look at that window where they were sleeping, those two beauties, the blonde and the one with black braids. Just a nice thought to hold onto, the day they would beckon him, beg him, and let down their nightgown straps for him. He could do them both easily, easily. When it was time.

He roared through the empty nighttime streets. He could see the girls' bedroom window in his mind, a high rectangle, with a dim glowing light behind it. They must sleep with a little night light, a little glowing owl, or a plastic Mickey Mouse plugged into a socket. They both had bigger tits than Ginny, though they didn't have her sweetness, they weren't angels, and they probably couldn't forgive him for the things he might do.

Fuck it, the cops were flashing him. He saw the lights in his rearview mirror, red as a bomb exploding in his head. Shit! He was done for.

AN IMPRESSION OF MICHAEL'S TEETH SAT on the nighttable. Alone, without his busy lips, his red beard, his flashing eyes, the teeth seemed to be a death's head grinning at her, terrifying her with its skeleton smile. It was 5 a.m. and he wasn't home. The new baby—Adam—breathed on the pillow beside her. Michael's teeth were distorted and ugly, detached from him like that, not so much crooked as askew, like stalks of corn bent by the wind and leaning upon one another. The casting material was a pale white-yellow; the teeth sat in bloodless gums without a smile to cushion their skeleton's thrust. Skin and bones; Michael was only matter, the new baby was only skin and bones, and born not even from her body.

"I don't want that around," she had said when Michael presented her with his mouth in chalk.

"An ash tray," he said, opening the model and showing her the concavities of palate and floor-of-mouth. That seemed more terrible to her, the idea of ashes gathered in the death's head. "It can remind you of me when I'm not home." But what it reminded her of was his ape's origins, that lipless clacking, those yellowed pointed spears designed to rip peel from banana, skin from fruit.

Ginny touched the baby's scalp, warm and pulsing, slightly damp, hot. A song of Joan Baez came to her mind:

> *Oh, little did my mother think,*
> *when first she cradled me,*
> *The lands I was to travel in,*
> *the death I was to dee.*

She lifted the baby onto her chest, felt comforted. The clock frightened her. Where could he be? She thought of the baby's mother sleeping in her bed without this child. She thought of her own mother in her widow's bed. She thought of her father in his grave.

The phone rang. Michael's teeth grinned at her. She answered.

"Ginny—I'm being tested by Jesus," Michael said, his voice queer and spacy. "It's only a test. Not the real thing . . . "

"What are you talking about, Michael? Where are you?"

"Come get me out of here. Bring money. I'm here with common criminals. This is not my fate."

"Oh God, Michael," she said. Her eyes rested on the new baby; she pitied him, herself, all the world.

"Life is a nightmare, you know," Michael said.

Ginny gathered her strength for whatever lay ahead.

"I'm coming," she said. "I'll be there."

She hardly had a neighbor she could count on. Next door was Mrs. Flanner and her cats. She didn't trust her; she didn't trust anyone. If she couldn't trust Michael, her own husband, who could she trust? But she couldn't take the baby to jail on his first night home; it could mark him for life. Maybe the bars would make an impression on his mind, like birds were supposed to get impressed with the images of their mothers, and he would think jail was his mother. Ginny knew she was getting out of control in her thoughts as she threw on her clothes. But this was too much to ask! *Michael*, she thought, *this is too much!* She wanted to kick something, but of course she didn't. That was the difference between her and Michael; if she wanted to do something that was crazy, she didn't do it, and if he wanted to do something crazy, he did.

She wrapped the baby in his quilt and went outside to knock on Mrs. Flanner's door. Their apartment house was just like a motel—rows of colored wooden doors, the doors thin as cardboard, the walls thin as paper. Michael had promised they wouldn't be here forever, but maybe they would be, now. She could smell the sea air, the one good thing about this place. They were only two miles from the ocean, and at night the fog rolled over the city, bringing the ocean smells with it—seaweed and salt, and the dark mysterious smells from the ocean depths. It was almost dawn; if she lingered another few minutes the sun would be up and then it wouldn't be so bad to wake Mrs. Flanner. At least it wouldn't still be the middle of the night.

Ginny had thought her and Michael's troubles would be over once they got out of San Francisco. She thought it was the people there that had had a bad influence on Michael—all those druggies, that's all they ever thought about. Turning on, tuning out. She remembered one night when they had just stopped in to see her friend Kitty, another art student, and Kitty was going up on LSD with some friends. "I wish I could visit with you, but I'm tripping, I'm on my way. I couldn't turn back if I wanted to. Come on in and join us. We have plenty."

"Let's go," Ginny had said to Michael, but he was already inside the apartment, taking off his jacket, popping himself open a beer, getting high on just the idea. He was so grateful for drugs. He loved them like she loved the sunshine. He thought they were God's gift to human beings. He thought people had to have *something* to get off on, something to block out the orders of the big shots and the *shoulds* and all the other crap that came down on them.

"Hey no," she had said, pulling on his arm. "I don't want to stay." Inside Kitty's place it was stuffy and hot. Dirty, too. She had the sense of a forbidden circle existing in there, all those bodies melting back into pillows and cushions and mattresses on the floor. "Hey, Michael, I don't want to *do* this." She thought of all the other times she had sat just outside the circle, bored, miserable, while Michael was turning on with grass or peyote or whatever they were passing around that night. And afterward, always, that isolating silence, and sometimes a candle burning in the dark, and sighs and occasional words, "Oh man," or "Wow," or "Far out." Apparently they all thought it was the most interesting thing they could do, but she never could go with it; she tried, Michael made her try, she just got palpitations of the heart. Except when he made her take LSD that one time. The things she had seen. That was the worst. She didn't want to think about it now.

But that time at Kitty's, he had finally left with her, furious. "Why not? Why not? We were *invited?* It was a goddamn party!" And then he drove home so fast, up and down those hills that he nearly got them killed. "I thought you wanted friends," he said between his clenched teeth, going 90 miles an hour. He stopped the car suddenly. "Let's go back, I want to do it. I have to. I *need* to." But she had said no; just no, that she wouldn't. And he had said, "Then fuck you."

When he stopped in front of the Sexual Freedom League house, he wouldn't park, wouldn't get out of the car.

"Aren't you coming in?"

"No."

"Where are you going then?"

"To kill myself." He drove away like a maniac.

For three days she had cried. Just collapsed there in the room and cried, and then one night some creep came in, one of Michael's buddies, some greasy creepy jerk, and he tried to make it with her. She was tempted, because, with Michael gone, she was nothing anyway. She was garbage. But in the end, when the guy was close enough so she could see the stubble on his face, she gagged. She told him to get lost.

When Michael came back, finally, after a week, she felt so relieved she didn't ask him anything, not one question. He was clean and refreshed and wearing a new Hawaiian shirt. He smelled sweet, like he had used some perfumed talcum powder. He didn't yell at her. He seemed to have forgotten their fight. He didn't do anything but claim her as his own and ask her would she please make him a great big *chile relleno.*

Ginny rang Mrs. Flanner's bell. It took a long time and then the old woman came to the door in a torn chenille bathrobe.

"I have an emergency," Ginny said, "or I would never bother you at this hour. Michael's had a flat tire. I have to pick him up. You knew we were going to get the new baby today. Well, here he is. This is the long-awaited baby. His name is Adam. Could you watch him for me for just a little while? He's all fed, but here's an extra bottle just in case . . . "

"I'm honored," the old woman said, taking the baby. "My, my, my, you did get a cute one." She examined one of the baby's fingers. "What a delicious child," she said, her cats coming to the door and rubbing between her legs.

Ginny had the thought that the old woman was like the witch in Hansel and Gretel, and as soon as she was out of sight, Mrs. Flanner would cook and eat the baby. *I'm as crazy as Michael,* she thought, *we deserve each other.*

MICHAEL WAS IN A HOLDING CELL with a bunch of drunks. He was crouched like an animal—banging his head against the floor, then against the wall of the cell, then against the floor.

What was she doing here? She had a new baby at home, she was a Jewish girl from a nice family, what was she doing in a jail with a bunch of drunks? Sometimes it came to her clear, all at once, what a mistake this marriage was. Michael was like an alien from outer space; she didn't understand where he was coming from, what he was about. There was the smell of vomit coming at her in waves.

The officer said, "Your wife is here, Fisher."

"Oh God, Ginny," he wailed. "Oh God—forgive me!" He came to the front of the cell and held onto the bars. He was a wild animal, she could see that. His eyes were bloodshot and he was filthy from vomit. It was caked on his beard and in the corners of his mouth.

Other men shuffled in the cell, like dark shadows. Michael, with his red beard, was like a flame, darting, dancing, begging, moving. He knelt on the floor in front of her and begged, prayed. He knocked his head against the bars. "I'll die if you don't forgive me," he cried. "I didn't mean it. It was just a fuck-up. I wasn't doing anything. I wasn't even drunk. I only threw up because of the stink in here, and because of what I'm doing to you."

You asshole, she thought. He was pathetic, she knew that, but she didn't know why she couldn't pity him. He was disgusting. And she was going to lose the baby now. No one wanted to give a baby to a criminal. Adele Ginsberg, the social worker, would find out somehow that Michael was a criminal, and they would snatch the baby from her arms.

He was beating his breast like a gorilla. "Please," he said, "I'll never . . . never again. I worship you. I can't live without

68

you." He began to cry. "You're the only thing worth anything in this shit-hole of a life," he said, crying. "Don't leave me. Get me out of here. You won't be sorry. Oh, God, I adore you. Who else would ever adore you this way?"

Ginny stared at him. It was true, it was perfectly true. He was her perfect love. That was why she took his shit. That was why she would always take it. She gagged at the smell coming from him. She turned to the officer. "How do I get him out?" she asked.

In the car on the way home, he knelt on the floor of the front seat, praying for her forgiveness. She couldn't talk to him. He was foul. She opened the window and let the fresh air blast her face. She had hoped all the trouble would end as soon as they got out of San Francisco. All those bad people gone, all those bad influences. He wanted to live near the beach so he could fish; fresh air and fishing, nothing dangerous about that. They had moved to their little motel-like apartment in Grecian Gardens, a city only two miles from the beach, near to Los Angeles, near to her mother. She had thought the bad stuff would be over. It had never been over. It just took different shapes, expressed itself in different troubles. It had never been over. In fact, she wondered if maybe it was just now really beginning.

"GUESS WHAT?" MICHAEL SAID. He had just come in with the mail. He was drinking coffee in the living room, and going through the pile of letters, reciting to her what had come—a pile of bills. Hospital, phone, gas, electric. There was a letter from Manny-the-catering-truck-man's lawyer, threatening Michael. Ginny was feeding the baby at the kitchen table, rice cereal with milk, spooning the mush into his mouth with a tiny silver spoon. He was very hungry. His dark eyes fastened on her like suction cups, waiting for the next spoonful. He seemed anxious, but also trusted her; he puckered his mouth, a little morning-glory opening up to sunshine.

"What?" she said. Michael talked all the time now. He had plans—big plans. She only half-listened. She was crazy with worry now that it was getting time to sign the final adoption papers. Michael's trial date was coming up; if he was convicted of drunk driving, they'd take his license away and then he surely could never work. Adele Ginsberg would find out; she'd take Adam away, or she'd tell that young couple that they should find a better home for him, a home that had a father who didn't babble all the time, and a mother who had had the sense to marry a father who worked and who had his head screwed on straight. She had fantasies of running away with Adam, packing him up in his little Carry-Cot, and taking a train to Alaska where no one could ever find her, not Adele Ginsberg, not the real parents, not Michael. Especially not Michael. Lately she dreamed of a life without his voice buzzing in the background, a grating drone, buzzing with plans to make them rich. He had figured out that getting rich would make her happy—and in a way he was right, because money would certainly solve nine-tenths of their problems. But it could never happen. She wasn't born yesterday.

"Look at me!" he commanded suddenly. "I want you to pay attention when I talk."

70

"I'm paying attention," she said, keeping her back to him. She scraped some rice cereal gently off Adam's cheek. The baby held his mouth open, sweetly, patiently, till she gathered a little hill of cereal on the delicate spoon again.

She heard a crash. She spun around and saw that the mirror on the living room wall had erupted into a sunburst of splinters.

"What happened?" she said, jumping up, and then she saw Michael's coffee cup on the rug, just under the mirror.

She stared at him. He had his chin thrust forward aggressively. "I said when I talk, you listen to me! You pay attention!"

"That was our good mirror. It cost a lot of money," Ginny said.

"Shit, don't talk to me about money, what's money? What counts is my getting some respect around here. If I say 'guess what?' I mean 'guess what?' especially if 'guess what?' is the most goddamn important thing to happen around here in twenty years!"

Adam was staring at the shards of mirror on the rug. The spikes caught the light of the sun, and sent them crazily careening off the ceiling.

"I'm listening," she said. His temper always made her wish she were somewhere else. Now that Adam was living with them, she felt ashamed for him to see his father carry on like that. She had a vision of taking one of those glass spikes and poking it into Michael's eye. God, she was getting to be violent just like him. Maybe she had lived with him too long.

She had learned it was best to ignore him at times like this. She turned her back again and went on feeding the baby. "I'm paying attention now," she said calmly.

"My mother sent a letter," he said, "and not that you deserve it or anything . . . but she wants to buy us a house."

Ginny was careful not to say the wrong thing. He could break up the place if she said the wrong thing. "How is your mother?" she said.

"Goddamn!" he shouted. "I said pay attention! Don't ask how *is* my mother if I tell you she wants to buy us a house, you cunt!"

Ginny wanted to hold her hands over the baby's ears. She looked at Adam to see if he had heard, if he could tell what was going on. The little dimpled fingers of his left hand were clutching her hand that held the spoon. He smiled at her suddenly, his face lighting up, a little rice cereal spilling down his chin, and he made a sweet sound, between a gurgle and a laugh. Ginny stood up and began to unlatch the high chair tray.

"Get in here," Michael ordered her in a low voice. "I mean it, get in here."

"I want to put the baby in his crib. He's all done eating. It's time for him to go down for his nap."

"I don't care if it's time for His Royal Ass to fly to the moon."

"Calm down, Michael. I swear, I'm listening to you. I'm paying attention. I heard every word you said."

"About my mother?"

"Yes."

"She wants to buy us a house and come and live with us in it. How do you like that?"

She paused, then she said, "I don't think it's such a good idea, Michael, considering how you don't get along with her too well."

"It's a *great* idea!" he said. "She's got it all worked out. She wants to get away from that wood-pulp smell up in Arcata, she wants to sell her trailer, and come down near the beach and baby-sit for Adam while you work."

"Oh sure," Ginny said. "I'm really going to let her raise my son. I'll be sure to show her where to plug the iron in in case he gets on her nerves."

He didn't catch on, he didn't remember how Agnes burned him, he was too wound up to remember. "It's the ideal set-up," Michael said, looking at her as if she were the most ignorant woman on earth. "It would free me up."

"For what?" she said. "For playing pool?" She knew she was pushing it, but she was only human. He had been talking about getting a job every day since she bailed him out of jail, but all he did was sit around and watch that guy on TV talk about investments and options and highs and lows and pork bellies and raw hogs. The man was a skinny old geezer in a tie, and he kept showing charts that looked like the zig-zags of lightning flashes.

Michael sat and watched him hour after hour, grinding his teeth, slapping his head now and then.

"Free me up to get a job, you fucker," Michael said to her. "Besides, she's willing to put up money to get me a first rate lawyer to get me off the drunk-driving charge. When you have to go back to work at the hospital, her being here will solve all our problems. Instead of me having to stay with the kid, my mother can babysit him, and you can work, and I can be free to develop some new themes."

"Like what?"

"Leave that to me. That's my job. I know all the answers. I'm King of the World."

"Oh, you are," Ginny said. "Sure you are."

Suddenly Michael stood up and pulled off his T-shirt. He did it in one sweep of his arms across his chest, and then there he was, with the red hairs on his chest glowing, his nipples like black eyes, and the light coming up like rainbows from the broken mirror on the floor. He beat his chest and laughed.

"C'mere cunt," he said.

The baby slapped his hands together.

He lowered his voice to a whisper. "C'mere, the King commands you."

"I'm busy, Michael," she said. Confusing shapes were moving in her head; she was sickened by him, and yet in her gut something else was happening, some pull toward him, as if his cock were a magnet, and her womb was a metallic net, streaming toward him over an electric sea.

"I'm in control," he said to her. "Just leave it to me. I *know* *everything*. I *am* everything."

He held out his arms.

"Oh God, Michael," she said, getting up and approaching him. "I don't understand you, I really don't."

"You don't have to understand," he said, as she came into his arms. "You just have to obey."

AGNES ARRIVED AT THE APARTMENT WITH three yapping white poodles. She blew in the door in a cloud of cigarette smoke, wearing her lumberjack outfit. Ginny had met her before, in Arcata, a logging town at the northern end of California which smelled of sour, acrid wood pulp. She reminded Ginny of a lumberjack—a tough-talking, smoking, cursing lumberjack. She wore a plaid wool shirt and blue jeans cuffed at the bottoms. Ginny was fascinated by her pointy-toed sneakers and white bobby-sox. She looked like a girl from the 50s but her innocent ankles didn't seem to fit at all with her bleached, yellow-white hair, or her cigarette-hoarse voice.

"Hey guys," Agnes said, dropping her electric facial machine down on the couch. "I don't look old enough to be a grandmother, do I?" Michael went out to her car to bring in more of her stuff, and Agnes said to Ginny, "Get me the real-a-ty section of the newspaper. We might as well get started."

"Don't you want to meet the baby?" Ginny asked.

One of the poodles was jumping up on Ginny and trying to stick his snout right into her crotch. She pushed him off. He skittered on the vinyl floor and crashed into the side of the kitchen sink.

"Listen, Ginny, you better treat my little darlings with velvet gloves," Agnes said to her sharply. "Those angels are worth a truckload of human beings. Give me a dog instead of a human any time."

"Do they bite?" Ginny asked.

"Not unless provoked," Agnes said. "So don't provoke them."

In bed that night, Ginny felt Michael rigid beside her. Sometimes he did that, stretched his body straight out like *rigor mortis*, like he was a board floating on top of the water. She wasn't supposed to disturb him, it was some kind of meditation he was doing to get his stress level down. He was always trying something new to calm himself down; deep breathing or staring at a silver nail he drove into the wall or some posture like the gurus got into. One whole Sunday he had sat around chanting "OUM, OUM," till it got on her nerves and she had just gone down to sit in the park till it was dark out. When he was done with these sessions he never seemed any calmer to her. He'd just be irritated that while he was in his trance she hadn't done the dishes, or watered the cactus or fixed some button on his Indian madras shirt. The way he flared up worried her. He'd start acting as if watering the cactus was the only thing she should have had on her mind and that it was some conscious desire she had to kill the cactus that was making her forget to water it. Water it! You weren't even *supposed* to water a cactus that much!

She was careful not to touch him in bed. He might accuse her of trying to interrupt his concentration. It was hard to live with a man she had to be so careful with. One minute he adored her, and one minute he was acting like she wanted to murder him. She hardly had any time to think about herself, or what she needed, or what she wanted, when she always had to be so careful about Michael. He was more trouble than the baby.

The baby. She smiled into the darkness. A baby was trouble, but it would grow up and get less troublesome. Adam wasn't like a poodle that would always be stupid, or like Michael, who would always be on edge and ready to blame her. He was going to grow up and be smart and understanding and brilliant and loving. He was the great hope of her life. Maybe it was worth having Agnes here, if she was really going to chip in and get Michael a good lawyer, and help them get a house where the baby would have a real backyard to play in, and his own room.

She would try not to worry that Adam was sleeping with Agnes and the three poodles in the next room. Michael wouldn't let her take the baby into their room for the night; he said he couldn't stand the sound of its breathing. He said it probably had bad adenoids. She said maybe it wasn't good for Adam to sleep in a room with dogs, and with cigarette smoke. But she couldn't argue with Michael when he got like he was now; rigid, nervous. His mother wasn't a good influence on him, Ginny was sure of that. Maybe he didn't even realize how much he didn't like her. But they were clearly enemies; they remembered wars she could only guess at. They had knowledge of battles that were beyond her imagining.

She sighed.

"Shit!" Michael hissed. "Don't jiggle the bed! Don't get me off my concentration."

What do you do in your head, Michael? she wanted to ask. He was no more understandable than a plank from a shipwreck, floating there on top of the waterbed. *What goes on in your mind?* Her mind seemed so simple compared to his. It just sat there, doing ordinary things, and only sometimes got a little depressed, or a little happy. Mainly it had lists of things laid out in it, things to do to keep life running. She liked to keep busy and not think of serious, dangerous things. It was as if there were two places she could be in her mind, and they were separated by a big curtain. In front of the curtain, in a well-lit place, were the ordinary things she had to do, wash the diapers, go to the store, play with the baby, cook dinner, go back to her job at the hospital. Beyond the curtain, way in the dark beyond, were the other things she couldn't understand—why she was born, why she had to die, what was the meaning of all this work and learning and suffering she had to do, what happened before she was born, and what would happen after she died. Ginny didn't want to peek around the edge of that curtain very much—it was better that it just hung there, heavy and thick, like a wall. Michael, though, was always playing games with it, running from one side of it to another, shouting back to her things he said he saw, what he thought would happen in the next life, what God was like. Ginny didn't believe in God; Jews didn't make a big deal about God, talking to him, begging him for private things—they felt it was a

76

waste of time. There were better things to do with your imagination, as far as the Jews were concerned. And with your time. Life was here and now. If you wanted happiness, you'd better get some here, for yourself, and for others, too. You didn't have to be afraid of hell to do good, and you didn't have to do good because you hoped you'd go to heaven and get your rewards.

Ginny's great-aunt Hilda had warned her against intermarriage. She had told Ginny that the first thing a Christian husband would say to a Jewish wife when they had their first fight was "Dirty Jew." Michael had never said anything like that to her. Thank God for that. Auntie Hilda also said that Jewish men were good family men, they didn't beat their wives or drink. Well, Michael had never beat her, not really, though he sometimes broke things pretty close to her, and he definitely did like to drink. He drank and he liked grass and anything that he thought could give him peace. He never got peace, though. He wasn't a solid man. He was always looking for something to hold him up.

Maybe it was his mother's fault. His mother didn't seem very solid, with all her dogs and her cigarettes. She didn't seem very reliable. All her talk about Christ and all the days she had spent in church hadn't made her a solid person. Ginny's mother, whatever her problems were, was at least reliable. She could get hysterical, but always calmed down fast and got busy keeping her house in order.

A mother had a very big job. Ginny took a long, slow breath, trying not to disturb Michael. She had a very big responsibility. She made a pact with herself that she was going to be the best mother for Adam that she could possibly be. It was the least she could do for taking him from his sane natural parents and bringing him to live in a house with Michael.

IN THE GUN STORE, MICHAEL ADMIRED a bullet-proof vest with velcro fasteners. It had a slip-out light-weight shield which was easily removable so the vest could be laundered. A feeling of gratitude came over him. He thanked his earthly brothers for being his keeper, for using their high human intelligence for developing inventions he could take advantage of, for having the fortitude to study difficult subjects and apply themselves to their drawing boards.

He was no slouch, either. He was a fast learner, always had been. Too fast. In school he couldn't stand how the teachers drawled their sentences, how slowly they proceeded from one subject to another. In seventh grade he used to rip off his teacher's clothes while she babbled *Turn to page 63 of your geography book, we will read the first five paragraphs.* His imagination was all that could keep him in the room all those hours. With her dress off, he would pull the hair pins out of her bun and pinch her nipples with them, twisting them tight over her pinkish-purple tits till she screamed for mercy. He could go on for hours that way. Tie her in the aisle, one foot to each desk, poke his ruler between her legs, use his compass with the point in her bellybutton, the radius being the distance down to her furry muff. Usually he could finger his cock through his pocket till the last possible minute, then raise his hand for a pass to the bathroom. Once some girl saw him slouched in his seat, rubbing himself, and she whispered to another girl, and before he knew it, the whole class was looking at him, with his cock big as a cucumber and nothing he could do about it.

Shit! People were shit, they didn't care how bad they made a person feel; even the teacher who he had begun to like a little because in his mind she had sucked him off a thousand times, sent him to the principal's office—and on the way he had gone to the bathroom and tried to get it down by jacking off, but his concentration was broken, he couldn't keep his mind on it, he felt afraid and ashamed, and he would have liked to kill that girl. He could even see her now, in his mind, as he stood in the gun shop; a cunt if there ever was one, in a lacy pink dress, and neat braids with ribbons at the ends, and those bitchy vicious eyes, right on him, between his legs on his most precious, most valuable, most kingly and beautiful part. Laughing, pointing. A man needed a gun to guard against people like her; every man should have a gun, to protect himself against cruel women who had no right to walk this glorious planet. A gun was essential. That's why he was here, that's why he had to have one; he should have had one years ago, and then he could have taken care of the whole bunch of them, his teachers, his mother, that girl with the braids, Irving Fuckface, Manny with his catering truck, the pickle-factory guy, all of them. A gun would wipe the smiles off their shit-faces. He had to get the gun now, before he had a police record. The way he figured it, he wouldn't have a record till the drunk driving business was decided one way or the other, so this was the best time. Right now.

He considered buying the bullet-proof vest, too, but that wouldn't be as easy to hide as the gun, and Ginny would find out about it and get all upset. Especially if he wore it. If he had one, he probably ought to wear it to bed in case some cop broke in looking for dope and took a pot shot at him. And if he wore it to bed, Ginny would start questioning him, the way women always did, push and push and nag and insist till the top of his head nearly blew off.

Women were a curse on the face of the earth. Sometimes he thought of what it would be like to be gay and be done with women forever; to have some guy's big stick hanging in his face, the guy's balls purple and veiny ticking like a pendulum over his face. But he couldn't get with it. The idea of someone else waving his wand, as big as Michael's, as commanding, was irritating to him. Also, he didn't want to give up the idea of tits. They were the one thing he could count on when his mind got over-heated and he needed to come back to something reassuring and comforting.

But women were unclean. Even Ginny said the Jews believed *that*, and if the Jews believed something it was probably true since Ginny said they didn't go in for as much crap as the Christians did. In the old days a Jewish woman who was bleeding couldn't fuck her husband; when she was through bleeding she had to go to a special bath house and show the woman in charge that she could pull a white cloth between her legs and it would come out white, without blood on it. Then, after her bath, and some mumbo jumbo prayers, she could come home and go to bed with her husband. By then it was ten days or so, and they were both horny as hell. It didn't seem like such a bad idea, in a way, because after he and Ginny did it every night for a month, the edge was off it. He sometimes was tired of her, if not for long. But just a little tired.

He thought maybe they should both become pious Jews. They could pretend it anyway. They could pretend they couldn't do it, and just talk to each other about doing it. That would raise the temperature, he was pretty sure. He was getting hot just thinking about it.

Fuck it, he remembered that his mother was living with them. He could hardly do anything with her there. Ginny kept holding her hand over his mouth when he'd start to grunt and push and groan. "Shh, Michael, your mother," she kept saying. If his mother went out for an hour, and he got Ginny in bed, she'd say, "Shh, Michael, Adam is sleeping." He'd like to shoot the whole goddam lot of them!

He stepped to the counter.

"Can I help you?" said the man who owned all the guns.

"I'd like to buy a gun," Michael said in his deepest red-white-and blue voice. "To help keep our country safe."

THEY HAD THREE LAWYERS NOW. Since Agnes had come to live with them, lawsuits were the main topic of conversation. She had hired a criminal lawyer to get Michael off his drunk driving charge as well as an adoption lawyer to make sure Adam's adoption papers wouldn't contain any small print clauses that would mean they might have to return him someday. In addition, Agnes had just "retained" (that was the word she liked to use) a plain regular lawyer for the grocery cart lawsuit: a shopping cart had bashed into Michael's car in the Safeway parking lot, making a big scratch in the fender, and they were going to sue. Michael wanted to sue for enough to buy a new car. When Ginny protested that the lawyer's fee would probably be very high and that the car was almost ready to be junked, Michael and Agnes looked at her as if she were a total moron. Agnes said you had to learn to take people before they took you. She had made a fortune, she confided, by suing as she went along in life. "You probably don't know how much I have," she said, "but it's more than you think. I don't live high because I like to keep a low profile. No one can get hold of my money that way, unless I let it go. When people know you have money, they stay up nights figuring ways to get it out from under you." Ginny didn't know whether to believe her or not. Sometimes Agnes cried poor, now she was crying rich.

She told them that once, in a Motel 6 in Sacramento, she had stubbed her toe, and sued for $50,000 because she claimed she wouldn't be able to work as a mail carrier and her future career was ruined. It happened that just before she hurt her toe she had taken the civil service exam to be a mail carrier, so she was able to prove that the accident had ruined her chances for the job.

Michael went around now imagining lawsuits he could throw at all the people who had ever made him angry. He wanted to sue Manny-the-caterer for not warning him about the dangers of going to a site that wasn't on his schedule. He wanted to sue Irving at the dental lab for not giving Michael fair and just cause for firing him. He was high on suing people all the time. He and Agnes would sit at the kitchen table, making lists of people they could sue and for what trumped-up reasons.

The whole business disgusted Ginny. She would be getting ready for work, where she made $5 an hour as a ward clerk at the hospital, and Michael and Agnes would be talking five million here, ten million there. Poor Adam sat there in his high chair, whapping his spoon down on the metal tray to get attention, but no one even glanced at him. Ginny had told Michael there were no two ways about it; she absolutely would not leave the baby with Agnes who might get so busy with her face in her facial machine that she'd completely forget that the baby was there at all. She'd made an arrangement with Mrs. Flanner for baby sitting, and Michael didn't complain. His mother was paying for everything and it meant the heat was off him altogether.

This morning Agnes was talking about her friend in Arcata who had taken some rich bastard for all he had in a lawsuit.

"Listen to this, honey," she said to Ginny, who hated to be called honey. "This gal was forty years old, a divorcee, who was trying to keep in shape, so she went bike riding every afternoon down the main drag of town. One day a wheeler-dealer big-timer in a cowboy hat pushed open the door of his Lincoln Continental without looking out into traffic, and smash! There went my friend Lilly's fingers. Crushed into a bloody pulp right against her handlebar. She put on a real show, you better believe it. She screamed and hollered for half an hour because she was no dope. She recognized that she had just bumped into her meal ticket for the rest of her life. Not that she wasn't hurt. By God, she was bleeding real blood, but she worked it out pretty fast in her head. She could see the guy was terrified right off the bat. She said he had a diamond ring on his pinky big as a doughnut. So she told him she was a concert pianist! Can you beat that? She told him she was about to make her deebut! And the main thing was—she could back it up. She had this friend of hers who was a bona-fide piano teacher and this friend swore on the Bible that she had been giving Lilly lessons for ten years, and of course Lilly split the take with this other gal, her friend. And it worked. She got what—I forget—a hundred thousand or so in the settlement. Never had to worry about working another day in her life. That's the way to live high on the hog. Sue the bastards. Go to court. That's where the money is." She looked at Michael. "It's not where *you* think it is, Mike, on Wall Street. That's hard work, that's risky. But lawyers and lawsuits. You just have to keep your eyes open for possibilities. That's where our bread is buttered. Lawyers know the score. Whatever they can get for you, they get twice as much for themselves out of it. And when you need them to get you out of trouble, you hire nothing but the best! That's why we're getting nothing but the best for you, Mike. Nothing's too good for my son. Nothing but the best!"

"I have to go now," Ginny said, taking a last sip of her cold coffee. She hated to see how turned-on Michael was by all this. His eyes were gleaming. He was getting hyper; knowing him, he would go out and smash another grocery cart into the *other* fender of his car, at the Alpha Beta or somewhere, and start a lawsuit against *them*.

She wiped Adam's pudgy fingers, carefully cleaning the dimples over each knuckle. The baby was like a breath of fresh air in all this smoke and conniving talk. She hoped he wasn't taking it all in; she was afraid it could spoil him, be a bad influence on his mind. Thank God he didn't have the genes of Agnes and Michael. Maybe his foreign genes would save him from being like them. She adored him more than anything on earth, more than her own self, more than life. She swung him out of the high chair and carried him, with his bag of diapers and bottles, next door to Mrs. Flanner. Michael and his mother hardly noticed. They were buzzing, buzzing about getting rich, and they were too busy even to wave to Adam. He didn't miss a thing, though; *he* knew who loved him. With those dark intelligent eyes, he knew everything.

"Hi, you have a good weekend, Ginny?" Dr. Zaltz asked her as he passed by her desk.

"Oh yeah, how about you?" she said.

"Sunburn," he said. "It's killing me. Know of any good medicine?" He laughed. He went off down the hall to surgery in his sterile green cottons. She watched him bounce along, in that funny walk he had, on his thick rubber-soled shoes. He was exactly Michael's age; he was the father of twin baby girls, who were gorgeous. His wife, Cindy, was a ballet-dancer. She often stopped by the hospital wearing tights and leg warmers when she was on her way home from the lessons she took with some old Russian princess. She was a small pretty woman with black hair wrapped in a tight high knot on her head. Dr. Zaltz was always delighted to see her. He hugged her delicately when she came to the hospital, as if she were a china doll. Ginny felt sad in their presence, almost like crying sometimes.

Dr. Zaltz had gotten his sunburn over the weekend on his speedboat. He and his wife owned a lake-front home up at Arrowhead, and when they went up to the mountains, they took their maid and housekeeper along to watch the twins. Sometimes, when the doctor was unwinding after surgery, he'd sit in the chair beside Ginny's desk at the end of the hall and tell her about the spa they were installing up there, and the sauna, and the solar heating pipes in the roof. Then he'd talk about where they were going at Easter, to someplace in Mexico where they had the best oysters in the world.

At times like that, Ginny thought she understood how Michael felt nearly all the time. Jealous. Angry. Crazy. She could control it; she would feel the needles of envy, and then she'd tell herself it wasn't going to do her any good to start carrying on that *she* didn't have a speedboat and a spa or had never had an oyster in her life, and then she would go back to work and calm down.

Sometimes she wondered why she hadn't married Dr. Zaltz or someone like him. Where did the ballet-dancer find him, and why hadn't Ginny been there? He was so talented, so confident. He was sweet and funny, too. He saved lives, and he joked around with the nurses, and he wasn't one of the doctors that had women on the side. He was just decent. And good-looking. And he probably never broke mirrors or called his wife a cunt.

Sometimes, sitting at her desk, stapling lab results to charts, and then running her feet off in the next second to take a *stet* blood test back downstairs, she would think, *How come I'm living in this same space as Dr. Zaltz, breathing the same air, my heart beating, using up my life at the same rate he is, and I'm getting $5 an hour and he's getting paid $100,000 a year?*

She didn't make a big dramatic thing of it, but it crossed her mind often enough. Didn't she deserve a ride in a speedboat, or a house in the mountains where the pine trees were bright green growing away from the smog, where the air was so sharp it could slide into your lungs without effort? Her lungs weren't perfect, one of them was compressed by her crooked spine, and she sometimes had to take very deep breaths to get enough air. It seemed unfair that her little baby, with his soulful eyes and his wise little mind, wouldn't get what the Zaltz babies would get in this life. The Zaltz babies, who couldn't even talk yet, and didn't know Russia from Africa, would have a luckier life than both Ginny *and* Adam had, just because their mother had married Dr. Zaltz and not Michael.

It was confusing, very confusing. She felt a sudden sympathy for Michael, love and pity for him, mixed together. Let him have lawsuits and lawyers. Maybe he'd get lucky. He believed in luck, and he believed it would be his turn, soon. And if he got lucky, as his wife she'd get lucky automatically. Sometimes she almost believed they were on the verge of big luck. Why not? Didn't she deserve it? She was as good as the ballerina–Mrs. Zaltz, as good as any movie star.

One of the technicians from radiology passed her desk and tossed a little packet of salted peanuts at her. He was a Mexican guy who was really sweet. He had five children already and he was only twenty-eight. "I hit the jackpot," he said. "You know the machine in the waiting room? Today it gives out two for one."

"Hey, thank you, Manuel," she said, looking up gratefully. When he had walked away, tears filled her eyes. Forget Dr. Zaltz; she would have been better off if she'd even married Manuel!

THE GRASS IN THE BACKYARD OF the new house was emerald green. The sun, coming at Ginny like a trumpet, made her want to dance, barefooted, in the bright air. Adam was asleep in his stroller under the patio awning. The smell of the sea air was fresh, salty, clean. She could even hear the pleasant drone of the plane which flew low along the shore, advertising The Country Western store and Blue Grass Records. She loved her husband Michael again, *adored* him. Somehow he had turned the bad end over and now they were at the good end. However he did it—and it was a great mystery—he was taking care of her finally in the way she believed in her heart he was supposed to.

When something like this happened, Ginny stopped attempting to understand if there was logic or sense behind anything. When she tried to comprehend how it had happened, it got completely beyond her and finally she gave up and believed that all her protests and her cautions had been meaningless, just as Michael had told her they were. She would have sworn this could never work out, there had to be some catch to it, some hidden secret which would rise up like a monster in a horror movie and destroy them. But they had been living here, so far, for two months, and the monster had not shown up.

Michael was stretched out in a yellow-striped hammock strung up between the branches of two eucalyptus trees. Behind him a row of oleander bushes sprayed out their yellow and white blossoms. Michael's eyes were closed; his beard and bare chest and thighs glowed in the sun. His chest rose and fell with each breath; she loved the powerful life-force in Michael. It seemed to inhabit him like a real creature, a spirit or an animal which actually lived inside him, nourished him, gave him the energy to accomplish his great plans.

Just look at us, she thought. If it had been up to her, they would still be in the apartment house with the paper-thin walls, and instead they were living in luxury, like Dr. Zaltz. A big house, three bedrooms and a family-room. A garage. A washer and dryer for the baby's diapers. A dishwasher. A sliding-glass door to the backyard from the master bedroom. Of course, Agnes had taken the master bedroom with its own private bathroom, but she deserved it. She had done all this for them. *Why* she had done it wasn't clear to Ginny. That was the aspect of it her mind couldn't follow. But the fact that they were here convinced her that Michael was truly smarter than she was; that his mind was more manly and more complicated. It convinced her that she should simply trust him and let him figure things out from now on. She saw finally that she only understood simple things, and got naggy and nervous when they didn't seem safe. But Michael was a man of the world, and knew how to wheel-and-deal in ways Ginny could never dream of. She should recognize it now and forever and let him be. She should always let him do what he wanted to do. In the end, he really knew best. That's what he was always trying to tell her.

Never mind how he did it. He did it. They were living like royalty. Like the King and Queen. Michael had said so. "Aren't I King Of The World?" he had said on their first night here. "Didn't I make things happen?" She wasn't mean enough to point out that Agnes had helped them happen, but why should she have? When he was happy, he was full of the fire that she adored; lately he was tender, sexy, bursting with hot wild things to say to her. Even though they had had to squeeze their water-bed into a small bedroom, it didn't matter, because at least their room was at the other end of the house from the master bedroom, far away from Agnes. Here they had some privacy. It wasn't really enough, not for Ginny, because when they made love, as Michael got hot and close to finishing, he started making his loud noises. She would have preferred that he control himself. She even worried that Adam might be able to hear, but how much could he understand just being under a year old? He was in the next room, right down the hall. He might think his father was sneezing or coughing instead of coming. That wasn't half as bad as Adam hearing Michael call her bad names.

She let the sun come through her cotton dress and warm her back. Agnes had gone down to the beach in her bikini, with a scarf tied around her hair to protect it from the sun. Michael was always encouraging Ginny to wear a bikini, and then later on he wanted her to graduate to wearing nothing at all. "It's our own back yard," he had said. "You can do anything here." He didn't understand that she didn't want Agnes to see her crooked back; definitely not Agnes, who already didn't like her for a thousand reasons.

But maybe she and Agnes could get closer now. The poodles slept in the master bedroom with her, and Agnes could let them right out to the backyard through the sliding glass door, so they weren't in the kitchen so much, with their slobbery pink tongues, and their pink penises slipping out of their undersides, and their dirty-looking rear ends. One of them still kept trying to stick his nose in Ginny's crotch; she hated that. Another slid along the floor, rubbing his anus on the rug as if it itched all the time. And they had fleas, too. But now they could be outside more, and she might be able to tolerate them better in these new circumstances.

She was trying to be happy. Happiness was a decision; Michael had read that to her from a book called "Getting Happy." Every morning when you get up, he said, you vote for happiness or unhappiness. You go into this little voting booth and draw the curtain and you pull the handle. *Happy. Unhappy.* It's your choice, Michael said.

She reached over from her beach chair and pushed gently on his hammock, so it rocked. His arms went up, wildly, flailing for balance, like Adam's arms flew up when he heard a loud noise, or when she rolled him too fast on the changing table. They were both hers, Adam, and Michael. She owned two men. It was a strange idea, but the thought thrilled her. She owned their bodies. She could lean over now and reach her hand into Michael's swim shorts and put her fingers around the soft tube of his penis and no one would arrest her. His body was hers, as much as her own body was hers. Being married had given her that right. Adam was even more hers. His body was just an extension of her own. It didn't matter that she hadn't carried him in her womb. He was as much a part of her as her hands, her breasts. When she changed him and washed him she always kissed the whole length of him, from his warm sweet forehead, to his nose, to the hollow under his chin (which she blew in to tickle him,) to his powdered chest, to his belly-button, to his precious bobbing tiny cock and balls, to the ticklish bottoms of his pink sweet feet.

Well, for today at least she had voted for happy, had pulled the handle marked happy in the voting booth. Things were working out. Agnes was busy all the time phoning lawyers, making deals, but—Ginny had to give credit where credit was due—she had worked this out. Ginny didn't exactly understand it, but it had something to do with her getting a tax write-off, and putting her name on the deed along with Michael's and Ginny's so that in case she got sued, (she seemed worried that someone was going to sue her soon), they wouldn't be able to touch the house because she didn't own it alone, she owned it with her son and daughter-in-law.

Leave it to the grownups, Ginny thought to herself. Grown-up matters always bored her, *that* kind, anyway. Money and numbers and financial junk. That was a horror to get into; like Michael's investment programs—that old man with the bobbing Adam's Apple, pointing out the ups and downs of the stock market.

Just give her sun and her baby, and the smell of the flowers and the trees and the ocean breeze. Maybe life was working out. Adam's real parents had signed the adoption papers without changing their minds about a single thing. Adele-what's-her-face had never shown up again. Ginny and Michael had gone to court with Agnes, all of them dressed up like an Easter parade, and the judge had signed the baby over to Ginny for life. She would never have to worry about losing him again. And one of the lawyers Agnes hired got Michael off his drunk driving charge by having him plead guilty to reckless driving, and all he had was a year's probation and had to drive carefully. Agnes was their fairy-Godmother. She paid off Manny-the-caterer for his coffee pot, she paid the hospital bill for Adam's birth-mother. Ginny thought maybe she could learn to love Agnes. Agnes had produced Michael and she certainly loved Michael. At least today she did.

He swung slightly, his leg twitching, in the hammock. He opened his eyes till they were two slits. On an impulse, she stood up and kissed him, on his forehead. He grinned at her, squinting into the sun. "Go get into a bikini," he murmured, "I want to see your tits hanging out."

"Oh Michael," she said. She smiled.

"I mean it," he said. He reached under the hammock for his can of beer and found it empty. "And bring me another can of beer," he said.

"Oh, you don't want to drink *now*, do you?" Ginny said. "It's a high, isn't it, just being out here? Maybe later we could take Adam down to the beach, and fly a kite and have lunch there."

"Hey," he said, trying to sit up, but having trouble because of the curve of the hammock. "When I say jump, you *jump!*"

Was he kidding now, or not? She hoped he was because she was feeling so good. But her heart had started pounding; she could never be sure with him. His mood could change so fast, she never knew what to expect.

"Let's go in and have lunch," she suggested, standing up. "You can have a beer with your lunch."

"I want it *without* my lunch! I want it now, bitch! I want it out here and I want it this minute!"

"Oh, Michael," Ginny said. "Please don't."

"Are you my wife?" he roared. "If you are, you better god-damn listen to me."

"I am," she said, "but sometimes you really make me wish I weren't."

He leaped out of the hammock so fast she jumped away and smashed her ankle into one of the bricks around the flower bed. She thought he was going to hit her. But instead he wrapped his arm around her shoulder, and buried his beard in the neckline of her dress.

"Let's go inside for a quickie before lunch," he said. She could see the rise in his shorts, his penis moving up, and there would be no stopping it.

"I have to take the baby in. The bees out here . . . "

"Yeah," he said into her ear. "That's what I said, the birds and the bees." He stuck his hand down, between the crack of her buttocks, pushing the cloth of her dress in tight there. She had to go inside with him. There was no other way. She couldn't pretend to understand him, but there was only one way to keep the peace and be safe; she had to do what he wanted. There never was and never would be any other solution.

IT WAS HARDER THAN EVER TO get away. Now that he was finally out of their clutches, Michael drove very fast toward Fashion Mall. He felt the women watched him like a hawk. He thought about that. Did it mean the women were like a hawk watching *him* or that he was like a hawk the women were watching? Sometimes, while in the backyard, in the hammock, Michael would hear a squeal in the sky and look up, shielding his eyes with his elbow, and there he would see a great bird circling round him, tilting its huge wings against the sun, banking, coming down lower and lower, closing the size of its circles till it was nearly upon him for the kill. *Take me,* he would think. And he would almost feel it happen, the shadow over him blacking out the sun, the sudden cold, the chill of the wind made by the bird's beating wings and then the feel of its talons gripping his thighs, tearing his flesh.

And into this would come their babble. *Would you come in and open a jar of baby food?* He was having a religious experience, flying over the earth in the claws of a winged creature, and they were pulling him down with their stupidity, their female chatter. He felt he could kill them at moments like this. More and more these days he felt he could kill. It seemed a simple solution to terrible problems. Animals in the wild did it all the time. The hawk, above him, killed without conscience for its pleasure or need. Why shouldn't he? Was he superior to natural creatures because he didn't kill, or were they superior to him because they did? If the elephant, King of the Jungle, killed, why shouldn't he, King of the World?

His mother and wife often disgusted him. He'd look at them and see nothing but rot and decay; his mother's teeth were rotten and yellow; if she were that far gone on the outside, what must she be like inside? It was probably time for her to die and make room for some new and clean human being like Adam. And

Ginny—she was still young, but sometimes he would come into the bathroom in the morning after she'd just been there, and he would smell the smell of her insides, something raw and bloody in the air, and he would wonder how he could ever touch her, bury his face in her belly, come inside her with his kingly cock.

He was beginning to like very young girls; children. They had no rot in them. They were almost brand new. He pulled into the lot of the shopping mall and parked, thinking he would just buy a slice of pizza and watch the teen-aged girls in their T-shirts, but instead he began watching the young girls, especially one very young girl. She was eleven, maybe twelve, with long golden hair held back by a pink ribbon tied on the top of her head in a little bow. She was alone, carrying a yellow plastic bag from the Earring Tree; he followed her into Pets For Everyone and stood behind her while she peered at some puppies in a glass cage. He stood so close he could see the golden downy hairs on the back of her neck. When the puppies climbed over one another, she giggled, and the sound of her sweet young voice gave him a sense of wild hope. She was still all clean inside, pure, free of decay. He got closer until the curve of her rump in the silky striped shorts actually bumped his thighs. "Oh, excuse me," she said, turning around briefly so that her hair spun against him. She moved closer to the cage. "Sorry."

He didn't trust himself to talk. He backed off, and followed her as she walked through the store to where the parrot was snapping open sunflower seeds with its hooked beak, then to the cage where the orange-footed finches crowded ten on a perch, then to the rat cage and the mouse cage and the fish tank.

The water dish in every cage was foul with dirt and crap. The newspapers shredded on the floor of each enclosure were wet and brown with droppings. In every fish tank, a fish or two floated, belly up, bloated, on the surface of the water.

Michael thought about how every living thing just kept eating and fucking and shitting and dying; what was the point of it all? A flower or a tree could just sit there and get fed by the sun and the earth; it never had to move, never had to earn a penny. A dead man just slept in peace. But living human beings had to scramble day and night, struggle just to get comfortable. This magnificent, innocent, sweet, unspoiled young girl would suffer

92

just like everyone; if the crazy hunger hadn't started yet, it soon would. She would always feel need, need, need. And for most of her life she'd be searching for some hopeless thing to calm her down; she'd race forever over the face of the earth, looking for money or a meal or a lay.

His heart went out to her. If he were a hawk, he would carry her over the mountains in his talons and drop her in his nest and feed her for the rest of her life, like a little baby bird. She could spread her golden hair out in the sun, and he would fly around the world, getting her the things she needed. He could even come to this mall, and snatch up things in his razor beak, whatever she wanted: fashion-designer sweaters, earrings, yogurt sundaes, giant chocolate chip cookies.

When the girl pushed open the doors to the long empty hallway where the rest rooms were, Michael followed and pretended to be taking a drink from the water fountain. When she came out of the Ladies' Room, he had his fly open and his cock sticking out. He was waiting to catch the look on her face with the camera of his mind. He would nourish himself on that picture. He needed it to shut out the babble of the women at home.

At first she didn't even notice, which pleased him. She looked at his face and didn't respond; didn't even recognize him from the pet store. But then she saw it; he saw her see it, look at it, a quivering redcapped mushroom. He felt the knowledge creep through her like a smash of high voltage, flaring through her nerves till it flashed into her brain like an explosion and blew her to pieces.

She covered her mouth as if she wanted to vomit.

Yes, he thought, even this golden child had vomit inside her. Women were foul even at their sweetest, most fragrant, most ethereal. He was lucky to be a man, lucky to be strong, and to have this hidden weapon attached right to his groin. He was luckiest of all creatures—he had *two* weapons, his cock and his gun.

The girl ran away through the air-conditioned hallway, to where the crowds of shoppers were, to what she thought was safety. She only imagined she was running to safety, but Michael knew no place was safe and soon she'd know it. She might someday mark this moment as the instant she was ruined for life, but he was only an instrument for the inevitable. Sooner or later the knowledge had to come to each person. At least he knew she would never forget him. Good. He didn't want to be forgotten. He tucked himself in, and exited through the fire doors into the sunshine.

Where should he go next? To the girls on Banyon Road. They weren't young enough for him anymore, but they had more flesh, bigger thighs, bigger tits. He couldn't really give them this kind of thrill because they had seen cocks before, they had probably each blown a hundred guys because that's the way girls were these days. Agnes had warned him that girls couldn't be trusted. No one really could be trusted, least of all Agnes. But he needed some entertainment before he went home. He needed it because his head was getting tight. He needed it fast.

"JESUS, MICHAEL, WHERE HAVE YOU BEEN?" Ginny sat in the living room, in the dark, in her bathrobe.

"At church," he said. He thought that answer was a stroke of genius. What could a wife say to a husband who's been to church?

"We almost called the police."

"You moron!" he said, stamping his foot. "*Never* call the police, no matter what! Do you think they have the answers to everything? They don't know shit! And goddammit, I don't want you cunts on my tail about where I am all the time. I'm a grown man! I can take care of myself." He was definitely strung tight. The girls on Banyon Road hadn't been there. He had waited for hours in his car, but the light in their high bedroom window had never come on. Then he had gone to an adult book store and bought a book called *Whips And Chain Games*, but it was boring. He could write a better book than that. There was no quality in anything these days. People were out for a fast buck, they made everything shoddy. He thought he might write a porno book himself, but he didn't even have a typewriter. Maybe he could get Agnes to buy him one, but then she'd be leaning over his shoulder all day, asking what he was doing. How could a man write hot juicy scenes if his mother was looking over his shoulder all the time?

Get rid of them, he thought. Then he remembered that his mother was providing the do-re-me for all his leisure time. Without her he'd be pounding the sidewalks again. Begging assholes like Manny and Irving for the chance to make pennies an hour. Just when he felt like getting rid of women, he realized that he needed them for his survival!

"Michael," Ginny said. "I have bad news for you."

Fear thumped at him. He felt his ears get red. They'd been following him! The security guards in the mall had got a description of him from the girl and they were going to arrest him.

They'd been tailing him all afternoon and night, and now they would have him. He'd go to jail and he'd be fucked in the ass by some six-foot black.

"Where are they?" he whispered, jumping back. He ran for the door. Luckily his gun was hidden in the car.

"Michael! Where are *who! What are you talking about!*" Ginny's face was like a white balloon. He couldn't make out her features at all, he could only see this floating white ghost balanced on her neck. "Are you drunk?" she said. "Where've you been? Are you on something?"

The cops weren't here, then. He relaxed a little. His head was clear as a bell. Ginny's face began to come back. He was glad to see it, in fact. He wished she would laugh, though. It had been a long time since Ginny had laughed. He couldn't remember when the last time had been.

"Here's a joke," he said. "Two Jews were coming down the street . . . "

"Go to bed, Michael," she said. "I'll tell you the bad news in the morning when you're not crazy."

"If I'm crazy now I'll be crazy in the morning."

"You want me to tell you *now?* I will, then. Your mother is selling the house. She has a buyer. We have to be out of here in thirty days."

"What the fuck—?"

"It's true. She's going to make $30,000 profit. She knew the house was a good buy at the price she paid, and she planned all along to turn it over. She just didn't tell us. She had it listed with a realtor as soon as she bought it. She showed me the realtor's ad in the paper. They call it a beach house. Would you call a house two miles from the ocean a beach house?"

"She's nuts," Michael said. "She can't do this to us."

"She's going back to Arcata. She misses her cronies in the trailer park. She misses playing poker. And she said she's tired of Adam's crying. Her dogs liked it better up north. She's already called the old woman she rented the trailer to and told her to get out. She wants us to sign papers."

"We'll never sign them."

"We have to, Michael. She owns this house."

"But we're on the deed. She can't make us sign."

"She's paying for everything," Ginny said. "Don't you understand that? Without her, we're dead."

"Without us, *she's* dead," Michael said. "I'll get the best lawyer. She can't sell the house unless we want to."

He could feel something happening in his jaw. Even his mother was screwing him. Even now, when these days they had long excited talks about lawsuits, when she praised him once by calling him "a son after my own heart," when she had even remembered Eric Feldmutter and once again told Michael that *he* should have been the Eagle Scout, after all that she was going to screw him. What about his goddamn hammock? How could he watch the hawks flying if he didn't have his hammock out in the yard? His head was blowing up. The balloon from Ginny's head was now on his neck, and it was blowing up. If it popped his brains would be all over the rug.

"We'll show her," Michael said. "We'll teach her a lesson."

"How?" Ginny looked terrified.

"I'll take care of it," Michael said. "I'll take care of the whole thing. Don't I always take care of everything?" He took her wrist and twisted it till she agreed.

"You do, Michael," she gasped. "Yes! Yes! You always do."

THE FUMES OF NAIL POLISH BURNED Ginny's eyes. Agnes was polishing her toenails with her foot up on the kitchen table. Her poodles were rooting around under the table, brushing against Ginny's ankles; the perverted one was trying to wiggle his nose against the zipper of her blue jeans. He always seemed able to pick up some kind of scent, even if Ginny had just showered and washed herself with soap and water. She wondered why dogs were attracted to the private parts of humans. She had seen pictures of people having sex with animals in some of Michael's magazines. He was buying more of these magazines lately, and showing her pictures of people getting spanked with hairbrushes and giving each other enemas with long rubber tubes. She could think of nothing more disgusting. When she had been a little girl, she had a lung infection once with such a high fever that her mother had to give her an ice cold enema to save her life. She could remember the feeling to this day; that stretched-out burning feeling in her butt, and the water gurgling through her, hurting and filling her insides till she wanted to throw up, and then her mother making her hold it in, even though it was leaking, dribbling out onto the sheets, because the cold water was supposed to cool down her insides so she didn't fry to death from the fever. She had felt all out of control, helpless and hideous.

Michael had just suggested the other night that she give him an enema, for fun, but she said that if he thought that was fun, he'd probably think drowning was fun, too. He said he agreed, that he thought drowning probably *was* fun, would she like to go down to the beach and try drowning with him? But at least he didn't force the enema business on her. Thank God for that.

She really didn't want Agnes to move back to Arcata. Not that she and Agnes were bosom buddies, far from it, but she felt safer with Agnes around. It wasn't just that Agnes had been paying

98

the bills and the lawyer's fees and the babysitter; it was her physical presence, the knowledge that she was across the living room and down the other hall, and Michael knew it, too. It kept him in line. He hadn't broken any mirrors or tossed any plates in the new house; he hadn't cooked up any oleander tea, either.

The plan was set for today. Poor Agnes wouldn't know what hit her. Even now, unaware, she held up her little bottle of purply-pink nail polish and offered it to Ginny.

"Try some," she said generously, in her hoarse tough-blonde voice. "It'll knock your socks off."

"No thanks," Ginny said. "I like colorless." She was finishing her toast and coffee. Adam was in his walker, rolling around the kitchen, honking the red horn on his steering wheel.

"Don't let him run over the toes of my precious poopsies," Agnes said as a matter of course. She said it all the time. Adam never once ran over the dogs. He could steer perfectly. Ginny had a sense of the day he would take off on his own wheels, *baroom, baroom*, and he'd be gone on his cycle, down the road, straight out of her life.

"You think I've got an even tan?" Agnes asked. She turned her back so Ginny could see what showed under her nylon halter-top. What she saw was Agnes' perfectly straight, even spine. The woman had a perfect body and she didn't even know it or appreciate it.

"It's great," Ginny said.

"I want to get black as a nigger," she said, "so when I go back to Arcata, they'll all die of envy." She talked about going back north as if she were just going down to the 7-Eleven and wasn't going to be making them all homeless as a result of her decision.

"Too much sun can give you cancer," Ginny said. "Skin cancer won't kill you, but too much sun will wrinkle you prematurely. I don't think you'd like that, Agnes."

"Hell no," she agreed. She put her other foot up on the table. Her legs were muscular and agressive looking. Ginny followed the line of her thigh up to her crotch. This woman had given birth to Michael from between her legs. Agnes knew all about the experience of birth and Ginny would never know. Even though Agnes had been through a lot and her husband had died young, she didn't look as if she had suffered very much. Maybe suffering wasn't a thing that showed. Maybe it lived inside a person, secretly, and eventually the person got used to it or forgot about it. Or in Agnes' case, maybe she turned it over to Jesus to do for her. That was the one nice thing about being Christian—Jesus lifted all burdens from the shoulders of the faithful.

Well, Agnes' faith was about to be put to the test. Michael said he wanted to pile it on till "the woman goddamn *felt* something." The blow-up was set for this afternoon. Michael was at this very minute in the garage, getting his attack ready. Ginny didn't like Michael's plan, it seemed too violent. She wondered if they just couldn't sit down and talk to Agnes as if they were all human beings. But Michael said they *weren't* all human beings, that his mother was a witch.

Agnes had already told them to look for an apartment. She warned them to keep Monday afternoon open, which was when they had to sign the escrow papers; the three of them had an appointment with the new buyer. It didn't seem to bother Agnes at all that she and Michael and the baby would be out on the street, that they had no money for rent, that Michael didn't have a job, that Ginny wouldn't be able to buy food *and* pay the baby-sitter out of her salary from the hospital. Nothing seemed to concern her but her toenails.

Ginny knew that in the dimness of the garage, Michael was hammering together a box to put his mother's dogs in. He was excited, almost happy, about his scheme. It sounded stupid and dangerous to Ginny, but she didn't tell him that. If Agnes was going to be gone, and Ginny was going to be left alone with Michael, the last thing she wanted was to have him angry at her.

"All finished," Agnes said, wiggling her toes at Ginny. "Time to hit the road while the sun is high." That's what she said every day when she left the house to drive down to the beach. "Time to hit the road while the sun is high." She packed up her food, two cans of Coke and a bag of Dorritos.

"You ought to get the baby down to the beach more often," Agnes said. She was drawing an orange mouth on her lips, with a thick greasy lipstick. "The fresh air would do him good." It was always a great relief to Ginny that Agnes didn't offer to take

Adam with her. She could never have let him go with her. Agnes would fall asleep, and Adam would toddle into the ocean and drown. Ginny could see his face in her mind, blue and dead, his eyes passionless, open but non-seeing.

"Have a good time," Ginny said guiltily, as Agnes knelt and kissed her poodles on their dirty black noses.

"Cheers, darlings," Agnes said, waving her tote bag. "See you all at suppertime."

When his mother had driven off, Michael dragged all of Agnes' possessions outside—her clothes, her color TV, her electric vibrating body-massager—and dumped them on the grass. Then he rushed back into the house and got on the phone. In twenty minutes the locksmith arrived to change all the locks on the doors. He was a little old man in a blue hat who had no idea what was going on. While he was drilling and screwing, Michael dragged the tall wooden box he'd been building in the garage out to the front lawn and dumped the three poodles in it. They fell in with a thud, scrambling on one another trying to get out. Ginny could hear the sound of their claws scraping the sides. She had the sense that someday she would be in a big pit, too; everyone who was ever alive would be in it, scrambling to get out, and wouldn't be able to.

When the locksmith left, Michael ran outside again and tossed all of his mother's gauzy nightgowns into the air. They fluttered, like weightless, mindless, pink and black birds, till they settled, motionless, on the grass. Michael said, "All we have to do now is wait." Ginny looked at his eyes and saw that they were vibrating in his head. He didn't see her at all. He was grinding his teeth.

She thought she heard the sound of a helicopter and, afraid to go inside with Michael, she kept Adam out front on the lawn to watch it. It wasn't a helicopter at all but the Goodyear blimp looking like a warhead that floated ominously by, vibrating the still air, blocking out the sun. She realized that the clicking she heard in her head wasn't the rotor-noise of the helicopter but was the chattering of her teeth as she shook with fear. The blimp drifted over them like some slow poisonous fog. She hugged the baby against her body and asked herself, *How much longer can I stay with him? What would it take to make me leave?*

THEY HAD TO PUSH THE COUCH against the front door and hold it there. Agnes kicked at the door and Ginny had a vision of her polished toenails breaking off like the china toes of a doll and shattering to pieces.

"Michael, you son-of-a-bitch, open the fucking door! This is my house and you know it."

Michael, leaning forward over the couch with Ginny as they pushed it hard against the door, turned to her and gave her a crooked, lewd grin. He didn't care that the neighbors were probably listening to every word. Now everyone would know their business. One of the advantages of living in the new house had been that no one knew how crazy they were. In the old apartment, everyone who lived there could hear Michael, daily, yelling through the thin walls, and she never was able to look at the other tenants' faces when she had to pass them outside.

"Michael! Open this goddamn door! I got you off your drunk driving, you bastard! I got you out of debt! I got you a chance to stay in this gorgeous house, like a free vacation. You dragged my best nightgowns in the dirt! You little shit! I don't believe this!" Agnes' voice cracked in hysteria. Then she began talking in a low mean voice, as if she had put her face on the ground and was growling through the crack at the bottom of the door. "Ginny, tell him to open the door. If you know what's good for you, tell him to do it right now. I got you your baby free and clear and I can take him away from you. I can tell the adoption agency all about Michael, I can go to those poor trusting parents, those innocent kids who gave their baby to you. I can tell them how crazy Michael is, and what he's done. You don't know half of it, Ginny. You don't know what he did when he was in elementary school. You can bet he never told you that stuff. Open the door. Michael, I swear, if you don't open it, I'll tell your wife what I caught you doing when you were baby-sitting. Do you want her to know that? *Do* you Michael?"

Ginny looked over at Michael who was still leaning against the couch, pushing it hard against the front door. His fair skin was flushed; his forehead beaded with sweat. She hadn't realized how his hair was getting thinner, how his hairline was receding. She always thought of him as being very hairy, with his beard so thick and red. Now he looked less handsome. His pink skull wasn't pretty.

Seeing him in that light alarmed her. If she didn't admire him, what would be left? His handsomeness had always comforted her. Women looked at him when she was with him and she had always felt proud. She thought that other women must think she was lucky to have such a good-looking, handsome, sexy man at her side. She cherished that idea, that someone else might think she was lucky. She knew she wasn't lucky at all and she felt she needed to deceive the world so she could imagine, at least sometimes, that she was. If she admitted to herself that she was totally unlucky, then she would have to blame herself for all the mess in her life. Not only would she still have the mess (for she would always have that), but she would have to take the blame, suffer her own self-hate because she had brought it all on by her own stupidity, or greed, or laziness—all the things she knew she was.

"What did you do in elementary school, Michael?" Ginny asked her husband as he stood there, panting and sweating, while Agnes threatened to come back with the police. Michael just grinned at her. His teeth looked like the ashtray-impression of his teeth he had given her when he worked in the lab, his skeleton's teeth. She felt she didn't recognize his mouth.

"Was it bad, Michael? Did you do something really bad?" She tried to think what it could be, but nothing came to her that could be so bad. He had looked up some little girl's dress? He had put dog shit on his teacher's chair? He had peed in his pants? Nothing seemed that bad.

Agnes was yipping outside, like one of her poodles. She was scratching on the wood of the door with her nails, as if she wanted to claw it down. "I'll get you for this, Michael. You can't get away with this, you know! He can't get away with it, Ginny. I have ownership papers for this house. I have the best lawyers. I have money and you kids have nothing. I'll get you out of here so fast you won't know what hit you."

Michael laughed. He let go of the couch and went to the place beside the fireplace where he hid his grass. It was in a little wicker cabinet that had a plant on it. Ginny watched him roll the dried grass in the cigarette paper.

"Don't do that now," she whispered. "If your mother calls the police you can't be high! Why do you need to get high *now?*"

He kept grinning. Nothing would stop him. He always liked to have a buzz on, even when it was important to be able to think straight. Adam was in his walker, with his fat little bare feet on the floor. He was watching all the activity with interest. He skittered himself across the room like a spider, came to the couch and put his hands out, pressed them against the cushions, as if to help.

"Look at the little bugger," Michael said. "He's on our side."

He lit his joint and inhaled. His eyes were on the ceiling as he waited to go up. Ginny heard Agnes start her car. She went to the window and saw Agnes gunning the motor of her little red VW. Clouds of black exhaust rose up into the sky. Then Agnes jumped out of the car like a spastic puppet, her arms and legs jerking. She gathered up handfuls of her clothes from the lawn. She ran around in her halter and shorts, with her fine suntan, picking up her facial machine and her vibrator and her magic-fingers heating pad. She threw them into the car. Then she raised her fists to the sky. Ginny looked from Michael's mother over to Michael. He was floating away in here and Agnes was having a fit out there.

"God damn it, Michael!" Ginny said, giving up on protecting Adam. It was useless to whisper these fights in his presence; he had to learn about real life sometime. Besides, there was only one kind of language Michael really understood. "Put out that fucking joint and get your ass in gear because you need to get a job or we're going to starve. *Damn you!* You need to get a job and you need to get one right this fucking minute!"

"PAULA," GINNY SAID, "HI. Guess who? It's me, in trouble again." She laughed. "Do you think you can lend me a thousand dollars? We don't have a bean in the house and we have to make a mortgage payment." She felt the weight of the phone in her mind; it was a phone that had the buttons in the handpiece; Agnes had bought it because it was modern. To Ginny it felt too wide, it made her hand uncomfortable and reminded her of a wide sanitary napkin that rode between her legs and wouldn't let her forget it was there.

"What's Michael up to now?" her sister asked. It wasn't an accusation, it was a patient inquiry. Her sister had always had great patience with her.

"It's a long story," Ginny said.

"Why haven't you been in touch with me?" Paula asked.

"Because Michael doesn't want Grant knowing anything."

Michael had once warned her, "If I ever catch you telling your sister what I do, you're in for trouble. I don't want that psychologist-husband of hers figuring me out! Those guys don't know anything! All they do is talk, and they can't fix one fucking thing." They had stopped going to visit Paula and Grant, because Michael thought Grant was an asshole. One time when they had been invited to have dinner there, Michael had stopped at a liquor store on the way and bought his own six-pack of beer. In Paula's house he had snapped off the pop-top of one of the cans and sat on Paula's good sofa with the can balanced precariously on his thigh.

Grant had said, graciously, and even in a friendly way, "Hey, there's a coaster right on the coffee table. How about setting your drink down there, Mike?"

"Listen!" Michael had said, "You think I'm some two year old or something? I know what I'm doing."

Grant had been wearing a knit-shirt with a collar and tan chinos; he looked like a college boy. "Don't be defensive, Mike," he said calmly. "I just want to save Paula mopping up a spill."

"Shit!" Michael had said, banging down his beer can on the good oak surface of the coffee table, "I'll just go out in the yard with the little kiddies and then you won't have to worry."

How could she have kept on visiting there with Michael? She was always having to apologize for his actions. Grant had told her she *didn't* have to apologize for him, that Michael was an adult and she wasn't *responsible* for his actions. But the truth was she was responsible for marrying him. So they had stopped visiting—her sister, and everyone else.

"Do you want me to bring the money over?" Paula asked now on the phone.

"Just mail it," Ginny said. "It might even get here tomorrow. We'll be okay, but there's a mess going on with Michael's mother. She's hiring some hot-shot lawyer to try to get the house away from us. She's living in Star Villas—that's a singles complex about two blocks from here. In the meantime, we have to pay this month's mortgage payment to show good faith or something. We own two-thirds of the house according to the deed, and Michael thinks we may have to buy her out."

"How can you buy her out on your salary and with Michael not working at all?"

"Tune in," Ginny said, with a weird laugh. "Stranger things have happened."

Ginny sang one song to Michael now, day and night. *Get a job! Get a job!* It killed her to see him sitting home drinking beer while she did everything. She had asked for the 3-11 pm shift at the hospital, which meant that she had the morning to grocery-shop, do the baby's diapers, play with him, talk to him, and nag

Michael. Each day when she left the house at 2:30, the baby was napping. She gave Michael an exact list of what to do with him, what to feed him, how to watch him in the yard. Because there was no money for a baby sitter, she had to take a chance on leaving him home with his father.

Sometimes, at the hospital, she would have an image come to her—a lightning flash of a vision—of Michael stoned out of his mind, and the baby wheeling out the door in his walker and into the street, right in front of a speeding car.

One night she told Michael of her fear, and the next morning after breakfast, he took a beach chair and planted it right in the street, next to the curb. He sat down there with a book by the Maharishi Mahesh something or other, some Indian guy with a white beard, and whenever a car passed by, Michael would leap up and shake his fist and scream, "Slow down, you fucker!"

When Ginny said she didn't think the neighbors would appreciate that, Michael turned on her. "You women don't know what the hell you want! You don't want these jerk-offs speeding down our street, do you? So I'm taking care of it!"

"I just want you to make sure Adam doesn't go into the street," Ginny said, feeling helpless, knowing he wouldn't understand such a simple thing. "I don't want you to make the world perfect. I just want you to watch *him*."

"But the world *needs* to be perfect," Michael said. "If it were perfect we could all be happy." He looked at Ginny as if she were the least perfect thing in the world, and she thought that maybe Michael was right; the world deserved to end.

"I'm working on the world," he assured Ginny. "I know what this world needs, I just have to figure out how to get it."

"By reading that book?" Ginny asked him. "Written by that guy holding the little flower?"

"That's your trouble," Michael said, waving the book at her. "You don't have a spiritual center. You don't know how to get quiet inside. The absence of desire is the only true happiness."

"All I desire is food on the table, Michael."

"You Jews," he said, "you don't ever stop thinking about what you want."

"Don't say it, Michael," Ginny begged.

"You Jews—" he said, his eyes flashing. She knew he was

getting on a roll. She would never be able to stop him. "You Christ-killers. My mother was right. Marry a Jew and they want a pound of flesh from you."

"How can you say that about me?"

"Because it's true! My mother said it's true and my mother knows everything about Jews."

"Don't! Please don't, Michael!"

"You," Michael roared, standing in the road, pointing his book at her, shouting so all the neighbors could hear. "You dirty Jew!"

During the night, Ginny was aware of the waterbed rolling wildly and sending waves into her chest and belly. She opened her eyes and realized that Michael was not there, that he had leaped out of bed so fast that the wake of the waves he left behind was still churning under her.

As the water quieted, she became conscious of a strange clicking noise. She threw back the covers and felt for her slippers. The house was completely dark. She went slowly down the hall and sensed Michael standing in the living room beside the fireplace.

Click! Click!

"What is that you're doing, Michael?"

"Nothing."

Click! Click!

Her breath caught in her throat. "Why don't you come back to bed?" she whispered.

Click! Click!

"Please."

He didn't answer her. She knew what the noise was; she had seen enough detective movies on TV. He was spinning the loading cylinder of a gun. *Where had he got a gun?*

"Please—come back to bed."

"We should move to the country," Michael said. "Build a fortress . Buy a thousand pounds of dried food. Beans. Rice. Ammunition. When the cities go, we'll be able to live for years. There's a guy on TV, an investment genius, who thinks that's the only way to survive. Build a bomb shelter. Arm yourselves."

His voice seemed to come out of the fireplace, deep and thrilling. "You and me, Ginny, we'll be the only ones left, the King and Queen of the world." She couldn't see him, she could only hear him. He came close to her, stood behind her and breathed his hot fierce breath on the back of her neck. Her hairs stood up.

Click. Click.

HE COULD ONLY THINK OF ONE thing now: the girls on Banyon Road. The girls. He liked the idea of their being girls. Girls were gentle and tender. Girls were sweet and submissive. Girls were like girls should be, delicate, graceful, sweet-smelling, accomodating. They would bend over backwards to please him. They were not like grown-up women who were bossy, demanding, domineering.

He pushed down on the accelerator. They had better not try to lord it over him, tell him the way *they* wanted it. He'd show them fast enough who was in charge. He felt for the gun in his jacket pocket; the barrel of his gun was long and thin while the barrel of his cock was thickening and expanding in concentric rings like a tree.

Good. He needed a good time. Ginny hadn't adored him for months. In bed all she could think of was Adam or Agnes. She wouldn't concentrate on the smiling buddha with his pungent cloud of incense, or the heating crucible of oil, or the intense body-massages Michael offered. She had an ear as big as a frying pan, cocked to hear his mother or the child. Even now, with his mother locked out for good, and Adam in his own room, Ginny was always tense, or tired from work. By the time she got home from the hospital after her shift ended at eleven pm, he had had all evening to work himself up, reading "Hustler" and "Big Mamas," whereas Ginny was wasted, hungry for a shower and sleep, and half the time talking about some guy who had spit up blood and died, or a woman with a breast shaved off who had got hysterical on the floor.

Not that she ever said "no" to Michael; she never said no— she'd open her arms and let him roll into them but he didn't have her grateful attention any more. She was a hole and she let him in, that's all it was. Fuck, he didn't have to take that, did he?

He suddenly felt tears begin to roll down his cheeks. He felt astonished. Just when he needed to be the toughest he could be, he was sobbing like a woman. Even his own body turned on him, springing surprises on him. He was a victim everywhere; a man double-crossed in life and double-crossed in his own body. All he ever did was wait to see what was going to happen to him. He felt he was nailed to a tree waiting for the locusts to attack, or the plague to erupt. He had an ulcer, he was sure of it. And hay fever. And of course the rot which waited everywhere. Inside him, at this instant, though he was strong as a mountain, some little cell was dividing, shaping itself into a hand grenade which would explode one day soon and wipe him out.

"I have to hurry," he said, wiping away his tears with the back of his hand. "Oh Father," he said. "Oh Dad, you fucker, where are you?" His father had died young; he had *never* had him. Everyone had a father, but not him. It wasn't fair. A father could have taught him the tricks, the manly, lucky tricks that other men knew. Agnes hadn't known shit. She hadn't taught him anything worth knowing.

He hated her. She had ruined him. Shit on her, and on all women who fucked around with their toenails and never saw the big picture.

The girls on Banyon Road were too young to be tainted with rot. He had to get back to thinking about them because his cock had shrunk to the size of a worm, and he was feeling so bad, so very bad.

He sat in the car outside their bedroom and watched the lit rectangle of their window. He felt himself changing form like the mad scientists in the horror movies on Channel 11. He tipped his head back and gulped the potion; he grew fangs, claws; his eyes became slitted like a panther's. Tears rolled out of the slits, drops of oily fluid that stained his fur, his golden fur. But then he stopped crying. It was good. He was feeling better. He should have been born an animal and not a man because animals could act and not have to explain their acts to their mothers and wives. Animals never had to lie. He hated to lie because he was a good man. He wanted to wipe out pain on earth. No one ever gave him a chance.

At least he had a right to wipe out his own pain. *Get a job. Get a job.* Did she think it was so easy? He talked his head off, selling himself, showing them his good points, and they didn't take him. He went from one place to another. He shined his shoes. He followed the ads. He did what Ginny said; he didn't chew gum, he slicked his hair back, he trimmed his beard—but he wouldn't shave it off, God no, they couldn't make him do that, those hippie-haters, those fuckers in suits and ties with their fat wallets and their expense accounts. He knew they would never phone him with an offer. And he knew why. It was because he didn't have an automatic phone answering machine. Because if they called at home and he was there, ready to grab the phone, they would know how anxious he was, that he wasn't independent and sought after. They would know he wasn't a prize catch if he was waiting by the phone, desperate. He told Ginny he wanted to go to Sears and get one and Ginny said he was mad, they didn't *have* $200 to waste when he was right there to answer the phone. He said that was the whole trouble, she was like a pig, stubborn and stupid. Fuck her! Fuck them all! All he needed was a goddamn answering machine to be a success in the business world, and she stood in his way.

He threw the car door open. He was King of the World, and he had to show them. And he would.

The screen door of the girls' apartment was locked. Through the grids of wire he could see through the living room to where the lights of the bedroom and bathroom were gleaming brilliantly. He heard the laughter of the girls. He felt his eyelashes blink across the screen with a cool scraping sound that played in his head like music. The stereo was on, loud, in the living room. He wished he could work it so they could dance a little first, turn down the lights and dance, a slow dance, her head under his chin, smelling of shampoo. Which one did he want first, the blonde or the one with the long dark braids? Maybe two of them was too many. He didn't know for sure if he could last. When he was young, when he lived in San Francisco, in the days he was on acid, he could do it three times in a row without a blink; but now he wasn't sure. He was nervous; he had stress in his life. He had read that stress can slow a man down. He wasn't sure he could depend on himself, trust himself. He hoped his crying jag was over; that was unmanly. Maybe this wasn't the best time to carry out his plan. He wondered if he hadn't thought it out carefully enough. Did he really want two at once? Where would he put one if he was busy with the other? What he really wanted was two at once, one under him, one over him.

His throat felt sore. What if he had strep, and spread it to the girls? He didn't want them to think badly of him. He was a man of morals. He wanted them to respect him. Maybe this wasn't the best time after all. He'd get some penicillin and make sure his throat was better, and he'd come back in a few days. He hated the thought that one of *them* might have a vicious germ in *her* throat. If his magnificent cock was going to get sucked, he wanted absolute guaranteed cleanliness, health.

He moved and the screen door rattled.

"Who's there?" said a girl's voice, fearfully, and then he had no choice but to make his shadow on the screen into steel, no choice but to break through the soggy netting with one wild bash of his shoulder. By the time the other girl had run in to see who was there, he had the screen door and the wooden door closed, and his gun out. He spoke with the tongue of a rabid creature. He could feel saliva lathering his lips.

"Get in the bedroom."

One was hiding behind the other; they were stuck together like two cookies.

"Take off your clothes!" he hissed. He didn't even want them to take off their clothes; he'd hardly had a chance to see them in a good light. He wanted to look at them, memorize their faces, ask them to dance, a slow dance, something to build on. He wanted his arms free to embrace them, but he had to hold the gun. Why hadn't he thought of that? He didn't want to do it one-handed. He had a sudden idea for the perfect weapon; he had just invented the ideal appliance. Necessity was the mother of invention. It would make him a rich man. An attacker should be able to wear his gun around his forehead, wear it like a surgeon's light. The device would leave a man's hands free, yet the gun would always be focused on the victim's face. A string attached to the trigger could be held between the teeth. It was the idea of a genius! Michael felt elated, but he knew he wasn't keeping his concentration; his cock was dying out like a shooting star. He was so busy inventing this tool, he couldn't focus on what he wanted from the girls. One of them—the one with dark hair, was in a white terry bathrobe. Her hair was wet and lay on her shoulders like seaweed. The other one, the one with big tits, was wearing some kind of striped caftan, and he couldn't make anything out, not even her nipples.

He swung his gun. He swaggered. "Take off your fucking clothes now," he said. *"Now!* I'm not playing games." He wondered how the words came to him so easily. He didn't even have to think them; they sat on the edge of his tongue, like his own name, and he said them perfectly.

He noticed that there was a yellow plastic lamp in the shape of a duck on one of the bedside tables. He saw a bride-doll like his sister Taffy had had, on a shelf. He saw a whole collection of dolls from foreign countries. He and his sister Taffy had shared a bedroom for years, and he had stared at those dolls, hating them, every night of his life.

"Get on the bed," he said. "You first." The girls were climbing on each other like spiders. They wouldn't let go of each other. "You!"

The black haired girl untied the belt of her bathrobe, and let it fall open. He snapped the belt from its belt loops and told her to put her hands behind her back. Then, holding the gun between his chin and shoulder, he tied her hands behind her. She was whimpering. He loved to hear her whimper. He loved to see the two of them cowering. They were big proud girls, healthy and young, and he had brought them down by a wave of his gun. He could do anything he had ever dreamed of with them, first with one, then with the other. Maybe he could make the blonde give him an enema. Maybe the dark haired girl would ride him as if he were a horse. She would gallop him around the room. Ideas came to him like poetry. He felt the gold elephants mating in his pocket as they were meant to do. Their tusks clicked like swords. He grinned.

"Oh please, oh God, please don't, oh please, don't hurt us, Holy Mother of God." The dark one was sobbing, her robe hanging open to show her breasts, her nipples, her belly. She had tufts of black hair all over her belly, up the line of her navel. She was as hairy as a man. She was sobbing, begging, stumbling about in her bunny slippers while the blonde, silent as stone, and as cold-looking, had lifted her caftan over her head and folded it and placed it at the foot of the bed. He was right about her. She had huge tits. She didn't say a word. Her face was hard and mean. She was staring at him as if he were a snake. She didn't take her eyes off his face, but lay down on the bedspread and let her legs fall open. He had the sense of chicken legs, white and cold, slimy, splayed open, on the kitchen counter. Her nipples looked red as iodine, bitter and dark.

"Oh please, oh no, Holy Mother of God, spare us, I will pray for your soul." The dark girl was babbling, babbling. He kept staring at the collection of little dolls from many countries. He tried to open his pants—his belt buckle, his zipper, he was messing it up. He wanted to slow-dance to sweet music, but one of them was babbling like a madwoman, and the other one was mean as poison. He didn't know the words to get them to adore him. And he wasn't fierce enough. He tried to trumpet like an elephant but he couldn't do it. He tried to get back his anger, thinking of his mother, his wife, but he couldn't even remember them.

"I'll be back, you bitches," he said, zipping up his fly. His voice was quivering. The splayed chicken legs shot together, the babbling stopped. "But I'll be back and you better be ready for me," Michael threatened. "Because when I come back, you'll be fucked like you've never been fucked before."

"WHY DON'T WE TRY TO HAVE a nice day today, Michael?" Ginny suggested. "Maybe we could go whale watching with Adam. Dr. Zaltz told me he went with his family and it was a lot of fun. We could just drive down to San Pedro, and buy tickets and get on a little boat. It doesn't cost that much. It's such a beautiful day."

"You know money is no object," Michael said from where he was, naked, doing deep-breathing exercises on a spiky hemp mat on the floor. "From now on, money will never be an object, ever again. I told you last night I've invented something that will make our fortune. All I need to do is put it into production. As soon as we win some of our lawsuits, I'll be able to get a factory to manufacture it."

"What's your invention?" Ginny asked. She was trying to show some interest in his projects, because he said that's why he had failed in everything—she wasn't supportive of his ideas. *Why do you fight me so much?* he always begged her.

"Never mind," he said. "You don't have the mental capability to understand it. It's for a technical application."

The baby toddled to where Michael was puffing out his chest like a blow-fish and put his hand down on the springy red-gold filaments of hair which glowed over his father's heart. Michael grabbed the baby in his hands and held him up in the air over his face. The baby laughed with delight, a string of spit falling from his lips and threading its way down to wave in Michael's face. Ginny feared that if the saliva hit Michael he might get furious, even throw the baby down. He was more unpredictable in the last few days than ever before. His moods swung from one extreme to the other. One minute he was talking wildly, full of energy, swinging his arms and stamping around the house, his eyes glittering, and the next he'd be slumped in a chair, his head down, trembling as he ground his teeth.

Ginny didn't want to spend the weekend watching him; she wanted to go out into the sun and smell the sea air and watch the whales. She was sick of worrying. They were going to court soon for a trial about who owned the house; Agnes had served them with papers. Michael was sure his mother didn't have a hope in hell. He was confident they would win. He was confident about everything, especially about getting a job. He had bought an answering machine on their charge card, and was home all the time now, waiting for the phone to ring about a job. The machine had a special feature; he could listen to whoever was leaving a message without the person's knowing it. He hovered near the phone, waiting for it to ring so he could test this special advanced feature. When Ginny pestered him about starting to earn some money, he said, "Don't worry, if worst comes to worst, I'll sell my blood." She was sorry she had told him Paula had loaned them a thousand dollars. That took the heat off him for another month—he could sit around chanting and holding his breath to the count of thirty. He was talking about building himself a bed of nails, like the ones the holy fakirs slept on in India. He wanted to learn to control his body so he wouldn't have to eat or pee or breathe if he didn't want to. He had told Ginny about a ritual in which holy men died by their own free will. They simply sat down in the lotus position and instructed their souls to enter the universe. When people came over to look at them afterward, the only thing left was the husks of their bodies, sitting there, empty as butterflies' cocoons. Michael said it was the achievement of the greatest goal in the world; death by pure willpower. Only truly holy men could do it. He was working on it and someday he would do it himself.

It sounded crazy to Ginny. Why would anyone want to die if he was healthy? But when Michael talked about it, his face was suffused with color and animation. He seemed to enjoy thinking about death. The whole idea of dying seemed like a grand challenge to him. But he said you had to start small, like he was starting, on a spiky hemp mat from Cost Plus Imports, with a naked body and by counting breaths. The point would come, he said, when he would be able to exhale and never desire to inhale again. He could die by choice instead of by violence. What could be better?

Not talking about death at all, Ginny thought. Going out in the world and breathing in sunshine. Buying a ride on a boat instead of buying answering machines and the services of lawyers.

"Hello from your Captain," boomed a voice over the loudspeaker. Ginny held Adam tightly on her lap as the small boat bounced its way over the waves and out to sea. She was sitting on a splintery green bench, feeling the sun warm on her back and shoulders. "I've had a radio report from up around Santa Barbara that a family of California Grays is coming this way, so we should be sighting them before long. I'll keep you posted folks." The staticky sound clicked off.

"Look at the big ocean," Ginny said to Adam. She pulled the hood of his little jacket forward and kissed his nose. She would teach him about the world. *This is the sun. This is the sky. This is the sea.* Michael was pacing up and down the length of the boat. He was wearing a blue wool watch cap pulled down over his ears; the rim of it covered his eyebrows so that his face had a strange, cut off look—it was almost half a face. He was talking to himself. His eyes stared straight ahead, not seeing the ocean, not seeing anything. His lips moved in strange, jerky twitches.

The loudspeaker rattled and came alive. "Porpoises, folks! Look to the right."

Ginny hoisted Adam to her shoulder and moved toward the side of the boat. There, in the glistening water, they saw porpoises, leaping in great silvery arcs, seven or eight of them.

"Michael, look!" she called. He was sitting alone on a bench. His eyes came back from some distant place. He looked confused. "Look, aren't they beautiful!" Glassy-eyed, he came up beside her and the boat tipped slightly as everyone crowded to one side. A young woman, standing beside Ginny, admired the baby. "What red cheeks he has," she said. "Oh—he's adorable."

"What's the best way to hitch-hike?" Michael said to her.

"What?"

"I mean, if you were desperate, and it was freezing cold, raining hard, and you didn't have a raincoat. What would you do?"

"I don't know," the young woman said. She laughed.

"You'd strip naked," Michael said. "It's the only sensible thing to do. You'd stand there in the road in your naked body, and you'd be picked up faster than if you just stood there dressed, trying to hitch the regular way."

The girl looked at Ginny. "What is he, some kind of joker?" she asked.

"The thing is, even if you got very cold without your clothes, you'd probably only have to wait a few seconds, and you'd lose less heat than if you stood there dressed, and had to wait longer. Not to mention that you'd get attention pretty fast if you stood there with your boobs hanging out."

The girl stepped back, and then walked very quickly to the other end of the boat.

This joker, Ginny thought. *He's mine. I'm married to him. God, I'm stuck.*

The great fish were still flying up out of the sea. Michael had pulled his watch cap down over his eyes completely. He was talking to himself. His mouth, like a black hole in his beard, opened and closed rhythmically.

When the family of whales appeared, spouting, coming out of the sea like three mountains, Ginny was clutching Adam against her, filled with nausea. The sight of Michael's face was so alien, so horrifying, that she was getting sick to her stomach. It was lucky, in a way, that she was sick here, on the boat, because no one would ever have to know the real reason. She made her way to the tiny, dirty restroom, which smelled of rotting fish and spoiled bait. She threw up into the toilet. If anyone asked, she thought, wiping her mouth with a filthy towel, she could always blame it on being sea sick.

HE WAS SO SORRY, God, he was sorry. He had to tell the girls on Banyon Road he was sorry so they wouldn't think badly of him. What if they thought he was one of the *really* evil people? He had heard on the news last night about a man who held women as sex slaves and sold their favors to men coming out of porno shops. The man picked up the girls in video arcades and pretended he wanted to buy them a drink. Then he chained them down in his van, and starved them, and sold them to men till they were skeletons and then killed them when they were too skinny to be of any use.

As evil as he was, in a way Michael had to admire him. Let someone else do the work and you be the brainpower behind the idea. He wondered what kind of terrible childhood the man had suffered; it must have been bad, even worse than Michael's, because Michael didn't have that low a mentality. He knew where to draw the line. That's why he was going back to see the girls now, in broad daylight, to say he was sorry, so they would end up having a higher opinion of him. He didn't want his *karma* getting messed up with bad vibrations. He parked his car on Banyon Road and smoothed his beard in the rear-view mirror. He was looking good; he had lost some weight and had a gaunt, intense look that he liked. He was looking like those gurus who meditated in India till they were ready to leave their bodies behind. He imagined the bodies, hard shells, dry and crackly and brown, sitting there on the ground with no one in them. He wondered if, when they were burned, they went up in a single flare, like dry leaves. He wondered what it would feel like, to vacate your body. Or to burn to death. Or drown. There were so many ways to die. He would only be allowed one death and be cheated of experiencing all the other kinds. He felt cheated all the time, by Eric Feldmutter, by his mother, by all his bosses, by . . .

He walked faster up the street now to visit the girls. They were lucky he wasn't like that man who kidnapped women and used them as slaves. He was compassionate and sincere—they would see for themselves when he knocked on the door and apologized. They might even ask him in, make him some coffee, turn on the hi-fi. They would be so impressed by his beauty and sincerity, that they would want to get to know him better. He grinned. He saw himself reflected in the shiny side of a red car. Good posture. Strong shoulders. The signs of strong character in his chin.

He thought that if he ever wanted to have a sex slave himself, he'd have to get a different car, a van at least, or a truck. In a closed truck he could have three or four slaves; three or four cots back there, and then he could take on a whole load of men and make good money. If he waited outside porno movie houses the men would already have shot their wads inside; but outside porno bookstores would be perfect. The men could read hot stuff inside, but they couldn't get relief in there. Then, when they came out, there he'd be waiting, with pussy inside for sale, tied up and ready to go. How much could he charge? It would be the perfect business. No overhead, except the truck, and no upkeep, not if you starved the girls. Some men might even get turned on by a skeleton, you never knew what worked and what didn't. Some men liked pregnant women. Some like two-year old babies. He, for one, preferred women without signs of rot. A skeleton wasn't his idea of fun.

He could see the girls' bedroom window now. He slowed his step because he needed to think and get exactly the right words in his mouth. *I came to apologize for the other night . . . I'm sorry I scared you . . . I'm a nice guy, no kidding . . . Would you like to dance? Look, I'm harmless. I don't have my gun with me. It's buried where the sun never shines. Really, I swear it is. It was just a joke the other night, a prank. I'm just a regular guy. I have a wife. I have a little baby. No kidding. I don't need to do this, believe me. I get all the fucking I need.*

A car slowed beside him in the street. It was one of those white dog-catchers' trucks, with little compartments in which to lock up dogs. A picture flashed in his mind of Ginny's dog Whisper on the day that it was paddling out to sea to drown. He could see its puzzled, drowning eyes. He could feel in his own body, as if he were a psychic, that moment when the dog went under, down, down, the sensation of choking as the water came into its lungs. Son of a bitch, it was the moron dog's own fault. He could have turned around and paddled back to the boat, but he had his mind set on dying.

The dog-catcher had come out of his truck now, and was standing in the street, holding a length of rope. It had a loop at one end. The man looked a little stupid to Michael.

"Hey, you see a big collie go by?" the man said. His voice wasn't steady. He was tall and nervous looking. He kept glancing over his shoulder. "Big mean bitch? Dangerous?"

Michael squared his shoulders. He could handle dogs. Probably better than this guy could. He could easily be a dog-catcher. Why hadn't he ever thought of that? Maybe he would get a job as a dog-catcher.

"I'll keep my eyes open," Michael said. "She bite someone or what?"

"Worse," the man said. "We have to round her up or she'll kill."

"Rabies?" Michael asked.

"Worse."

"Trained killer? One of those mean guard dogs? An army dog?"

"Yeah. We've got a bulletin out on her. Don't be surprised if you hear sirens around here. We're trying to surround her."

Just then two police cars came up the street on one side, and another one came up the other side.

"The cops are helping me look," the dog-catcher said, and Michael caught a tone in his voice he didn't like. A lie. The man was talking too much.

"Well, I have to be going," he said, and just then the doors of the squad cars flew open all at once, and six cops rushed at Michael. He saw a flash of revolvers, and black thighs. Shit. One of them was bending back his arm till it nearly broke. *What the fuck!*

"It's him, on the same goddamn street, for Christ's sake!" said the dog-catcher. "Would you believe anyone would be so dumb?" The dog-catcher was flashing a picture at the cops; it was a drawing. It looked like Michael a little, a guy with a beard, with his sharp eyes. "He was coming back to finish the job!" the dog-catcher said proudly. "I just found him walking down the street, just like that. He matched the description so close I didn't think I could be wrong. So I radioed right away."

"Yeah, well we thank you," the cop said who was breaking Michael's arm. He felt handcuffs go on him. So that was the end of that. No slow dancing, no slave girls, no time to make a good impression. He was caught and done for. And he was no worse than any other man, just unluckier. He knew the cops were just as guilty as he was; the dog-catcher was guilty; in their minds they had all raped those girls and owned slaves who they starved and sold to other men, and they had tortured their own Irving Fuckfaces and murdered their mothers.

Michael was as wise as God. He was the mind of God. He knew what was in the hearts of men and he pitied them all, cried for them, buried the husks of their bodies as they flew up to God. He was going to jail now, and what lay ahead was so terrible, so hideous, he wasn't even sure the King of the World could bear it.

WHEN THEY WERE NEWLY MARRIED, they had frequently played a game called *Whose fault was it?* It took up a great deal of time, and on weekends when there wasn't enough money for booze or pot for Michael, or even for a movie, they would find it a grim entertainment. When it was Michael's turn for *Whose fault was it?* he blamed his father for dying young, and his mother for everything else. If he wasn't successful, rich, lucky, powerful, it couldn't be his fault, so it had to be theirs.

Now that it was very late at night and Michael was not home, Ginny needed a way to pass the time. Her stomach was tight with fear. Adam was sleeping, and the windows were all black. She lay in the chilly waterbed in her aqua chenille bathrobe and played *Whose fault was it?*

She started with an easy question: Whose fault was it that the waterbed was cold? The heater had given out a week ago, and Michael had looked up "Waterbed Heaters" in the Sears catalog and had promised to order one. Every day when Ginny went to work at the hospital, she reminded Michael, politely, to remember to call Sears. She suggested it each afternoon just as she was leaving, sticking her head back in the door and saying, in a lilting cheerful voice, without a shred of accusation in it, "Please remember, Michael . . . call Sears." She didn't say that the muscles of her back were tight and aching from the cold; or that her neck was stiff. She didn't say that she felt she was sleeping in a cold muddy swamp every night. She didn't tell him that she had dreams of sinking to the bottom, her arms and legs entangled in strands of strangling seaweed till she froze or choked or drowned, thrashing hopelessly while the life went out of her. In one dream, Michael stuffed her and her precious dog Whisper into a green glass Coke bottle, and threw them overboard.

Sleep, which had been her one escape, her rest from life, her peaceful disappearance from troubles for a brief, blissful while, had now escaped her. If she slept, she woke at once, listening for the dreaded *Click, Click* of the gun, the hairs on her arms electric with the sense of Michael's being gone from bed. A few nights ago she had heard the *Click* and was certain Michael was coming down the hall with the gun pointed right at her, but when she roused herself she could tell he was sleeping, hot as lava, on his side of the bed, and the noise was from Adam's room as he drew some plastic toy across the rails of his crib. Then, just last night, she had wakened and knew at once, from the icy void beside her, that Michael was gone from the bed. With her eyes as cold and hard in their sockets as marbles, she stared into the blackness, listening. She heard a drawer slide open in the kitchen. She heard the metallic click of utensils, then the rasp of a knife being pulled across the cutting board, its serrated teeth sawing wood.

"Michael . . . " she had called, her voice quivering. "Get me a drink, too, would you?" Then she prayed. *Let him be fooled. Let him think I don't know what he's doing.* The knife drawer closed. She finally breathed. She heard him shaking the corn flakes box, the dry rattle of the last few flakes dusting the waxy paper sides. Then the rubber suck of the refrigerator door opening, and the slosh of the milk container. But she didn't sleep, not in those icy waters. Soon after she heard the back door close. In the dark, she made her way to the window and she saw him at the far end of the yard, digging! Digging what? Her grave? He was down on all fours, digging like a dog, throwing dirt up behind him, flap flap, the lonely gravediggers' sound of earth falling on earth. *About to bury what?* She couldn't ask him. And she couldn't sleep, not even after he had shuffled back to their room and fallen, like a dead tree, smelling of soil, onto the frozen surface of the bed.

Whose fault was it? Maybe it was the fault of drugs. Maybe they had been born into the wrong generation. Other generations had had to work for their highs, wait for their thrills, and when the thrills came, they came maybe years apart, much too long a wait for someone like Michael. He had no patience at all. He was a person who couldn't, under any circumstances, say "no" to such easy joy. Ginny had seen the miracle at work in the hospital—a cancer-ridden man moaning with pain, eyes black-rimmed from too much radiation therapy, his fear bringing the walls in on him. And then the nurse would administer a shot of Demerol, and instantly heaven came floating down like a soft veil. In five minutes the man would be at peace, restful, able to smile, then to sleep, free of pain.

Michael kept trying to sell the idea of this pleasure to her. She could only resist so much. *Don't you trust me?* he always used to ask her when she refused a pellet of peyote, a joint, some acid. *Don't you want to let me lead you into the greatest moment of your life?*

Somewhere she still had the notes he took the night she agreed to go along with it. Why not look for them? She would never sleep, anyway, not till he came home. Where *was* he, oh God, where was he now? *Whose fault was it?*

They had gone to The Green Unicorn in Haight-Ashbury; Michael had assured her it was the best place to trip on acid. The people there were sympathetic. If someone hit a bum trip, they wouldn't freak out or call the cops. If anything, they would be helpful.

Ginny rummaged in the box of documents she kept in her nighttable drawer; it was where she kept Adam's adoption papers, and her marriage license. And there she found the ragged notebook pages in Michael's scrawl. She settled back to decipher the words:

Ginny says she feels she's floating up the hill. Says her jacket is like cement. Sees hole in boy's pants. Picks a rose and eats a petal. Says it tastes like satin. Then wax. She spits. Kicks a green bottle. Says it is a giant grasshopper, then its head falls off. Then its legs. Cops pass. She says, "Wind my clock." In The Green Unicorn, the wooden seats turn into foam rubber, she slips down under the table, puts fingers into tea, dips fingers into candle. Hot wax, fire. Starts to talk about walls. (Now I am writing her words:)

"Walls, bleeding and cracking. That's a very sad wall friend. Words are written on it, I can't see, I'm crying. Oh yes, it's a burlesque show . . . it's a very sad wall. It's breaking up and bleeding. There's one eye up there, it's so sad. Two dwarfs are kissing each other. Oh God, they're devouring each other. That makes me sad. They're eating each other and kissing each other, the eye is right above me, sometimes they're in full face and sometimes in profile. I didn't know it was my face. It is my face. Except I really don't know what I look like. Sometimes I'm Bridget Bardot, or Sophia Loren. I'm having this thing with Sophia

127

Loren. Like a newsreel, my brain hurts. Michael wearing a headband, Michael with my face. Layers of thin things you can see through, to layers of white and blood, heart of the matter, Christ, ugly on cross, I want to see inside people, see their systems working, like clocks with gears. The clock is stopping, war is killing the children. I still haven't read the wall, it's not producing . . . if only the dwarfs would stop devouring one another!"

Ginny looked at the black windows and remembered the dwarfs eating each other. She knew it was her and Michael, who else could it be. *But whose fault was it?* She could have left Michael in San Francisco, pulled herself out of his magnetic field, gone on to be someone, do something with her life. But she had been a coward, and lazy, and spineless. She could blame it on her father who died without saying goodbye to her; or on her mother who had made her weak. "You don't need to carry that heavy box, you need to rest, Ginny. Sit out in the sun. Why should you study so hard? You'll get tired out." Sit and rest, her father told her. We'll take care of you, her mother told her. So she believed she was supposed to be taken care of, all the time.

Well, it was over. No one was taking care of her. All she had was black windows and a frozen bed and a little baby who *she* had to take care of, and a sick husband who was worse trouble than the little baby. His crazy mother, Agnes, with her poodles lived a few blocks away, cooking up lawsuits against them, and it was four a.m. and Michael was never coming home again. She could blame him but what was the point?

She watched the phone. She held the crumpled papers from her acid trip in her hand and she stared at the phone, willing it to ring. She was so tired of waiting. If it didn't ring in the next half hour, she was going to climb into Adam's crib with him, and press his warm damp body against her icy skin. Maybe that way she could get to sleep. And in the morning she would think of moving with him to Canada, so when he was old enough to go to war they couldn't get him.

She stared at the phone till she made it ring. It didn't move at all when it rang, though the sound was loud enough to split her head open. She picked it up, ready to hear Michael's weak, pathetic excuse for being so late, his groveling apology.

"Yes?"

She heard a voice so strong and loud she held the receiver of the phone as far from her face as she could. She watched the voice come out like thunder. The phone trembled.

"Mrs. Fisher?"

"Yes."

"This is Lieutenant Kresge, calling from the county jail."

Whose fault was it?

"We have your husband in custody."

You were speeding. You were drunk. Oh Michael. Not again.

"On what charge?"

"I'm sorry to tell you this, I really am. Your husband was picked up this afternoon. We just got a positive identification from the girls. I'm so sorry to have to tell you this news, but your husband is charged with attempted rape."

MAN HELD IN RAPE TRY

Police Friday arrested Michael Fisher, an unemployed dental technician, as he returned to the Banyon Road apartment complex of two women he is believed to have attempted to rape on February 11. An animal control officer driving past the apartment complex said he recognized the suspect from a prior description and called officers for assistance. Detectives said they are questioning Fisher regarding other sex-related cases in the area.

There was Michael, on the first page of the Daily Star, famous at last. His picture now lay staring at the sky on the lawns of all the houses of their neighborhood. His face on the mug shot had a look of passion on it, as it sometimes did when he climbed on top of Ginny after he had oiled her body and was ready to slide home: mouth slightly open, nostrils flaring, tongue protruding in deepest concentration. His eyes were hard and narrow, having the wild desperate intensity of a creature focused on survival, or of an animal who is cornered.

Holding the newspaper in her hand, Ginny sank down on the ground in the front yard, feeling the sharp grass prick her bare thighs. She tucked her nightgown down in the space between her legs. Adam, who was holding onto the door frame, let go of his support and came reeling toward her in a snaky path, smiling his new cocky smile now that he was walking. He approached in jerks and starts, pitching forward, flailing his arms, getting on course again, zooming toward his destination—when he found his balance—like a windmill. He was wearing his blue corduroy overalls and tiny bright red sneakers. As he reached her, his knees gave out and he fell down across her legs with abandon. His head dove into the newspaper and he laughed.

God forbid that Adam should ever see that picture! His father's face! His rapist father. She swooped the newspaper from under her son and flung it as far as it would fly; it scattered over the grass, flapping and unraveling like a bird peppered with shot.

Adam thought it was a game and started creeping toward the sheets of paper. The sound of gravel underfoot brought Ginny's head up. A man was walking by on the street, tossing rolled-up ads onto each lawn. He was young, but dressed in shabby clothes; at first she thought he was a black man, but then saw that his face was only stubbled with dark growth. He dragged his feet, letting his eyes stay in one place as if his head were on a pivot. His eyes were between her legs.

She felt her lips draw back; she felt an ugliness coming over her; how dare that man look at her like that. *Fuck off!* she thought. If he *ever*, if any man ever, looked at her like that again, she would kill. If Michael ever tried to touch her again, if he ever tried to have sex with her, she would kill *him*.

The man was holding in his hand the rolled-up ad, a long cylinder, low down, pointing it at her.

"Don't you throw that junk on my lawn!" she yelled. "I don't want that stuff flung on my property. You throw it and I'll call the cops!" She sounded hysterical, but what did it matter? The neighbors already turned their backs when they saw her outside; they had heard plenty, they knew all they needed to know. Fuck them, fuck them all. She had been up all night after the phone call from the police, and she hadn't eaten, and she hadn't been able to understand any of it. Rape. Two women. Being questioned for other sex-related cases. *Her husband.*

What was she to do next? Feed Adam. Change his diaper. Just this morning, after she had powdered him, she had kissed his belly-button, and his bare tummy and his tiny penis. His genitals were so soft, so vulnerable, so complicated with their many parts and shapes and colors and textures. They lay between his legs like a little toy, intriguing him so much that he often reached down and felt for what was there, pulled, almost roughly, at those irridescent, innocent parts. It was such a leap of imagination from those delicate tender shapes to what she knew of Michael's parts in their frequent state of excitement: distended, purple, veined to bursting. Would Adam someday point his penis at a woman like that man had just pointed his rolled-up ad at her, like Michael had pointed his cock at those women, and threaten her?

Her pulse was beating against her eyes so hard she had to cover them for fear a fountain would burst out and drench her lawn with blood.

What should she do? The policeman had said Michael was being held on $10,000 bail. Why would anyone want to let him out for any amount of money in the world? Let him rot in jail, she thought. And then began to cry, stupidly, helplessly, not quietly. She grabbed the baby in her arms and ran inside. Then ran outside again, to seize the newspaper, smash it into a ball against her, streaking her cotton nightgown with newsprint and making her fingers black.

Inside the phone began to ring. What if it were Michael? What would she say to him? Or her mother! She could never face, see, talk to anyone she knew, ever again. Shame. It covered her like a burning cloak, it seared, took fuel from her dry heart, flared.

Adam tottered to the phone. He fell on it, victoriously, and its shimmering ring splattered and was silent. From the floor came her sister's alarmed voice, tiny and distant, calling her name.

"Hello! Hello! Is that you, Ginny?"

She lifted the phone from the rug and held it, silent, against her ear.

"What's wrong?" Paula said. "Is anything wrong?"

"Oh God."

"Tell me. It's Michael."

"Yes."

"He's gone."

"Not exactly."

"You asked him to leave? You told him *you'd* leave?"

"He's been arrested, Paula."

"Arrested. For what?"

"I can't tell you."

"You don't know?"

"I know, but I can't say it."

"He can't have murdered someone."

"Worse."

"This is crazy. How could anything be worse? Was he driving drunk? Did he hit someone?"

"Rape, Paula."

"*Rape?*"

Ginny began to cry.

"I'll come over," Paula said. "I'll leave right now. I'll be there in less than an hour. Hang on. I love you. Hang on and I'll be right there."

"MOVE IT! Move it back there!"

"Move it along, ladies. You wanna be here all night?"

"Hey—can't we wait inside or something? My ass is freezing out here."

"You know something better to do with your ass? Come over here and we'll talk business."

Ginny braced herself as the wind flapped in cold bursts off the concrete walls of the jail building and battered her sore body. She had been standing on line for two hours. Every twenty minutes the guards let 75 women go in and then the door clanged shut.

"What's yours in for?" a Mexican woman behind Ginny asked the black woman standing in front of her.

"This time?" The woman's purple painted mouth pulled into a round hole, puckered as if a draw-string ran through it. "Let's see—this time it's just a drug bust. Last time it was felonious assault." She laughed. "What he do to me at home don't count as nothing. But he takes a swing at some dude who asks for it, they put him in jail." She laughed again, opening her mouth so that the wind filled it and she coughed. "Shit weather for standing out around in," she said. "What's yours in for?"

The Mexican woman was wearing a black sweater with rhinestones all over it. She looked like a starry night.

"Mine was tired of us eating beans. He hit a gas station. They were wired up with some alarm. And I'm pregnant, too. Again. My mother's at home now with the other three kids."

"I don't have kids," the black woman said. "Praise the Lord."

"Listen—I love my kids," the Mexican woman said. "What joy have I got *but* the kids?"

"We had kids he'd throw them out the window. Just as well this way." The black woman touched Ginny's shoulder. "What's yours in for, honey? This your first time here?"

134

"Yes," Ginny said.

"You get used to it. It's not so bad when you know the ropes. It's no different than waiting on line at the Food King."

The two women opened a warm space for her in the absence of wind between them. She could join them by telling her story and make friends! But even here Michael kept her from having good friends. If only he had been busted for drugs or had mugged someone. She was too ashamed to tell them what he had really done. They looked like women whose men were faithful to them; they had big breasts, shining black eyes and soft, vulnerable lips.

"A car," she mumbled. "He stole a car."

"He'll be out in no time then," the Mexican woman said. "Don't you worry."

"Move it! Move it up here!" The guard up at the front of the line was banging a club on a metal railing, and the women ran forward into the gap made by the crush of visitors who had just entered the building.

"We'll be next," the black woman said reassuringly. "We'll all be nice and warm, soon."

Ginny moved forward with the line. She felt herself thinking about where she was with two parts of her brain. Her head was split down the middle like a cookie called a "black and white" which her mother used to buy for her in the bakery when she was a little girl. The black side was chocolate, dark and sweet, buttery and clotted with lumps of fudge; the white side was lemon-vanilla, cool, almost tart, iced with a smooth glaze, pure, perfect. Half of her wanted to be on the dark side with these dark sweet women, to be part of their warmth, their wisdom, their comforting knowledge. And another side of her, her cold, white, pure, superior side, her mother's side, scorned them. She didn't belong here with these low-class individuals. She was only here by a quirk of fate. She could have married a doctor, a lawyer, anyone . . . she, unlike them, could be living like Dr. Zaltz's wife,

135

with maids, with summer houses, with sailboats, with ski trips. It was purely an accident that she was here, outside the jail, in the night wind, with the wives and sweethearts of robbers and murderers. The accident that had brought her to this moment was itself a mystery—it could be blamed on the random choice of her taking the art class where she had met Michael, or, going further back, on the particular sperm of Michael's father which had fertilized whichever egg of Agnes' that had shot out of her ovary on the critical day. Or maybe it had to do with some odd little twist of the curves in Michael's brain. Sometimes, in the market, when she saw packages of cow's brains, she stared at their white convoluted roadways and wondered how such an inert and hideous thing could command the body of a cow, tell it where to move its graceless spindly legs or where to dip its square heavy head to find the water trough. Everything was accidental. Michael said it wasn't, that every act was destined, plotted by a Grand Designer. In the last few weeks he had begun to believe he had once been, in another life, an African who had been captured, like Kunte Kinte, and shipped to America on a ship. He had discovered a thin red line around his left ankle, which he was certain was the place the chain had been fastened. Ginny told him it looked more like an infected mosquito bite.

"Hey, why can't you *support* me, you ignorant bitch!" he had shouted, kicking the coffee table so hard that a chip of wood flew off.

Why then was she here to visit him? Did she *want* to visit him, this man, her husband who was now a prisoner in jail? Why had he done what he did? Would he tell her why? What would she say when she saw his face? *Why*, when he had her at his beck and call, day and night, when he could do with her as he pleased, do it whenever he wanted to, *why* would he want to straddle another woman, hang over her and do that private, personal married thing with a *stranger*?

"Move it, move it! Slow down, lady—you don't need to shove like it was the last train out of Siberia!"

The guards were counting the women in. Ginny made it, just barely, the second from the end of the line.

She was marched around the huge room as if she were the one who was a bad person or a criminal. Blasts of hot air blew down on her head from grates in the sooty ceiling. The women walking in front of her were being directed, one after the other, to slide into glass-enclosed slots. Ginny entered her cubicle, took a seat on the wooden chair, lifted the grimy phone receiver as the printed instructions on the table told her to do.

She seemed to be in a hall of mirrors. Each woman, within the dusty glass barrier of her cubicle, appeared to be a reflection of all that she was feeling. Each face she glanced at was suddenly her own face—hard, taut with apprehension, edgy with some sudden doubt. Outside in the cold, the women had seemed relaxed, accepting of their fates, almost light-hearted, but now she saw that their faces were really tinged with anger. None of them wanted to be here. None of them wanted to be alone on the outside, waiting for their men, waiting to have a normal life again. Their men had made victims of them just as they had made victims of whomever they had robbed or mugged or murdered.

Her heart nearly stopped beating as the criminals filed in. The presence of the men changed the nature of the room suddenly, shattered the breathy hot air with the jerky muscular swinging of their arms, the pounding of their shoes on the floor, their heat and commotion and most of all their restrained power. Ginny saw them as if they were bombs, waiting to explode.

When Michael took the seat opposite hers in his glass cubicle, when he lifted the receiver of his black phone, in that moment just before he said a word to her, she felt his destructive aura and saw herself as a person who had sacrificed her life for his. His face was wild; all his tremendous energy was blowing up his head. His eyes bulged. He pounded on the glass and puffed his question into the phone as if he had been waiting to exhale it for an hour.

"So what is this going to mean to us?" he demanded, as if his acts could be assessed right here and now, without a judge or a jury. He asked the question as if his mind could be put immediately at rest by a soothing word or two from her.

She tried not to receive his feelings. A shell was beginning to form around her, not as hard or clear as the glass box which defined her space, separate and safe from him, but made of a sinewy, protective material, like nylon netting, something that she could breathe through.

"Bail me out!" he begged, moaning, not seeing her at all, only seeing his own need in the reflection of his face on the glass. "You've got to get the money. I can't stay here! You know that. Anyone knows that. Even my mother wouldn't want me here. Try to get the money anywhere; my mother. Your mother. Your sister. I'll need the best lawyers, nothing but the best."

His eyes were rolling, although he had not yet looked at her, not once. "Find out when's the soonest I can get out. It's not safe here."

He had no sense at all that she was living through this, too. "I don't think you should get out," she said softly. "I don't want you out, Michael."

Finally he looked at her.

She was grateful for the hard glass between them. "I think you wouldn't do well at home, Michael. You need help. You need to figure out what's going on with you."

He stared, his eyes like ice chips.

"They'll kill me here," he said. "I'm a pretty boy. You know that, I'm so pretty you could eat me up. They want to eat me, Ginny. I heard them talking last night. They'll get me and trade me around. They'll *rape* me."

The word made her nipples contract.

"You've got to let me come home."

She shook her head.

Michael slammed down the phone. His face went to pieces. His eyes, which looked at her from two different planes of his head, rolled.

She hung up her phone and sat there, trapped in the cube, staring at him. By the time the twenty-minute bell rang, releasing them from each other, he seemed blind. He staggered away, herded in with the other men, head down, stumbling and swaying till she could no longer see him.

138

GINNY TURNED INTO THE PARKING COMPLEX at Star Villas. She drove up a long ramp, turned right into the underground parking structure, then climbed level after level with the sense that she had entered some kind of automatic ride in an amusement park. She got dizzy turning the wheel. Obediently she kept following the white arrows, up and up and up, till she wondered if it wasn't a cruel joke, if at the top she wouldn't drive out on a plank and plunge miles below to the city.

Star Villas, the sign out front said. "The fun-place for singles!" What was Agnes *doing* here! Why hadn't she taken her lawsuits and her facial machine and her dirty white dogs and gone back to live among the sour tree pulp stench in Arcata? Well, her fun life was about to suffer a rude jolt.

"Your son was a bad boy." Ginny was getting the words ready. When she was six years old, a boy named Joseph had hit her on the back with a short rubber hose and forced the breath out of her. When she could finally stand, she knocked on the door of his house and turned to show his mother the red raised swelling on her back. "Your son was a bad boy," she had said and the woman had laughed at her and slammed the door shut.

What wounds could she display to Agnes? Where were the marks of this marriage? Ginny reached the top level of the parking structure where tenants' boats were stored on trailers in marked stalls. There were no cars up here—it was deserted. She parked and killed the engine.

The poodles scratched at the door and yipped madly when she knocked. What was she going to say to someone who wasn't on speaking terms with her, to someone who was her enemy? The woman had hired lawyers to hurt her, to evict her from her house, to cheat her. Did the kind of news Ginny was carrying automatically create a truce in this war?

The door pulled back. Agnes had her head wrapped in an orange towel. Without her painted mouth, with her skin-colored bathrobe hanging on her, she looked ravaged, ashen. The pom-poms on her slippers trembled. She wrinkled her nose in confusion.

Let her wonder, Ginny thought. Let her stand there. One of the dogs jumped up and stuck his nose between Ginny's legs. She kicked him away, hard, and he ran whimpering, tail tucked under, skittering in the slate entryway.

"It's me, Agnes. Don't call your lawyers. I have something important to tell you. It's about Michael."

"He's been in a car crash!" she said. Her pale eyes blinked. She waited for affirmation; clearly she could imagine no other reason for Ginny to be at her door. Ginny waited to be asked in. Let her be in suspense. Let her feel guilty. Let her think that her son had died. Died of the aggravation his mother had caused him. But Agnes didn't look guilty or even too worried. She patted her towel. Ginny had the feeling she was wondering what to wear to the funeral.

"I wouldn't be here, except that Michael is in jail for attempted rape."

She watched Agnes' eyes narrow. They ticked there like faded wooden beads in her hollow head. What could a mother say to such news?

"It must be a trumped-up charge," Agnes said finally, exhausting in her narrow brain all the alternatives. "Of course you know that." She stepped back to let Ginny in.

I turn him over to you, Ginny thought. *I'm through. I give him back. You made him, you take him now. He's yours, body and blood. I'm not related to him.*

She felt she had just had a revelation. She was not *related* to Michael; they were blood-strangers. They were nothing to each other.

"He wants to be bailed out," Ginny said. "He wants you to go over there with $10,000. Frankly, I wouldn't do it," she advised. "He's all screwed up, Agnes. He's nuts, he's dangerous.

140

Your son, *your son*," she said, and paused—"your son is a mental case."

When she came up the walk to the house, she paused in the front yard, inhaling the smell of orange blossoms from her neighbor's tree. The night was vast, blank, full of meaningless stars and eerie moonshine. Dr. Zaltz had shown her a cartoon torn from a magazine in which two men were staring up at the sky, and one was saying to the other, "Whenever I look up at the stars, I realize how insignificant they are!" Puzzled, she had smiled at him and he'd explained the joke—"Not that we're insignificant, but *they* are, get it?"

And the stars *were* nothing, she realized. She wasn't a doctor or anything special, but even so, she was more real, more full of life than any fancy far-off empty star.

"Is that you?" Paula called. She came to the door carrying Adam on her shoulder. "Are you okay? What happened, did you see him, what did he say?"

The baby's polo shirt was stiff and sour with spit up milk. His cheeks were fatter than moons. Poor child, to have to face the news someday of what his father was. She didn't deserve to have him because she had known the truth when she first adopted him, known that Michael was wild, dangerous, even mad. Hadn't she gone to great pains to deceive Adele Ginsburg, the social worker? Whom had she cheated? Not Adele, who must now be prancing down someone else's walk with her snooty nose in the air, but her own precious boy. She had done a great injustice to his sweet in-love parents, to the girl who now wore Ginny's plastic digital watch, saw it blink and flash away the hours in which Adam was not with her.

Mistake after mistake, selfish, stupid, thoughtless thoughts. "Paula?" Ginny said to her sister. "If we came from the same mother and father, how come you knew how to do everything right and I knew only how to mess up everything?"

141

"Hey, Fisher! You want to fish with me? You want to stick your pole into my muddy stream?"

"Hang your pole out the bars, Fisher! Let's have a look at it. Bet it's a pretty one."

Michael was busy, busy, with his bedsheet. The voices came hooting at him, from within his head, and from the tier. He could tie a good knot. He was the best nautical-knot man in the Boy Scouts. He could tie any knot faster and more accurately than anyone else. He could have been an Eagle Scout if not for Eric Feldmutter. Well—Eric Feldmutter would bother him no more after today. No one would bother him after today; he should have done this years ago and saved himself all the crap he had endured, all the shit he had put up with. He tested the knot; it was good. It was the best. Now if only the sheet would be long enough. He thought it would be. It was tied to the end support of his bunk, right up against the bars of the cell. The catwalk outside the cells was only about two feet wide. When the door slid open automatically for mess he would be ready. Peace, he thought, and then said it aloud, "Peace!" Three tiers up. He hoped his neck would snap at once so he wouldn't be hanging there like a chicken, his eyes popping. For once he didn't want to know about the details. This surprised him because he had always been curious about the physical effects of existence on the body. From the time he had first seen his cock stand up, he was fascinated with the human body. He should have been a sex-scientist; by now he knew so much about the ways to get hard, by a high-intensity flash in his head, by leaning forward against the spinning washing machine. Merely by holding his breath a certain way he could direct the air to his cock and blow it up like a sausage balloon. Too bad, sad, he would miss that, maybe the one thing he *would* miss. That, and Ginny. But fuck her, she would pay, she wasn't bailing him out, and now she would be a

142

fully depressed person the rest of her life.

He had a little time. He re-read the note he had written to her. He had felt kinder when he wrote it:

Ginny, what have I done to you? Get out of the city, there's so much evil and danger. From age 12 tell Adam that jail is the most terrible thing in this world. I'm sorry I broke your heart. I believe there is life after death. Get the best psychiatrist! The world is a terrible place. Nature is beautiful.

The voices were coming at him again, blinding him so he could hardly read.

"Fisher, hey, Fisher. Watch out in the exercise yard. I'm going to be there, Fisher."

"I hear you do it real good, Fisher."

Three minutes till the bars slid back. He tested his knot. He read his other note, the one he wrote before he made his absolute and final decision:

Acquire confidence
Gain courage
Banish worry
Realize potential
Create a happy family atmosphere
Root out resentment
Face life with enthusiasm
There's no place like home!

Too hard, too complicated, to carry that stuff out. He had no strength to try that hard any more.

"Fisher, I got a lollipop for you to suck!"

He knew the world should have been blown up long ago. *Kaboom! Blammo! Bang!* Get rid of the dumb gorilla moron bastards, even get rid of himself, King of the World.

Shit, a guard was looking in. Right at the sheet, right at his exquisite knot. Michael could see the news dawning on his blank ape-face, his cloudy moron-eyes cleared, sewage water settling in two holes. Then the guard jerked like an epileptic. He danced this way, that way. He had no key to the cell. In thirty seconds the door would slide open. The magic was about to happen.

Michael slid the sheet over his neck. The guard jumped away, running, jerking like a spastic.

"Fisher, Fisher, kiss my ass!"

Mom, I'm sorry I broke your heart. The Lord is my shepherd, I shall not want, he maketh me to lie down in green pastures, he leadeth me beside the still waters, he restoreth my soul, he leadeth me in the paths of righteousness for his namesake. Yea though I walk through the valley of the shadow of death, I will fear no evil. For thou art with me, thy rod and thy staff shall comfort me . . .

The bars begin to slide back on their oiled track. He could smell the vomity smell of tomato soup coming from the mess hall. *Thou prepared a table for me in the presence of mine enemies, thou annointed my head with oil, my cup runneth over. Surely goodness and mercy shall follow me all the days of my life and I will dwell in the house of the Lord forever.*

Michael lofted himself over the tier rail and dove, arms outspread. He flew away from his pain, like an angel, like an eagle.

A MAN AND A WOMAN WERE attacking one another with foam rubber bats in the waiting room at Mental Health. One bat was pink and one was green. Whap! Whack! The man and the woman went at each other, teeth clenched. Two small girls sat on the plastic couch watching them. One yelled, "Hit him, Mommy! Hit him as hard as he hits you at home!"

Ginny pulled her feet in to keep them from being stepped on. The man wore huge blue nylon running shoes, and drops of sweat or saliva were turning them darker in little dots. Ginny glanced at the receptionist, who sat behind glass in a little room, answering phones. The woman slid back the glass window and said to Ginny, "Don't let it worry you. It's routine. They do this for ten minutes, then they go back inside and talk to their therapist some more."

Ginny had an appointment to see a therapist named Annie. Paula's husband Grant had insisted that Ginny see "a professional."

"You're not doing that well," he had said to her on the phone yesterday morning, just after the night she had visited Michael in jail. "From what Paula tells me, you need help. You can't get through this on your own. Believe me. I want you to see someone."

"What for?"

"To talk."

"I could talk to you."

"I don't think so," Grant had said. "You probably have things to talk about that would be easier with a stranger than with me. It's not recommended that we treat our own family members."

She didn't know what he meant. With him, she could start from where she was, he already knew Michael and their troubles. With a new person, where would she start?

"I don't think I want to see a stranger. I'll be okay." But Grant had made phone calls, made this appointment for her, got her a month's leave of absence from her hospital job. He was such a nice smart guy. So cool and together. How come Paula had found him, and Mrs. Zaltz had found Dr. Zaltz and she had found Michael? Maybe she could ask the therapist that.

She went up to the receptionist. She said, "What do they ask you in there? I mean—when you see your therapist?"

"Oh—not much. Just how you feel and all that. I wouldn't worry if I were you. It's easy. Most people like it and feel better afterward." The woman slid the window closed.

How did she feel? She watched the husband and wife striking each other with the bats. She felt like stone. Since seeing Michael at the jail, she had started turning numb. She noticed it when she first kissed Adam in his crib last night. She couldn't feel his warm skin on her lips. At night, in the waterbed, she didn't feel the waves. When Paula, who was staying with her for a while, served her coffee this morning, she drank it fast and scalded her throat. That was when Paula called Grant and made her speak to him.

"Hit him real hard, Mommy!" the smaller of the two girls screamed.

"You can go in now, Mrs. Fisher," the receptionist said.

Ginny stood, and the man in blue running shoes knocked into her.

"You asshole," Ginny growled. "You dumb creep!"

Annie the therapist weighed at least 200 pounds and was spooning won ton soup into her mouth from a white carton with a wire handle.

"Come in, come in," she said, wiping her chin. "Want some?"

"No, thank you," Ginny said. White limp noodles hung over Annie's soup spoon, dripping.

"Have a seat."

Already Ginny didn't trust her. How could this woman understand anything about her? About her passion for Michael, about her bad luck with him? This woman had probably never been adored by a man. Maybe it wasn't fair of Ginny to judge her; she felt she was looking at Annie with her mother's narrowed, critical eyes—"an ugly old maid, poor thing." That's what her mother had always said about nuns—they took the veil because they were ugly, and no man would have them. "Think about it," she had urged Ginny, when Ginny had tried to protest. "They all have bad skin, and eyebrows that connect over their noses. They have round faces and round eyeglasses."

Annie was rounder than any nun Ginny had seen. The flesh of her buttocks hung through the opening at the back of the chair, her thighs over the sides; her chins were like ruffles of pink dough hanging down over her voluminous breasts. She had tiny shaven whiskers around her first loop of chin.

"So tell me about it," Annie said, sucking in soup.

Michael was crazy, but he was precious to Ginny. She wasn't going to lay him out for this woman who couldn't understand the slightest thing about life, or love. She decided, for Grant's sake, to tell the bare minimum.

"We met in an art class," she began, "and now he's in jail."

Spare rib bones lay ragged on a paper plate on Annie's desk. She had swung her chair around to face Ginny, and Ginny was transfixed by the seam in her pants, which bulged forward over her belly. The woman could not bring her thighs together.

"What I gather from all this is that you're a Jewish princess," Annie said, "and you exacerbate Michael's pathology. You want to grind him to a pulp till you get the things you want. You can't let him be the way he is and it's the only way he *can* be." She tossed back a strand of lank straight hair. "So there's only one thing to do and that's to cut him loose; don't hang around, don't give him hope. If he's to survive, he's got to be free of you."

"If *he's* to survive? How about me? How am I to survive?"

"You? You won't have any trouble." Annie laughed. Ginny felt the woman's eyes on her face and saw what she saw: a thin pretty woman, a woman with every possibility in the world. What Annie didn't see were her fatal flaws, her weakness, her ugly crooked back.

"I have a lot to think about," Ginny said, standing up.

"He's a nut," Annie said. "That's clear as day to me, and by now should be to you."

"A nut?"

"Crazy. Bonkers. Does a sane man do what he did?"

"I guess not."

"So keep away from him. Go find a Jewish doctor to marry. You'll do better next time around, I'm sure. So let's work on that—right?"

"Okay," Ginny said, moving toward the door.

"I want to see you once a week," Annie said, rocking back so that the springs in her chair groaned. "And next time we'll talk about Voc-Rehab. It seems to me you're a smart girl, you have Jewish genes, like Einstein, you know? So you can do better than a job as a mere ward clerk in a hospital. We'll talk next time about retraining you for a real career. Okey-doke?"

"Okey-doke," Ginny said. She escaped into the hall. *My God*, she thought.

"I hate to be the one to tell you this, Ginny," Paula said the instant she walked in the door. "The jail just called me. Michael made a noose from a bed sheet, and even though a guard saw him doing it, he couldn't get into the cell because he didn't have a key. When the cell door opened so the men could get out for dinner, Michael leaped over the railing from the third tier."

Ginny sat down so hard on a kitchen chair that her spine crackled. Paula was squeezing Adam as if he had no shape at all, as if he were a down pillow. The baby didn't seem to have a face anymore, nor did Paula. Ginny saw herself in a black suit, kneel-

148

ing in a cemetery in the midst of a brilliant green meadow. There were flowers all about, glistening in the sun, fragrant. Her hair, black and thick, absorbed the heat from the sun and warmed her bones. She felt a sense of peace as she never had before. "So that's how it is," she thought. "Now it will be quiet."

She reached for the baby and took him, prepared to press her face into his softness, feel the feathery caress of his skin— but he jerked violently in her arms, pushing her away. His head was like a rock, heavy and fierce, and his body writhed powerfully, like a snake's. His heels whacked against her hip bones as he kicked her.

"Let me have him back," Paula said. Her sister's face looked very old. She looked older than their mother.

"Michael broke his hip in seven places," Paula said. "He had a concussion. They've taken him to the county hospital jail ward."

"Oh no," Ginny moaned. The cemetery disappeared, and instead she saw herself back on an old battlefield, well-known, littered with debris and bodies. All the bodies were her own, in different ages, from the time she was a child till now. The enemy was Michael, and he inhabited the bodies of all the enemy soldiers. He threw hand grenades at her in all her forms, and her bodies burst open, spewing jets of blood, like Bonnie's body in "Bonnie and Clyde" when they machine-gunned her down.

"Ginny, drink this," Paula said, giving her a glass. She shook her head. She didn't need anything to go up, this was the biggest turn-on of all. She felt as if she were on LSD in the old days. Nothing would hold still, everything was twisted. She longed to get back the meadow in her mind, the cemetery, herself, lonely in a black warm mourning suit. The peace, God, she wanted that peace.

"He may be a vegetable," Paula said. "They don't know yet, he's not conscious. He couldn't do that right either."

"Don't criticize him," Ginny said. "It's my fault. I wasn't nice to him."

"You weren't *nice* to him?!"

"I've never been nice enough. I can't accept him the way he is and he can't be any other way." Ginny said. "I've *never* been nice enough. That's always been the whole problem."

You, WHATEVER YOU ARE TO ME, but never again my soul-mate—this is my last letter. If you don't write after this one, may you burn in hell. Not ONE word of forgiveness have I heard. I love Adam. You don't think so, do you? But my worst moment came when I imagined that someday he could be where I was. I NEED YOU TO TAKE CARE OF ME. If there's a trial and you tell the judge you'll take me back, they may let me off. A man needs somewhere to go. I have only a constant burning need for you. IT IS KILLING ME. EACH MOMENT HAS BEEN HELL. WHY DO YOU THINK I TRIED TO DIE? If anyone else had hurt me so bad and so often I would have felt like killing. Fortunately, I have no violence except for myself. I need my family behind me, a good job, psychiatric treatment, and you waiting for me. If you were sick or dying, I would stick by you. I can't take this separation any longer. I FEEL I NEED CON-STANT SEDATION TO HANDLE MY GRIEF. Don't hurt me anymore. I didn't love you enough or wasn't man enough to han-dle that big ugly world out there. Soon we can have a sweet life. I will suffer and I will grow. We have to learn to be a happy group. Don't run away, please give us a chance. I'm a man who's down. It can only happen with your blessing and faith. Don't hurt me anymore. *If you don't fall for this I will be lost!*

P.S. I don't want anyone else nursing me. I would like you to buy some special pretty clothes. You may redeem yourself for your part in this tragedy by loving and taking care of me now, or we will never see each other again. LET ME COME HOME! OH PLEASE, OH GOD, I DREAMED I WAS A LITTLE BOY CROUCHED DOWN IN GOD'S HAND. GOD WAS MY FATHER WHO LOVED ME AND DIDN'T DIE. SOME-ONE—OH SOMEONE PLEASE TAKE CARE OF ME! NO MATTER HOW BAD I WAS, I CAN'T BE THAT BAD.

HOLD ME SOMEONE, HOLD ME, IT HURTS TOO MUCH TO BEAR.

SHE SLEPT AT NIGHT WITH ADAM balanced on her belly in the waterbed. They were swimmers in a secret sea. He clung to her, face down, with his arms hooked around her ribs and the hard knobs of his heels locked against her thighs. She sank peacefully under his solid weight, grateful to be screwed to life this way, to be held in place, kept whole, rocked and comforted by the rhythm of his hot rapid breathing and the slight rock-a-bye roll of the water beneath.

With his skull just under her chin, she could reach out with her tongue and fish up a few of his fragrant hairs. She would keep them in her mouth for reassurance, sucking on them, trying to keep her mind still so she might sleep. Paula had gone back to her family. Ginny's mother had come to stay for two days and become hysterical. "He ruined your life! The bastard ruined your life!" Her mother became wild when the mail came and Ginny read his letters and cried.

"Let me cry," Ginny had said. "I need to cry. If you can't take it, go home."

Cursing Michael, cursing the day he was born, cursing his whore-mother, his tramp-sister, Ginny's mother ranted, hopped around the house sizzling like a sausage, ready to burst from her skin. She complained that the baby whined like a moron, could it be he was retarded? Who knew what kind of people had had him? He wasn't flesh and blood, and a person could only trust flesh and blood.

"You should be glad he isn't Michael's flesh-and-blood," Ginny had said. "Go home, Mother. Help from you is worse than no help at all."

She floated through the days, holding Adam against her all the time, never letting him wander away from her. When she bathed, she locked him in the bathroom with her, putting on the bath mat his set of circus animals—the plastic arena with its yellow wooden ladders tottering toward one another, the red-nosed clowns, the elephants and lions who hung, like mutations, gripping the ladder with horrifying hook-shaped forelegs. Sometimes she sat on the mat with Adam, naked and dripping, and played with him, letting the rigid acrobats swing dangerously high on the trapeze, taking away the safety net, letting the pink plastic man in white tights and the woman in her silver-glitter suit clash in mid-air and spin clumsily to their tragic ends on the unforgiving tile.

These little things she did seemed all she could do. She had resigned from her job. Dr. Zaltz had sent her a bouquet of red roses and thanked her for her good work and wished her luck in the future. Once a week she went to see Annie at Mental Health, keeping Adam on her lap as a shield while Annie, her thighs bigger at each visit, counseled her about digging out, breaking free, making it on her own. She didn't want to hear about being on her own. It made her gasp for breath. In the meantime, Annie arranged for Ginny to apply for welfare, attesting that she was a single parent without visible means of support.

At home she ate and breathed and waited for night when she could finally lower herself into the roil of the membrane-held sea, attach the child to her securely, and sink down into dreamless sleep.

On one of these days Agnes came and pounded at the door.

Ginny could smell her perfume as it seeped through the hardwood door. Her heart skipped as she thought of what her mother had said about this woman.

"What is it?" Ginny cried, her voice a thin, sharp bolt.

"Hey—let's have a little truce here," Agnes croaked in her hoarse, whore's voice. "No hard feelings. You and I have a few important things to work out. I have some really good news for you. And I want to see my little sweetie-pie, I bet he misses his sweet little Grammy."

Ginny unbolted the door. Agnes stepped in wearing a peach-colored gauze dress and high-heeled lucite sandals. In the front of each shoe was embedded what looked like a small real lizard.

"Number one," Agnes said, tossing her purse on the brown plaid couch, "Let me get right to the point—as of today this house is yours and Michael's. I have bigger fish to fry, big things are pending, this house is peanuts—under a hundred-fifty thousand—and my lawyer tells me it's best right now for Michael's case that you two own the house as a couple without any complications. You mind if I sit down?"

Ginny was studying her face; certain veins in Agnes' forehead were very prominent; were they signs of mental illness which she had passed on to her son? How could one tell who was mentally ill and who wasn't? Was Annie, the therapist at Mental Health, mentally *well?* Wasn't it odd that she kept describing Michael as "nuts," "crazy," and "bonkers," instead of what he really was—"paranoid schizophrenic" or "psychotic"? Wasn't a trained therapist supposed to have better words for Michael's condition? What would Annie say about Agnes, whose lips were now moving like the mouth of a fish underwater, pursing and popping; little air bubbles were coming out, rising up like helium balloons, bursting on the ceiling.

"I'm so proud of my son," she said. "It was all a setup, you know—he was framed. He's always had a hard time in life. He could have been an Eagle Scout but he never got in with the right people. Never." She looked Ginny in the eye. "Oh well, that's the way the cookie crumbles." She opened her purse and took out a silken-wrapped package of cigarettes. The silvery paper had flowers and vines on it.

"No smoking here," Ginny said. Her voice sounded like it had come from a helicopter, or even from heaven. It boomed, it rang in her own ears.

"So what if I die young?" Agnes said, but she held the cigarette, unlit, her fingers shaking. "I visited Michael—he told me you haven't been there. He hasn't heard from you. Not once. Not at all."

Ginny began to touch Adam's hair with her tongue. It tasted of talcum powder and baby shampoo. She licked a strand till it was wet.

"God, they give you a shit time down there. First of all, Michael's all wired into the bed. The boy is in agony. They don't even let visitors in. God—they have him in the jail ward, you'd think he was a dangerous character. If they knew my boy they'd know he couldn't hurt a fly. And there's no such thing as a private talk. I had to look into a little glass window with bars on it just to get a glimpse of him. Then, if I wanted to talk, I had to bend over and put my mouth to a hole in the door and shout to him."

Very gently, Ginny covered Adam's ears with her hands. Who knew what babies heard or could understand? She ran her index fingers gently through the swirls of his outer ear, tickling him so that he laughed. She laughed with him.

"My son is *suffering*!" Agnes said, stamping her foot. "Why have you forsaken him?"

"Who?" Ginny asked.

"Okay, I can see you won't cooperate. I'll get to the point and get it over with. We're suing the county for eight million dollars for negligence. Michael never should have been allowed to hang himself. My lawyer says we have a good case. No one was watching him. They're definitely at fault and liable. When it's all settled we'll be on Easy Street, Michael and me, so I'm going to just let you two have the house. I don't need the hassle of going to court and all that crap. I'll just get off the deed and turn it over to the two of you. The important thing is to show the judge that Michael has a loving home to return to. *In a home that he provided for his family*! He didn't commit a crime, *you* know that, he never did *anything*! He was framed. Those girls had it in for him. They were crazy, the *story* they made up! So the sooner this is all settled, the better. The main thing is—you have to testify that you're taking him back."

"Who?" Ginny asked.

"Are you high or what? You look like you're on something. Jesus! My son is in hideous pain. He's crying for you like a two year old. He's in that ward with hardened criminals. One man had his testicles cut off in the prison shower. He's a murderer, and he's in the next bed to Michael. It's not good for him." Agnes opened her purse again and took out a bag of M & M's. "I left Michael a half dozen bags of these, and here's one for my

155

little sweetie-pie." She ripped the bag with her teeth. Into her palm she poured a little pyramid of candies. Immediately they began to stain her palm orange and brown. "I'm sweating like a pig," she said. "Begging you this way isn't easy for me. Michael's only chance to get off is if you tell the judge you'll take him back. He's getting out in a couple of weeks. The girls aren't pressing charges, you know. So he can get off with just the time he did—if you say you'll take him back. When the cast comes off he'll be an invalid for months. He'll be on crutches. He has a stainless steel pin in his leg. He'll need constant care, and he wants only you for his nurse. Listen, are you heartless or what? He's the most desperate man you'll ever see."

Agnes popped the melting candies into her mouth. She sounded as if she were chewing on broken glass. "The thing is, if you won't take him back, I'm ready for that possibility, believe me, I'm not counting on your generosity. Your people are not known for their generosity. If necessary, I intend to take him back to live with me in Star Villas. I'll nurse him. He'll soak in the hot tub there, and he'll have the swirling waters to bring him back to good health. All I ask of you is that you come to the hearing and promise the judge you'll give Michael another chance, that you love him, and you're sure what happened will never happen again. You don't have to *do* what you promise, of course. But I'm leaving the way open for you. You thought I was going to fight you tooth and nail to get the house back, didn't you? Well, you can just have the house—what do I need a tract house for if we're taking the county for eight million! And guess what? Michael's going to get Social Security Disability. God knows why but the shrinks who examined him think my boy is *disabled*. That's one over on them, isn't it? But who's going to turn down $1000 a month or so? It'll pay the mortgage with some left over beside. So he's going to have a free living for the rest of his life without ever lifting a finger. Listen Ginny, if you take him back you'll never have to worry again. You won't have to hound him to get a job *ever* again. This is a *windfall! Completely tax free!* All I want you to do is tell the judge you have every intention of being a good wife to him and standing behind him and supporting him in all his endeavors."

"Is that all?" Ginny asked, opening the door and waiting for Agnes to leave.

"You should also say you gave him full sexual attention; I know when I was living with you the two of you were screwing all the time, so it's proof he didn't need to go raping any women. You just have to tell the judge you gave him everything he ever wanted." Agnes walked toward the door, pausing to get her heels balanced in the backless shoes. The lizards embedded in the lucite had open eyes. "I *hope* you gave him what he needed," Agnes said, "because even as a boy he had very powerful sex appetites. I'll tell you something—when he was about twelve, he baby-sat for a little girl next door, and when I went over to bring him his schoolbooks so he could study and do his homework, I found him in the crib with the little girl, and he was over her with his pants down." Agnes smiled. "So long, kids," she said. "Enjoy the M & M's."

"Take this, Mrs. Fisher," the receptionist at Mental Health said, handing Ginny a pink foam rubber bat. "Annie wants you to practice while you're waiting. Hit the furniture, hit the walls. But hit."

"No thank you," Ginny said. "I don't like to be violent."

"Well, obviously it's time to start, don't you think?" The woman, who wore harlequin eyeglasses on a little pearl chain, and who had blue-white hair, urged the bat at Ginny through the glass window. "Take it, take it. I'm not a psychologist, but if I learned anything from working here, it's that you have to express your feelings or you go nuts." A man reading "Psychology Today" on the plastic couch looked up. "You want a bat, Mr. Ricardo? Maybe you and Mrs. Fisher can release a little anger while you're both waiting."

"Why not? Sure," he said. "Good idea." He took the offered bat and whomped Ginny suddenly on the backside.

"Hey!" Ginny jumped away and then turned to face him furiously. "I don't even *know* you." He was a short little man of about fifty, wearing plaid polyester pants.

"Hit anyway," he said. "You'd be surprised how much better you'll feel afterward." He smacked her again with his bat.

"Go ahead, Mrs. Fisher. It's therapy. On the outside, the cops would come and get you, but in here, it's just therapy." The woman closed her little glass window and began to make a phone call.

"Whomp!" The bat landed on the top of her head.

"Shit!" Ginny yelled, whirling around and fending off Mr. Ricardo's next blow. She fenced with him for a few seconds and then got in a good hard hit across his shoulder.

"Keep it up!" he cried, ducking under her blows. "Do it harder."

She pummeled him with all her strength. He turned his back to her and dropped his bat, protecting his ears with his

158

hands. She kept smashing the bat against him, gasping for breath. Even when he said, "Hey, that's enough, murder is *out*,"—she kept whacking him till she was covered with perspiration. When she finally stopped, she was aware of Annie filling the doorway to the waiting room, smiling.

"All*right*!" Annie said. "That's what I like to see, a little movement. A little passion."

Mr. Ricardo took the opportunity to stagger back to the couch and collapse.

"Thanks, honey," Annie said to him. "You just did her a world of good."

"Yeah, maybe I should go into psychology," the man said, panting.

Annie motioned for Ginny to follow her down the hall. "Come on kiddo, I have a surprise for you. Presents!"

"Presents?" Ginny kept close behind Annie's huge hips. The workout with Mr. Ricardo had flooded her with energy and a sense of well-being. She hadn't felt so good in years. "*Presents?*" She had a flash that Annie was dressed as Santa Claus and had glued a white cottony beard to her triple-chins.

"You will no longer exacerbate his pathology because soon you will be your own person and will have no need for him to fulfill you." Annie wedged herself into her office chair, fanned herself with a file folder, then rolled to the closet and pulled back the door. "Voila!" she cried. "The future awaits."

"What will I be?" Ginny asked.

"To begin with: a thing with which to begin." Annie leaned forward and pulled a typing chair from the closet. She sent it whirling on oiled wheels across the floor toward Ginny. Then she reached in and extracted some articles from a shelf. "And now: a typewriter, and now: a dictaphone, and *NOW: le piece de resistance*: the stenotype machine!"

The equipment, piled high and balanced on Annie's thighs, quivered and clanked their coverings as she laughed. "Hey, not bad, not bad, eh?" she asked Ginny. "I did good for you, no? I showed your file to the director at the office of Vocational Rehabilitation; I showed her your test scores—you're a smart cookie, Ginny; some IQ you have. Einsteins of the world unite! (Did you know I'm also a Jew like you?) So you're in the ball game—some poor Mexican girl just gave up school and turned back all her equipment, she couldn't hack it. And Helen over at Voc-Rehab was going to send it to storage when I said 'I have just the girl for you!' So here it is, your future—all in my lap. And you get to keep it!"

"I get to keep it? They're giving me this stuff free?"

"Free if you work your ass off and become a court reporter. Free if you go to school, and do your thing, and make good grades and someday graduate and take yourself off the welfare rolls. Free if you can become a self-supporting, tax-paying citizen!"

"Is it hard at school?"

"You bet your sweet boobies it is. But it's better than being some little ward clerk! You can make a hundred bucks a day doing court reporting."

Ginny opened the little black case of the stenotype machine. She ran her fingers over the concave black keys. They cradled her fingers, receptive and spongy.

"We have to get busy," Annie said. "We have to get you registered at school for the new session which starts Monday, and get the paperwork in order so Voc-Rehab can pay your tuition. We have to get this show on the road, kid, so you can stand on your own two feet."

Ginny touched the typing chair.

"Sit down in it. Get the feel of independence, kiddo. Your ass has never had it so good, believe me."

"Thank you," Ginny said, trying the chair. "Thanks very much."

"Don't mention it," Annie said. "Just bring eclairs next time."

DON'T BLOW IT. Don't cry. Don't beg. Don't blow it. Don't cry out her name. Do what the lawyer said. Look intelligent and capable. But not arrogant. Not humble, either. Don't show any anger, that's what they're looking for, some sudden irrational flare of anger. Just sit in the wheelchair as if I'm healing bravely. There's Agnes out there, looking concerned and loving. Shit! Why is she wearing that hat with feathers! It isn't good for me to be going to live with her. Anyone knows that. A man my age with his mother! But that's not the story we're giving the judge, that's not the story. Why doesn't the *Queen* look at me? Her face—that smear of misery. I wronged her. The King wronged the Queen, dishonored her, rejected her. Look over here, Queen. Ginny, Ginny, Ginny, *Ginny*. Look at me and you won't be able to turn me down. Look at my suffering face. Look at what I've lived through, a million hours in hell. Isn't that enough? You think you've had pain? I'll teach you what pain is!

Look at my neatly-trimmed beard. The nurse took pity and did me. Handsome? Handsome enough for you? Too thin? Is Jesus Christ too thin?. God knows he doesn't have a patent on suffering. Get it? *God knows*. Hey, don't smile, you asshole, you'll fuck-up. That's what they're looking for, some sign that I'm nuts. Inner voices. Sure I hear voices. I hear them all the time. How can a man live and not hear voices? The sounds of the thoughts in my mind. The voices are the thoughts in battle, going round and round till they blow out my ears. All the shrinks, asking coyly, smirking, after an innocent question like "Do you still have sexual feelings?" asking "Do you ever hear voices?" Looking at me as if it will be just fine and dandy if I do, *everyone does, don't they?* I can con any shrink, any time. Even they know it. It worries them. They can't get me on the fancy technicalities. I can act cool. I give the right answers, man. Just let Ginny give the right answers today. When the judge glances over here I have

161

to look like a man who never jerked off, who never belched, who never farted. Look at me in this blue jacket. Square shoulders. I look like a Coast Guard captain.

Hey gang! See my leg? It has a nine-inch metal stake in it. I'm bionic. I'm able to fly out of this chair and buzz every fucking one of you, with your smug little judging faces. You're free, you can just go home. I get sent to state prison or to the funny farm. Nothing's wrong with me, no more than with any one of you. Even *you* Judge Fuckface.

Only *please*—Ginny, Ginny, Ginny. Tell them you love me. Tell them it was all a big mistake. I didn't get to *do* it to those girls, everyone knows that, so where's the crime? It's no different than sitting on the can with Hustler and drooling, I just went one tiny step further, I went a little further along and got a little closer, but Jesus, I didn't do it, I went *back to apologize! A textbook case!* Let me spread my love and light. My brain scan was *normal!* That's a fact. I'm a regular normal ordinary dumb animal. But it wouldn't take much to really mess me up. I cried all last night. I wanted my daddy. I felt little and wanted to be held and loved by someone three times my size and cry out twenty-five years of hurt. As soon as I get on Social Security I'll be able to get trained into a high paying type work. Then I'll find the answers that have to be found, but can't be found. I'll never understand this world. It can be beautiful for us, but we know what *really* is going on out there.

Speak up, girl! Speak up! I can't hear what you're saying. Don't whisper to the great Judge Fuckface, damn you! You broke your promises to me at great cost to us all. Face over to me. I want to see your precious face. That hair, that hair, that vampire hair. Where is your laugh? Did it curl up and die? I forgot about you, I roared so loud that women fainted in the streets. Pain. What do you know about pain? I did this to myself. I need my family behind me, a GOOD JOB, the glories of life. I extend to you my sincerest apologies for the pain I've caused. My wounds can only be healed by the sacrifice of your life to my needs. The problem is I won't be as athletic as I was due to this leg. My mind is stuck on you; if you were dead I could accept that I can't have you. No other way will I ever accept it. *Take me back or else!* Look at the deputy, he has a wedding ring. Look at the bailiff.

162

They're all married. Everyone, Ginny, *everyone* experiences tragedy before they die. We've had ours. Let us be true to one another.

Don't stop talking so soon! What did you say? What was your
statement? God, Jesus, Buddha, what did you say to the judge?
Am I a free man or a dead man? You lied through your teeth,
didn't you? For money, for cash, for goods, you whore! For a free
house, which my mother is giving you. She said you'd do it. She
knows human nature. You don't deserve it. Look at me, bitch.
Look at me, cunt. I'm not showing anger, oh no, they're not going to see me snarling and showing these fangs. Look at this
sweet angelic face of mine. Look at these innocent blue eyes. I'm
an angel. The judge is sucking his big lips! Agnes' feathers are
flying! Thumbs up, thumbs up! I'm out, I'm out! Hot fuck! I'll
be staring in your window as soon as I can walk. You'll never be
rid of me. Look at me, Queen. Smile, *goddamn you!* I'm human.
I'm a human being. Smile at me or you're dead.

THEIR OWN HOUSE, their sweet house! The house held its walls snugly around them. It was their cocoon, keeping out the night, the wind, the chilling rain. It hid the stars and let them forget the coyotes in the dry brush of the hills, the snakes coiled under the leaves, the airplanes with their cargos of bombs.

"Big deal! So you're alone from now on!" Annie had said. "So are we all! And how much protection was he, after all? Was he going to keep out the big bad wolf, or was *he* the big bad wolf? Listen, kiddo, don't tell me you can't stand to live alone because we can stand *anything* unless we die of it!"

Ginny now lived alone with Adam in the house. She did what Annie had instructed; when the big fear came, she said to it, "Oh there you are, fear, I know you, old friend. Just pass through and let me get on with my life." The fear had different faces: growing old alone and no one, ever, to hug her; wondering what Michael would do when his leg healed and he could come for her; leaving Adam each day with the baby-sitter Annie had recommended, a girl who had been in a depression but now was better. When the what-ifs began to drum inside her head, she did what Annie told her, she put herself in a sweet place and held tight. It was called *visualization* and was something new in psychology. If you were sick, you visualized yourself well; if you were cold, you imagined yourself on a hot, sunny beach. If you were afraid, you put yourself in your mother's arms, cradled against her breasts. Ginny made her own adjustments in the technique; the thought of her mother's arms didn't do much good for her. She would rather imagine herself floating on a raft in the middle of the warm blue ocean. When doing it worked, when her heart stopped pounding and she actually got calm, she wanted to call up Annie and say, "Hey, you were right." Annie was really okay, she was good, she knew what she was doing. Ginny was sorry to have judged her so fast, the way her mother had judged nuns. Annie knew about pain. Annie knew about fear. Ginny's mother would have dismissed her as a fat slob, a gobbler without any self control. She would have condemned Annie to a mountain of white paper cartons full of won ton soup and spare ribs and ended the whole business right there as if that were all there was to the person. Ginny herself had been guilty of it. Sometimes— to her amazement—she thought exactly the same way as her mother, as if they were connected by perfect, permanent ESP. She felt she must have grooves in her own brain that were exactly like those in her mother's. Annie said everyone had tapes like that in their heads; people would open their mouths to speak, and out would come their mother's irrational voice, or their father's prejudiced remarks. "We can't always help it," Annie had explained, "but once we're aware of it, we can catch ourselves, and try not to project their interpretation onto the world we live in, especially if it's wrong and doesn't apply to our world."

Annie was smart and had good ideas. Ginny loved to do visualization. It was almost like magic. At court reporting school, Ginny visualized little pairs of wings on her fingers as they flew over the stenotype keys. She started out at nothing per minute, and could soon do 45 words per minute. She loved the feeling of coming into class with her little carrying-case, getting into her seat, fluffing through the fanfolds of narrow green paper. A sense of purpose filled her. The teacher, Mrs. Klein, dictated to them at a slow steady pace and eventually rolled out a little electrical board with flashing colored lights on it.

"This is a make-believe courtroom," she told the class, "When the red light flashes, it's the judge talking. The green light is the defense attorney, the blue light is the prosecuting attorney. Each witness will be another color. Remember to attribute remarks to the correct speaker."

Ginny sat erect and let her fingers fly. She had to learn words like *deposition, protocol*. The other students were serious, too—she had gotten to know two of them, a young girl named Kathy who was engaged to be married to a construction worker, and an Indian man named Prashkar, who was tall and thin, with the blackest hair she had ever seen. She was making friends, getting to know people. If anyone asked, she planned to say she was divorced.

She *was* getting a divorce. That was what she had decided. She knew the exact moment she had made up her mind; it was in the courtroom as she had seen Michael being wheeled through the door in his wheelchair, all dressed up in a blue suit. She was far across the room from him, but she could feel the power of his eyes drawing her, draining the strength from her. She could hear his voice in her mind, demanding that she look at him. She knew him so well, though she hadn't seen him in all the months he had been in the hospital. And she could feel her name on his lips, *Ginny, Ginny, Ginny,* like a chant, like a curse. She purposely didn't look at him. She couldn't trust herself to look at him. She did what she had to—lied to the judge that she definitely planned to take him back, to see that he visited a therapist regularly, to help reduce the stress in his life as much as she could, to care for him while he healed, and even to forgive him for an act she said she was sure he didn't mean to do.

She never looked once at Michael's face because not a word of what she told the judge was true. She *never* intended to take him back. She *didn't* believe he didn't mean to rape those girls; she believed that he did, that he meant to do it to humiliate her, and would probably do it again the first chance he got.

When she had told Annie that she was going to divorce Michael, Annie had held up her dimpled fat hands to form a megaphone and let out a big cheer.

"Yay, Yay, Hip Hip Hooray,
We are making progress today!"

Now that Michael no longer lived in the house, the neighbors smiled sweetly, almost pityingly, at Ginny. The woman next door, trimming rose bushes in her garden, waved when she walked by with Adam in his stroller, but never quite looked her in the eye. No one ever asked any questions, either; she was certain that the neighbors on her street had seen Michael's picture in the paper that day, or that someone else had been sure to show it to them. They were so polite to her now that it was almost as bad as when they had shunned her.

"Yook," said Adam, pointing to a cat.

"Yes," Ginny said absently. "Nice cat." She maneuvered the stroller down the curb and quickly crossed the street. The houses were laid out like a line of toy buildings—little red and green Monopoly pieces. Every house had a tree in the front yard. In every house was a husband and wife, and two or more children. Only in her house were the numbers wrong, a mother and not a father. The balance was wrong—she was living a lopsided life.

Prashkar, the man in her court reporting class, had called this morning and asked her to have dinner with him. In his formal, English-sounding voice, a little insincere, she thought, he had asked her for a date. She had said she didn't know if she could get a baby-sitter and would call him back this afternoon. Now she had to decide. A date—what did a woman who still had a living husband do on a date? What would there be to talk about? Her past life? Her crazy husband?

Well, soon she would not have a husband to worry about. Annie had helped her find a woman lawyer through Legal Aid and they had already filed papers of dissolution. In six months, if Michael did not protest, the marriage would be automatically dissolved. For safety's sake, at Annie's insistence, she had also served Michael with a restraining order which forbade him to approach the house, or even to call her on the phone.

167

The move seemed sensible. She wanted nothing to do with him, wasn't that the case? Then why—*why*—was she approaching Star Villas? The stroller was drawn along as if it were magnetized. She certainly wasn't going to *visit* him, she was just going to stroll by. It was a free country, she could walk on any street she pleased. He had been living with Agnes for two months, and Ginny had never thought of walking this way before. Why now? Why hadn't she heard a word from him, restraining order or no? On the night she knew the deputy would serve him with the divorce papers, she waited, alarmed, for his angry phone call. But there was only silence. Had he forgotten about her so quickly? Had Agnes finally convinced him of how bad she was for him, how rotten? Maybe he was just honorably fulfilling his part of the bargain Agnes had set up—that if Ginny made certain promises to the judge and he was released, he would then leave her alone forever.

But it wasn't like him to give her up without further struggle, especially after those letters, those terrible, crazy letters written from the jail ward of the hospital, especially after she had felt his burning eyes on her in the courtroom. He had always been so persistent. His silence wasn't at all like him.

"Yook, doggy," Adam said. His pulled his index finger from his mouth and pointed it, wet with saliva.

"Yes, doggy," she said, coming up to the driveway of the Star Villas parking structure, and seeing the low wall just beyond, which faced on the area containing the pool and spa.

"Airplane," Adam said. He made a zooming motion in the air over his head. "Zoom, zoom."

Ginny felt a wave of dizziness come over her. While a small plane buzzed low over the apartment complex, she could see the form of Michael's back quite clearly. She knew it was his back, not someone elses'—she knew the curve of his spinal column, the line of every vertebrae, the slant of his shoulders. He was seated in the spa, facing away from Ginny. The sun, at his face, outlined his entire form with a spectacular glow. His crutches rested against a yellow lounge chair within reach of his arms.

"Go, Mommy," Adam said, lunging forward in the stroller. "No stop!"

"Shh," Ginny begged. "Be quiet."

"Move!" yelled Adam.

Ginny saw Michael's head tilt, as if he had heard something. She knelt down and rummaged quickly in the stroller's carrying pouch till she found the bottle of apple juice she had brought for Adam. Although he drank from a cup now, he was always willing to suck on a bottle if she provided one. She pulled the stroller seat back and pressed Adam into a reclining position, stuffing the bottle in his hands, guiding the rubber nipple into his mouth.

"Nap time," she said firmly. She was shaking. "Drink this. Be very quiet."

When she stood up straight, she saw that a woman was in the spa with Michael. She had probably been there all along, but her figure had been blocked out by Michael's back. Now she was standing between his legs as he sat on the seat of the spa. The blue-green bubbles swirled around them. The foam from the air jets was wild as white water. The woman wrapped her arms around Michael's neck and pushed his head against her breasts.

Ginny gasped involuntarily. The woman was small, dark, petite, wearing a blue bikini. She had very short hair. Michael's head rose up just under her chin and then bobbed down again, to the place between her breasts. His hair flamed red-gold in the sun.

Jesus Holy Christ, Ginny thought. *How dare you fool around? You're still married to me!* She visualized a pink foam rubber bat. She turned it into much heavier matter—lead. She wanted to leap over the low wall and smash him on the head with it. She visualized killing him in the hot tub. She would use the bat with one hand, and with the other use one of his crutches—she would beat him senseless, till he died, bled to death, drowned, fell in a soft useless lump at that woman's feet.

"Oh God," she moaned. Adam, getting drowsy, let his eyes roll upward to find her face as he drank from the bottle. The baby's eyes lingered on her face, then slowly closed.

"Michael, you bastard," she whispered. "Your mother put you up to this. She fixed you up with that little *shiksa*."

Over the swish of the air jets, Ginny heard Michael laugh, actually laugh. *How dare he laugh after what he did to those girls? How dare he do this to her—again?* Something hotter, more dangerous and more acid than tears flooded her eyes.

169

"I have a date," she said out loud. "I have to get home and get ready." She spun the stroller around on its oiled ball bearings and began to run awkwardly along the street toward home. The bottle spun out of Adam's hands and flew into the street, clanking as it rolled. Surrendering to sleep, Adam let his hands fall quietly to his sides. Ginny didn't stop to retrieve the bottle. She heard it rolling along as she ran till it clunked against the curb with a hollow sound—a dull, wrong note—and then there was no sound but the frantic turning of the stroller's hard black plastic wheels on the cement.

A WAITER IN A RED JACKET bowed from the waist, setting a silver goblet on the table in front of Ginny. A circle of huge shrimps, pink-fleshed, red-veined, arched over a glistening scoop of crushed ice, while their tails rested in a river of blood-red cocktail sauce. Prashkar, the Indian, in a black suit and black tie, sat opposite her, watching intensely as she handled the several forks to the left of her plate, trying to choose the right one. His eyes were black, and his hair, black, and shining with grease, seemed to grow unusually low on his forehead.

"Will you have some wine?" he asked, holding up the bottle of burgundy which the waiter had uncorked for him earlier.

"Yes—sure," Ginny said. She would have preferred a Coke. With Michael she would have said, "Get me a Coke." With Michael she could always be natural; that was the essence of him, his absolute conviction that anything a person felt was okay, anything he needed, whatever it was, was okay, no apologies needed. Now she was on guard; she felt stiff, as if she had been dipped in a vat of starch. She moved like a metal doll soldered in one piece, brittle, rigid. If she wanted to pick up her soft dinner roll, dotted with poppy seeds, she had to move her entire body forward, not bending or curving any part, not going soft anywhere.

She was exhausted already. She had thought to herself, *Well, what can I lose? At least it's a free dinner.* But now she longed to be slouched at her kitchen table, smearing peanut butter on a piece of wheat bread, dotting it with red raspberry jam. She was ravenous for peanut butter and jelly.

Something should be talked about here; it was only fair that she make an effort at conversation.

"So how do you like our class?" Ginny said, finally. "How do you like our teacher, Mrs. Klein?"

"I am very happy to be in this country," Prashkar said. "It is a land of opportunity, and I am glad to serve God by getting a good education in a field that serves the law."

Jesus. Ginny took a gulp of the wine. She waited to feel the heat in her arms, melting her down. It never took much alcohol for her to get soft and wobbly. A half glass of wine could fold her in two; a full glass could easily put her to sleep. This evening was going to be like a long boring movie. She ate a shrimp, chewing on its tasteless, rubbery body. It was only the first course.

"At least they say we can make good money if we ever pass the state test," Ginny said.

"Yes," said Prashkar. "That is an interesting aspect of our study."

"Do you want to have a lot of money?" Ginny asked. "Would you like to be a rich man?"

"I don't know," Prashkar said. "Money is not a path to happiness."

"Well, it sure buys a fancy shrimp cocktail," Ginny said. "It beats McDonald's."

"Yes, that's true," Prashkar agreed. He tore his roll in two, and began, very deliberately, with a knife in his long dark fingers, to butter it.

When they pulled up in front of her house, Ginny had the crazy thought that she was a teenager out on a date, and that her father (but it was Michael, not really her father) was waiting for her inside, watching from the window. She better not stay out too long, it wouldn't look good.

"Listen—thank you for a really nice dinner," Ginny said, her hand on the cold handle of the car door. "It was very nice of you to ask me out."

She realized how silly she sounded, like a girl of fifteen would have sounded twenty years ago. She had never learned how to date—never had a chance. No one had been interested in her at all until she met Michael, and then, she never really *dated* Michael, she had been swallowed by him, absorbed, vacuumed up like a speck of fluff into the roar of his desire.

Prashkar's long dark hand landed on her thigh, his fingers closed around the flesh of her leg sharp as a crab's claw.

"You invite me in," he said. It was not a question.

"What for?" she said in surprise. They hadn't talked very much all during dinner, just chewed their shrimp, their steak, poked holes in their baked potatoes, letting the yellow butter run in rivulets over the ridges.

"To be alone with you." He smiled so that his large white teeth seemed detached, floating in the darkness of the car. His fingers massaged her leg. In spite of herself she felt something clutch in the pit of her belly, something drastic and strong, separate from her mind.

She tried to think with her mother's brain: *he isn't Jewish. He's not your type. He only wants one thing.* She shook her head as if a bat had got entangled in her hair. That line of thought was pointless. What did *she, herself,* think about this moment in her own brain? She was bored silly. The man was nothing but an irritation, flitting on the periphery of her true concerns—her worries about Michael, her wish to see and touch Adam again as soon as possible. What she really wanted to do was go inside, pay the baby-sitter, lift Adam from his crib and carry him into the water-bed where she could sink with him into her dreamy winy sleep, and forget completely about this foreign man. She didn't want to think about him at all, in any way. She wanted to think about Michael and how the sun had shone around him like an aura of gold. She wanted to prick herself on the pain of remembering that woman in the spa, who was only taking what Ginny had voluntarily discarded.

"Are you interested in marriage?" Prashkar asked.

Where was this guy coming from? She had the sickening realization that no one was coming from where Ginny was, from her particular set of experiences, from her reality. She would *never* find a man to "have a relationship with." Michael was bound to her in ten million ways; he was her only true love and he was crazy, mad, dangerous, violent. Yet she longed for him to oil her flesh, whisper in her ear, knead the sad thin bones of her crippled back. No one would ever love her like he had. She would always be alone. How could she stand that? Annie had said that you could stand anything if you didn't die from it. Would she die from this awful loneliness? Should she let this man into the house? His hand was inching up her leg, toward the hungry quivering in her groin.

"Listen, Prashkar," she said. "You don't even know me, you don't know where I'm coming from, you have no idea what's going on in my head . . . "

"You have beautiful dark hair, like an Indian woman," he said. "You remind me of my country."

He was hopeless. Someone might love him, some soft Indian girl in a silk sari, with a long soft braid down her back, with a red dot on her forehead. But he was like the man in the moon to her.

Suddenly Michael seemed so incredibly precious. He understood her. He was like God—he knew every thought in her head, he had always known exactly what she was thinking. Right now he knew everything in her mind; she could feel his presence close to her, his spirit enveloped her.

She flung open the car door and let the cool air bathe her face. "It's too soon for me to talk about marriage. I've only split from my husband recently and I don't really have my head together yet."

"That is a unique American expression, is it not?" Prashkar said. "You will please explain it?"

"Hey, not now," she said. "I'm feeling pretty woozy, too much wine or something."

She was frightened of how much she suddenly adored Michael. She had to remember some of the bad things; the cursing, the broken furniture, the foul cruel things he had said to her, the ugly sight of his face when he was stoned and further away from her than the farthest star. *Remember Whisper*, she instructed herself. *Remember those two girls and what he tried to do to them.*

"Goodnight, and listen, I really thank you very much for the dinner. It was really good. I'll see you in school Monday, okay?"

She clopped awkwardly up the walk, not balanced well in her dressy high-heeled shoes. She had the sense that her father was behind the door, waiting to welcome her in, to check her for damages, to say goodnight a little gruffly, but lovingly. The trouble was she didn't know who she was, a little girl, or a wife, or an old crone. And she didn't know where she was, in her own house, or in her parents' house, or in a lunatic asylum. Time whooshed around her like a whirlwind, not letting her get a grip on her position in life. She was huge and she was tiny; she was old and she was young. She had to take care of everything, and the truth was she wasn't able to take care of anything. At times like this, she wished she could sit down like a guru in the lotus position, command her soul to leave her body, and flash off, like a rocket, into the eternal oneness of God's mind. Like a snake who has shed her skin, she would be able to look down from the sky and see the husk of her poor, empty, mortal body, sitting there on the lawn. All the feeling parts would be gone, blood and guts and brain and heart. Nothing would hurt her and she would be free. And what was so bad about that?

In October, when Michael was strong enough to walk four blocks on his crutches, he delivered a letter to Ginny's mailbox, stopping once on the way to re-read it with satisfaction: *Why aren't you calling me?* There is nothing that insults me more than being ignored. *How dare you try to divorce me, implying with certainty that I am unwanted and no longer beloved?*

But don't despair—I have come up with the ideal way to resurrect our marriage. I am going to become Jewish! They can dock my cock. What do I care, I have more than enough, anyway. Once I embrace your religion, we can go to temple arm in arm on Friday nights, you in a fur stole. We can go to temple on Friday night and church on Sunday morning. We can have a rich and varied social life through our religion.

Money troubles are over. A windfall from a $50,000 (at least!) lawsuit is on the way. I had to have minor surgery on my toe, complications of my fall. I had three drinks of whiskey before and told the doctor and nurse that fact in front of a witness. Still, they insisted I take Valium, two five mgs, and when Agnes drove me home I lost all memory; however, I am told I remained on my feet for eight hours, yelling, breaking furniture, kicking at neighbors' doors in Star Villas, and had to be restrained by two maintenance men. I was finally taken to jail where I woke up in a padded cell covered with my own blood.

So: I know *malpractice* when I see it! It's worth at *least* $50,000. Stick with me, baby, and I'll make you rich and famous. But here's a warning: DON'T IGNORE ME. I'm mobile now. You can't escape me. When I get my full strength back, BEWARE. This is no joke, BEWARE THE MAD DOG. Take this seriously. If I can put a letter in this mailbox, I can also put a bomb in it. Don't ever cross the KING OF THE WORLD.

"So what else is new?" Annie said, flinging her eyes heavenward, bringing her puffy palms down in a rubbery slap on the mounds of her thighs. Ginny suppressed an impulse to tell her not to wear orange polyester stretch slacks, that they made her look like a cartoon character; she was aware that she must not veer so far from the expected track, that they were here for a purpose and they had limited time in which to explore the problems. That's what was called "appropriate behavior," being aware of the limits of the situation. It was what Michael had never had.

"So he's begging you and stalking you and threatening you and scaring you! So what did you expect, that he'd just fade away like an old soldier? Did you expect this to be *easy*, for God's sake?"

"But at first he didn't call me at all. I thought he was seeing the sense of the divorce."

"You want sense from a severely psychotic individual?"

"I don't know. Sometimes he sounds as sane as you or me."

"Hey—who says *we're* sane?" Annie leaned forward and punched Ginny on the knee for emphasis. She reached behind her to take from a shelf a tall paper cup with droplets of water running down its chilled surface. "If I were sane, would I be drinking this milkshake?" She bent her head and slurped noisily till the last of the chocolate air bubbles ascended into her mouth. "We all have our obsessions, sweetheart. What are yours, Ginny-baby?" She stared at Ginny, her lank hair falling into her eyes. "*Tell*, kiddo. *Tell*. If you can't tell me, who *can* you tell?"

Ginny stared around the dim little office, at the shelves full of stacks of folders. A plastic fern hanging low from the ceiling dropped a dusty leaf on the floor.

"It's the smog," Annie explained. "It rots everything." She reached up and scraped off a handful of leaves. "So let's get on with this. What do you really, persistently obsess about?"

"Michael."

"Aha, he's *your* poison."

"What do you mean?"

"I mean he's your *poison*, sweetheart. Chocolate shakes are mine. In our own ways, we each self-destruct. Not just you and me, I mean *everyone*." She blew into the empty straw, making a hollow, flat sound. "Unless we pull out in time, we finish ourselves off. Are you going to?"

"Going to what?"

"Save yourself?"

"I'm getting a divorce, aren't I?"

"Are you really? Want to bet he'll be back in your bed in no time?"

"Never," Ginny said, and at the instant she said it, she felt a violent thrill, remembering how he had thrust the side of his hand between her buttocks, sawing her through and through, into perfect oblivion.

"I saw that quiver in your eyes," Annie said, pouncing on her. "What was that? What are you thinking?"

"Nothing."

"Hey, you can't fool me, you know? I saw you get that shot of something, your fix. I saw you convulse, for God's sake. It happens to me when I think of chocolate covered cherries, with that runny red juice leaking all over my fingers. Tell."

"Maybe he's *not* crazy," Ginny said. "How do we know he isn't sane? He sounds sane to me, sometimes."

"So don't tell me what you're really thinking. It's your funeral. And look—of *course* he's sane at times. That's the problem. When he's lucid he seduces you into believing the logic of his delusions. The man is no dummy. Wouldn't this all be simple if he were a drooling idiot? You could keep him at your side on a leash, and feed him downers to keep him under control. But your hero has beauty, sex appeal, intelligence, he probably has a higher IQ than mine. He's a charmer from all you tell me, schizos often are—some of them are artistic, have good vocabularies, they latch onto a little philosophy here, a little druggy stuff there, maybe a little of the occult, a little Jesus talk, a little Werner Erhard, and they roll it all up into one great big psychotic ball and ask you to push it up the mountain with them if you want to be saved."

178

"He really needs me," Ginny said.

"Are you going to *buy* that? You think he needs a Jewish princess like you? Nothing could be worse for him! I've told you, you exacerbate his pathology. Don't tell me we're back where we started."

"No, we're not," Ginny said. "I just don't know what to do sometimes—at night I'm scared. In the daytime, it's okay. I go to school, I'm really getting fast on the stenotype now, I'm doing 85 words a minute, and I'm ahead of some people who've been doing it a year longer than me. But at night I think he might be coming around, I hear noises in the bushes, I think I see his face at the window."

"Close the shades. Wear earplugs."

"What if he's dangerous?"

"He *is* dangerous. That's why you're getting the hell out of his way."

"Okay," Ginny said. She had no more arguments in her. People were forcing her to decide things. Did they really know better, were they smarter, in some absolute way, than she was? Annie had guaranteed that divorce was the only answer. "You want to have a life? Then you have to divorce him and never see him again." Well, she would, she would. She *was*. She just sometimes forgot why she was doing all this, learning the bones of the human skeleton so she could spell them in court cases about accidents, sitting stiffly till her twisted back screamed in agony as she poked the keys of the machine. Didn't Michael tell her about some invention he was making that would put them on Easy Street? He had promised her a spa, a sauna. Maybe he could really provide her with all those things. They could travel, go to Hawaii, buy a retirement home in the mountains. Why should she give up that chance? How did Annie know it wouldn't happen? All anyone needed was a little luck. Or was that Michael's argument? Wouldn't being with him be much better than the terrible fear at night, accusations from Annie in this crowded little office, a million hours of dictation sitting on hard chairs? And at school Prashkar the Indian now sat at the far end of the room from her, keeping his stern profile turned away, his greasy black hair a reproach that made her shiver. When she was divorced, if she went through with it, she would have to date men She needed men the way Annie needed chocolate. She couldn't go forever without that sweetness. It had already been so long. She missed it, yet she never wanted to get herself worked up enough so that she would want to touch herself. It seemed to her that if she did that, she would betray Michael totally. Yet— she thought of the girl in the spa! *He wasn't exactly suffering any guilt, was he?*

She thought in circles. She always came back to the same place. With Michael she was lost. Without him she was lost. She couldn't stand to look at Annie's piles of flesh. Everything was sordid and people were weak. Was there anyone who wasn't weak? You'd make someone your hero or heroine, and the next day you'd read in the paper they were drug addicts, or they had committed suicide. Even people who were making it weren't making it. They hung on for dear life to God or Jesus or the head honcho Dalai Lama somewhere, or blanked themselves out with meditation or coke or pot.

When she left Annie's office she saw twenty businessmen walking in the streets, wearing suits and ties, carrying leather briefcases, and felt nothing but contempt for them. They hid their rotten cores. Michael, at least, had the courage to lay his out in the open for all to see. She had to give him credit for that. A man ought to be given credit for his good points, even if he *was* psychotic. Wasn't that only fair?

FEAR WAS HER CONSTANT COMPANION. Ginny thought she had heard the phrase on TV, or read it once in a book. The words seemed comforting, sounding to her like a prayer, or a story told long after a crisis is over when everything at last is calm and all danger is past. Right now, as she heard Michael's footsteps crackling on the dry leaves under the window, she formed the words with her lips. *Fear was her constant companion.*

Moving along the line of a moonbeam, she stepped out of bed. *Hello fear, old friend, I know you, just pass through and go on your way.* She recited Annie's formula but knew it would have no effect, not now when she was this terrified. Steadily, she glided toward the bathroom. Last year Michael had installed a deadbolt lock on the bathroom door because one day when she was late for work she had jiggled the doorknob to signal him to hurry, and the pushbutton lock had popped out and let her in. She had confronted him as he was trying to tie a noose around the showerhead.

"What the fuck are you doing in here?" he had roared, and when she said, in her confusion, that she just needed her hairbrush and her lip gloss, he had pulled the rope off the pipe and snapped it at her in fury, shouting, "A man can't even practice nautical knots in peace in his own home." She had started brushing her hair, tearing through the tangles till her scalp burned, while Michael watched her, hopping from one bare foot to the other. Finally he had said, "Never walk in on me again like that! And I don't like you painted up like a whore. You want some doctor to get you in the supply room and give it to you good? Don't put that crap on your face unless it's for *me*. And I'm getting a lock in here so you can't ever invade my privacy again!"

She was grateful now that he had put in the heavy lock. Her fear inhabited her like a whirlpool just under her breastbone; it sucked her breath down before she could use it. She had to breathe in little shallow gasps.

This was the third night she had heard his footsteps outside the window. She could see the shadow of his form, backlit by the moon, moving behind the partly open curtains. He paced like a lion in the phosphorescent light, back and forth over the leaves. How much fear could she stand? Each night she had gone from terror to exhaustion and finally to indifference. At the end of many hours she didn't care if she lived or died. Let him break in, let him do anything to her, even kill her, it didn't matter. She sank into hopeless sleep, lying on her back with her palms up, in surrender. And each morning the sun had come in bright and white to find her alive, with no proof that he had been there. Leaves were leaves; she was no detective. She didn't know how to prove the existence of footprints. Maybe he hadn't even been there. Or if he had, maybe he was tired of doing it and would never come back. It had to be boring to stand in a dark yard, hoping to force someone to love you.

She slid the deadbolt home. There. He couldn't get to her now, anyway, even if he prowled in the yard all night, even if he broke down the door and came inside. She could sleep on the bathmat. She could drink water from the faucet and live this way for days. If necessary, for nourishment, she could swallow Adam's cough syrup, chew on aspirin.

Adam! She had forgotten him. Completely! She had left him out there, loose in the house, sleeping and vulnerable. She must go out and rescue him, bring him with her into the tiled sanctuary. Even as she pictured herself tip-toeing down the hall, she stepped into the shower stall and clicked the glass door closed. Another barrier between her and Michael—another inch of safety. That's what she wanted, a place in the world where he couldn't get to her, not with his threats, not with his seductive invitations.

A twig tapped on the high bathroom window that was set in the shower stall. She saw the stick of wood in the glow of moonlight, distorted and gnarled, scratching on the mottled glass. She heard Michael laugh, and then was sure she heard the sound of the old redwood table being dragged along the dirt.

When his head appeared in silhouette, his beard thick as a bush, she ducked, took a sliver of white soap between her fingers for a weapon. It gave off a smell of rank, overripe roses.

Oh Jesus, she thought. *Go away. Die.*

"Let me in, Ginny," he said. "Or I'll huff and I'll puff and I'll blow your house in."

Die, she thought, trying out the word, the idea. Did she care if Michael died? He had wanted to so badly, so often. Was it the worst wish she could imagine for him? Maybe it was a gift, a favor. If right now, he was struck dead by lightning, fell off the table, onto the grass, she thought she could leave him there with relief, go back to bed, and sleep a deep and dreamless sleep.

"I'm chewing oleander leaves, Ginny." He made a loud slapping sound with his lips; she could hear him chewing through the window, or thought she could. "I'm your husband in the eyes of God, and no man can put us asunder. You know I could be poisoned dead in twenty minutes," he said. "It doesn't have to be by oleander tea, that's not the only way. It can be smoke from its ╲leaves, or sap from its stems and flowers. But the leaves are the most potent." He chewed again, making a wet, lip-smacking sound.

Go away, she begged him, beginning to turn to ice in the shower stall.

"I know a new way to make a fortune," he called. "It's a sure thing. No one else knows about this."

She slid downward toward the tile floor. Directly beneath her she saw a puddle of water which shimmered like mercury. She sat and let it soak through her nightgown, let it spread along her skin like ink on a blotter.

"It's best to let me in," Michael said reasonably, almost tenderly. "Isn't it better to have me in your bed than stalking you? Do you like to have me peering in the window? Would you rather find my body on the lawn? Hanging from a beam in the garage? I could slit my throat in the hammock, and bleed red clots all over that clean yellow canvas. I wouldn't mind. A few minutes of pain, that's all. It's nothing to what I'm going through now. Anything is better than living without you. My mother is poisoning my mind. You know how bad she is for me, how she screwed me up. I'm all better, Ginny. I have a therapist now, you know. This guy, Ross, he has PhDs up his ass, he told me I'm in extended adolescence. He says I'm showing real progress. I have to think of therapy as a relaxed adventure. He's straightening me out. I

183

never gave you enough slack, that's all. He says I have to let you go your way, I'll go mine. I won't be any trouble. I have plenty of money now, I'm a disabled man, Social Security pays everything. Just let me in. I'll sleep with you like in the old days. I'll rub you down. I'll fix your back and protect you. You'll never have to be afraid again."

She heard the sound of chewing. "I hope I don't vomit this, it doesn't taste that good."

She was so cold. The tile was cold, the water, holding the thin silky cloth of her nightgown against her, was icy cold. She noticed black strips of mold growing on the white grout. She put the sliver of soap in her mouth, and bit it, tentatively. She wanted to keep herself from saying the dirtiest words of all. She chewed a corner of the soap and swallowed it. She waited to see if it had cleansed her.

But it hadn't. She was still weak and bad.

She stepped out of the shower stall. She unlocked the dead-bolt. She went down the hall to the back door. As she opened it, Michael flew toward her with the speed of a bat, knelt at her feet, began to kiss her toes.

"Allah be praised," he murmured. "I am saved. I adore you. I worship you. I will serve you all my days."

"Come in, Michael," she said. "Spit out those leaves right now." She held out her palm, and he bent forward and emptied his mouth into her cupped hand. "That's a good boy," she said. "You didn't swallow any, did you?"

"You rotten backslider! You giver-upper! Shit, kiddo, and I had this present for you." Annie waved a box at Ginny. "You don't get it now, of course! I'll save it to give it to someone who really deserves it. But you can look at it, anyway. I snitched the brilliant idea from a New Yorker cartoon." She tossed the box on Ginny's knees. Ginny opened it and pulled out an oversized blue T-shirt with letters on it saying. "I WANT NATIONAL REC-OGNITION FOR ALL THE TROUBLE I'VE HAD WITH HIM."

"Cute, eh?" Annie asked. "Give it back. You disgust me." Looking sour, she shoved the box into one of her desk drawers.

"Don't get so emotional," Ginny said. "I thought a therapist wasn't supposed to get excited."

"Not get excited! Sweetheart, what have I been breaking my ass for all these months if not to get you as far from that psycho as possible? Didn't I get you your little stenotype machine? Didn't I get you your dictaphone? Set you up in school? Jesus, don't you have any gratitude? How could you let that ass-hole back into your life? Don't you ever learn *anything?*"

"I'm not going to give up *school*," Ginny said. "And I told him it's conditional, that he's on probation with me, just like with his probation officer. Look, I couldn't ever get any sleep. I was so scared I had diarrhea every day. I couldn't eat, I gagged on everything. So I let him come back, but only on about a hundred conditions. He's so grateful, he's so meek, you wouldn't believe it's him. *I* never saw him this way before. He made *chile rellenos* for dinner last night, with green chile peppers and a special bat-ter that he learned somewhere. I swear, he kisses my feet."

"Yeah," Annie said. She glanced down at Ginny's feet, which were in leather sandals. Opposite were Annie's feet, huge, puffy, stuffed into misshapen vinyl loafers. "We know what he'll be kissing next, don't we? Scratch that, I'm sure he has already."

"Why do you have to be so gross?"

"Because gross is what *is*, sweetheart, it's what we are, it's what runs us! And we might as well face up to it. You didn't let him back for his Mexican eggs, so don't tell me that's the reason. You let him back because you're weak, like I'm weak, like he's weak. You let him back because it's easier, right? Right? I see by your eyes, I'm right. It's easier. For a day or two, or a month or two, it will be easier. I grant you that. But then what? You think he can cure himself by biting his tongue? You think he can stay sweet and servile for long? The man has a chemical imbalance in his brain; at least that and maybe a physical abnormality as well. Something's all screwed up in there, and no amount of apologizing and promising to be good is going to keep that monster in his brain from rising up with all its claws and fangs again—and guess who's going to be sitting right there when the monster comes out to strike? Little, sweet, tiredout, I need-it-easy Ginny."

"Jesus," Ginny said. "How can a person talk to you when you're like that?"

"You didn't come today to talk," Annie said. "You came to confession, and you want to be absolved. Well, honeybunch, I'm not your goddamned priest, and I'm not going to tell you to go home and do ten Hail Marys and you'll be okay. Michael is a time bomb waiting to go off, and right now he's just ticking away, sitting there waiting to blow you up."

"He's not that way now," Ginny said. "He's so grateful to be back, I swear it, that he's in perfect control."

"For how long? How long do you think that can last?"

"As long as he wants it to, maybe."

"I give up on you," Annie said. "I know you took him back because you want a little fucking. I know you miss it. You're dying for it. I'm no dummy. Just because no one's fucking me doesn't mean I don't know what goes on between a woman's legs."

"You don't have to talk like that."

"Why not? Do you have tender feelings? Are you shy, Ginny-baby?"

"It's not called for."

"Who are you to say what's called for and what isn't? In this office I call the shots. What will it take to shake you up? A hand grenade to the head? Or maybe a pillow over your mouth? What was it you said he once described he could do to you? Stick your head in the toilet and drown you?"

"He was just saying he *could*, not that he *would*."

"Oooh, I see, there's a *big* difference, isn't there?"

"I thought you would try to understand," Ginny said. "I thought you would see that I couldn't bear it, being so afraid all the time. This way I felt I could keep an eye on him, know where he is all the time. It's better for him to be next to me in bed than to have him scratching around at the windows, terrifying me. At least I know where he *is* this way . . . "

"You're going to trust him with your son?" Annie interrupted.

"I have to," Ginny said. "He seems very tender toward him. He says he loves him."

"The way to a man's heart—and mine—is through his stomach. The way to a mother's heart is through her kid, right?"

"It's his kid, too."

"Oh, is it now? Did you forget how you got him? Was it under a cabbage you found him, or was it the stork that brought him?"

"I've never seen you this way, Annie," Ginny said. "You seem so out of control."

"No shit," Annie said. "So now you're interpreting *me*."

"I don't think your reaction is professional. I came here to tell you Michael is back with me now, and I didn't expect you to attack me."

"It's me attack you, or Michael *kill* you. And *I* don't go for the throat. I just try jabbing till you feel something."

"I feel plenty," Ginny said. "I feel that I told you all about my life and about everything, and you're doing like my mother used to do, attacking me because I'm weak. So what if I want to go to bed with Michael! That was the best thing there ever was about us, for God's sake! It was the only thing that *wasn't* poison."

"Maybe I'm jealous," Annie said. "Maybe I'm just as messed up as anyone or maybe I'm just having a bad day. I'm entitled to have a bad day, aren't I?"

"I don't think you are," Ginny said, hitching her purse over her arm and standing up. "I don't think you're supposed to indulge yourself in front of your patients."

187

"Aren't *you* the righteous one?"

Annie stuck her face forward, pushing it, splotchy and red, toward Ginny. It expanded, stretching and streaking like a balloon about to burst. She was hideously ugly. No one would ever hold Annie tenderly, or caress her with passion. She would never have a child, or sleep entwined with a man. Suddenly Ginny's own life seemed infinitely attractive to her, even with her worries and fears. She thought of Michael waiting at home for her now, grateful, submissive, humble, keeping the house in order, looking after Adam, mixing up some hot concoction with cilantro and chile peppers and sausage.

He had said to her the night she had let him in, "You won't be sorry. No one will ever love you the way I do. No one could ever adore you this way. It happens once in a million years." And he had taken her damp, chilled body to bed, and slowly, slowly warmed and thawed her till her blood was flowing like liquid rubies in her veins.

"I feel sorry for you, Annie," Ginny said. "I won't be coming back here. I hope you get some happiness in your life and I thank you for the ways you helped me. But I think you need help more than I do now."

"You're a dead person," Annie said.

"I'll be all right, you'll see."

Annie stared straight forward, her gaze formless and blank. She was like a blimp hanging without power in the dead air space in the room. Her color had gone gray. She looked like a sinking blimp in which all the lights had gone out.

"COME HERE AND WATCH THIS PROGRAM with me," Michael said. "This guy Milt Grosser really knows his stuff." He grabbed Ginny's arm as she passed by the couch with Adam on her shoulder. She was walking fast and Michael's move spun her to a violent short stop.

"Hey! Don't do that!"

"Sorry. Oh sorry, sorry, sorry." He put his beer down on the table and slid off the couch, kneeling at her feet. "I beg your pardon. I do beg your Royal Highness' pardon. I won't ever do that again. Believe me."

"Okay," Ginny said. She waited for him to release her.

"I didn't mean anything by it, *believe* me. I swear it. I just wanted you to look at this guy on TV. Forgive me. Will you? Will you?"

"All right. Don't make such a production of it, Michael. I just don't want to fall and drop Adam. So I don't like to be grabbed when I don't expect it. You made me lose my balance."

"My abject apologies."

"Okay."

"It won't happen again."

"*Okay*. I believe you. Please let go of me now."

"Only if you promise to put him to bed and come right back. I want you to get a load of this character. He's a wizard. A genius."

"I'm sure he is," Ginny said. She already knew more than she wanted to of Milt Grosser. Michael had been watching the program religiously. There was something sinister about Milt Grosser, in his dark tie, with his endless charts, his pointer, his monotone voice. Somewhere in the vicinity of his chest, where his heart should have been, were rows of computer symbols flashing by, signaling the prices of stocks as they changed from minute to minute.

"And bring in a pencil and pad," Michael demanded as she lay Adam in his crib, kissed his fragrant cheek. "I want you to start taking down his formulas."

"You take them down if you want to," Ginny called back. "I'm not too interested in that stuff."

"Dammit, you can *get* interested, can't you?" Michael shouted. "It's only a matter of life and death, you know."

"Watch it, Michael," she warned him in an even voice, as she came slowly back to the living room. "I told you I don't want any of that yelling."

"Right. Right. Sorry sorry sorry. I forgot, I have to kow-tow to you to stay in my own rightful home."

"You wanted limits," she reminded him. "You said so yourself, that you wanted me to impose limits on you, so you could keep control."

"I'm in perfect control!"

"Well, good." She sat down on the couch beside him. Milt Grosser was moving his pointer up the zig-zag mountain on the screen. He had a voice like a buzzing fly.

"Over the past month we decreased our position in stocks by 50%. My Discovery System identifies shortcuts that require little skill but that contain the effectiveness of the most advanced techniques. These shortcuts are honed together and gelled into a new format which I call the Discovery System. Last month alone we closed out the 20% of our portfolio invested in money market mutual funds. We believe that cash prices for choice steers will advance with relative ease, especially as tight pork supplies were aggravated by the spring planting season which caught hog marketings short and diverted some demand to beef."

Ginny got up. "Want some ice cream?"

"Sit down! Don't interrupt my train of thought with some idiot remark!"

Milt Grosser held up another chart. "As you can see," he whined in his terrible voice, "the cotton crop has a projected domestic consumption of 5.8 million bales. The crop is making good progress throughout planted regions although some farmers are concerned about cool temperatures. However, this will foster excellent root development and prove highly beneficial for the dog days of summer."

"Write down 'Cotton,'" Michael said gruffly. He held his hand up to ward off her comments. "I want to hear every word of this."

"The cash plywood market remains quiet but still under pressure of the contract grade at the mill level."

"Skip lumber," Michael said. "It doesn't interest me."

"In corn, we would suggest trading the summer contracts from the long side. Weekly corn exports approximate 50 million bushels, 15 to 20 more than the average weekly clearances during the first half of the crop year. With corn futures lower than a year ago, the price risk in owning corn futures seems minimized."

"Good," Michael said, his eyes rolling. "I like corn. People are eating corn tortillas all over the world. Corn is a sure thing."

"Michael, this has nothing to do with us. It's for rich people."

"We are rich people," he said, his eyes fixed on the screen. "You just don't know it. Be quiet now, he's doing soybeans. And I want to hear pork bellies."

She went into the kitchen and began clearing Adam's high chair tray. She heard Milt Grosser do Japanese Yen, cocoa, sugar, wheat, copper and live hogs. "Be sure now to send for my Discovery System newsletter with the up-to-the-minute recommendations in commodity research. Three hundred dollars a year gives you fingertip control of billions of dollars. Don't be pennywise and pound foolish. Send in your money today."

Michael clicked off the television. "Get the checkbook," he said. "We're sending in our money today."

Ginny had been writing checks earlier in the morning at the little desk in the kitchen. She had been trying to make it all work, the mortgage payment, the utility bills, the taxes, the homeowner's insurance. All they had for income now was Michael's Social Security Disability check each month. She had to finish her court reporting requirements, take the Certified Shorthand Reporter's exam as soon as possible, and get a job. They could hardly make it this way for much longer.

"We don't have three hundred dollars to throw away," she said.

"Throw away! You women! You don't know your ass from a hole in the ground."

"I won't have that kind of talk, Michael. You're living here on that agreement we made. I told you I don't want Adam hearing that kind of language."

"Right. Right right right." He was silent. She felt her heart quiver, and the whirlpool of fear began to spin in her chest. Her hold was weakening. He had been living with her for four months now, and his humility was sifting away, he was forgetting how he had begged and pleaded to be˜let back, to return home, to get away from Agnes.

Suddenly his arms were around her waist. He stood behind her, pressing against her, his knees pushing her knees forward. "I adore you, remember that," he said, blowing her hair from her ear. "But we have to beat the system. I want to build you that spa you need for your back. We'll never make it, just on disability payments. How long can we live that way?"

"We're living on it, we're just barely making it, Michael. We're lucky to have it."

"It's not luck, it's their fuck-up that I broke my body in a hundred pieces, and they're going to pay. Agnes says it's coming along, this lawsuit ought to net us 8 to 10 million for negligence, malicious wrongdoing, pain and suffering, and punitive damages."

"I've told you. I don't want to talk about that, and I'm certainly not going to count on it."

"Neither am I," Michael whispered in her ear. She could feel her knees go weak as he rubbed her breasts. "That's why I want Grosser's newsletter. We're going to study it together. We're going to work at this stuff till we're experts, and when we know every angle, we're going to sell the house, put every penny in gold futures, and then we'll be rich as kings. I *am* a king, you know, you've always known that, and soon I'll be able to live like one."

"Michael, we can't ever sell the house. It's all we have."

"It's nothing! It's shit if we don't have money to live right. Can't you ever make sense? Just write Grosser the check. I want it in the mail today. And when the newsletter comes, I want you to read it from one end to the other. I'm going to test you. I need your support in this, your brains, your intuition. That's one thing I don't have is woman's intuition, and, in this business, you have to be right on the mark at the right instant. You're going to be in this with me all the way."

"I'm not interested," Ginny said. "It's boring to me, all those numbers and charts. I don't understand any of it."

"Well you goddamn will if you put your mind to it."

"I'm already studying a very hard course, Michael. I have to learn law and medicine and anatomy and English, and I have to get up to 225 words per minute to pass the CSR in May. It's taking all the energy I have."

"I don't want to hear about your little dinky black machine. Gold is where it's at. Bad money drives out good money, and greenbacks are bad money and gold is the only good money. When the world ends, we have to have stacks of gold bars hidden in our hideout in the desert. We have to have stocks of food, enough to last five years. We have to have arms and enough grain to sustain us. And when the dust clears, we'll emerge from our shelter victorious. The King of the World and his empire."

"I hear Adam calling me," Ginny said.

"Write the check to Grosser first," Michael said, pushing her, with his arms still around her, tight as a python, toward the desk. "Write that check now and get it mailed by the next pickup."

THEIR HOUSE BECAME AN ALTAR. Gold was the God Michael worshipped. He found the gold elephants he had made at the dental lab and hung them from the light fixture over the water-bed. He hung them low, so he could reach up with his toes and tap them, sending them into a glimmering dance, their tusks clicking together as they spun. He asked Ginny to go to the library and check out fairy-tale stories about gold. He took Adam on his lap for the first time in history, and read to him the stories of King Midas and of the gifted Rumplestiltskin. Even if Adam arched his back and tried to slide away, Michael calmed him, read to him in a voice full of excitement about the story of the rooms full of straw that was spun into gold by the little dwarf, and the other story, about the father who valued gold so much that he turned his precious child into a gold statue.

"Daddy would never do that to *you*," Ginny said to Adam, but she wondered, the way Michael fingered the boy's hair, if he really *wouldn't*, had he the chance.

They were leading a life that seemed, to Ginny, to be possible. If she watched her words, tip-toed around Michael when he was touchy, tried not to argue with him too often, he was fairly content, watching Milt Grosser on TV, puttering with the engine of the car, watering the lawn, trimming the oleanders.

She called him from court reporting school at every break. "How is Adam? Have you fed him? Is everything all right?"

"Fine, fine." He was impatient. "I'm studying Grosser's newsletter. I have to go now. I want you to read it when you come home."

But when she came home she was exhausted, and had to transcribe all her stenotype notes and type them up in good form. She had to study the technique of taking depositions, had to memorize words which might be used in medical testimony, practice the spelling of all parts of the skeletal, digestive, urinary and reproductive systems. She studied her book on court procedures, trials, torts, contracts, wills and areas of jurisprudence. She wrote up a mock autopsy, carefully describing the organs examined in the surgical procedure.

"Come and read the mail," Michael would call to her, where she was bent over the typewriter, her back aching. "These brochures are full of priceless information!"

"I'm busy."

"But listen to this . . . " He would come into the bedroom and begin to read her an ad. "'Buy my Brilliant Black Box and you can expect seven out of ten winning trades . . . where you are rewarded by over fourteen dollars for every one dollar of loss! The secrets are only yours to know, locked into the Box, no one knows what you know but YOU, and everyone and his brother will not be taking the same trades you want to take. A ten year old kid can work this system. I am not some fly-by-night systems man, hiding behind a post office box. I am RELIABLE.'"

"What's his address?"

There was silence while Michael checked. Then his answer, "A PO Box in North Dakota."

"Well, Michael," she would say, and go back to her torts. But he would never be quiet. He was tireless.

"Listen to the rest: 'This is not some razzle-dazzle program where you've got to call your broker ten times a day. All you need to do is enter the day's high, low and close into the Brilliant Black Box, and out comes one, and only one, number, which will be your entry level for the following day.'"

"How much, Michael?"

"Only $1800."

"Let me study, Michael."

"He says he knows the cost of the Box is high enough to restrict sales; he's an honest guy. He says right here, 'I probably won't have more than 200 units sold, but if you are interested I suggest that you order one immediately, today, since—if you're looking for major explosive commodity moves—this is your answer.'"

"We have $78 left in the checking account, Michael."

"Can't you borrow it from Paula?"

"We owe her thousands already."

"Your mother?"

"Michael, if you let me learn this stuff, I'll be able to earn a living one of these days."

"I don't *want* you to earn a living. I want you to be Queen. I want you here for me, ready to come when I call. Not busy finger-fucking that machine day and night."

"Don't get started."

"You *get* me started. You don't have any understanding of basic economics."

"Maybe not."

"Will you ever learn that you can't make it in this world with some piddling hourly wage?"

"Maybe not. But just let's hold off ordering the Brilliant Black Box till I pass my CSR, okay?"

"That's all I hear, your CSR, like it was the only thing of any importance in the universe."

"I've worked very hard to learn this Michael. I want to try to pass the test. It's very hard to pass."

"When the bombs hit, they'll hit the cities, you know that!"

"*What?*"

"And if you're working in some court house, you'll be the first to disintegrate. So we have to move to the country as soon as possible."

"If I'm going to do court reporting, Michael, I have to live near a city."

"I'll buy you a fast, high-powered sports car, and you can commute. But the main thing is that we'll have to live far out of bomb range."

"Michael, when do you have an appointment with Ross again?"

"Thursday. Why?"

"Because I think you should talk to him about this hideout you keep telling me about. I think it's a problem area."

"I don't *have* problem areas anymore. I'm cool. I kiss the ground you walk on every single day that I am privileged to live in this oasis with you and Adam, my every need catered to."

"If it's an oasis, then why do you want to move?"

"Women understand nothing," Michael said.

"Talk to Ross about that, too."

"Ross, Ross my ass. You think he's Top Banana? He's just a guy whose wife is screwing around behind his back, who can't keep up payments on his BMW, who has a slipped disc from falling when he was rock climbing in Grand Canyon. You think he can fix everything in the world? Everything inside my misshapen head?"

"I don't know, Michael. But *I* can only concentrate on one thing at a time, and right now I have to study."

"You should be studying *this! This stuff!*" He waved a handful of letters at her. He came toward her and stuffed a letter in her hand. "Read, read this out loud to me!"

She read: " 'Dear Investor: I don't mean to scare you, but after reading this letter, I think you'll understand that our world is headed for a breakdown of awesome proportions. Not someday, but, if the signs are right, it should hit in late July, give or take a few weeks. You must take advantage of the time still left to begin making preparations to survive. Doomsday is coming. If you do nothing, if you procrastinate . . . if you continue to buy the liberal line of a healthy economy, you will lose EVERYTHING in the economic, social and racial inferno that is swiftly approaching. THE PARTY IS OVER. The only value havens are gold, silver, real estate, and art objects. Let me send you my Strategy Letter, and if you follow my recommendations, you will be among the top 1% of investors in America next year.' Jesus, Michael, I can't believe you're swallowing this stuff hook, line and sinker."

"You think I'm the fool? You'll see who's the fool, you'll see."

"I can't argue with you now. I don't have the strength."

"Gold is beginning to rise. We need to put the house on the market and sell it. We have to buy gold while it's still low enough."

"We can never sell the house—we'll be on the streets."

"We're selling. I'm having some realtors in to give me appraisals."

"Michael, don't push your weight around, don't get like you used to be. I don't have to take it."

"What choice have you got?"

"Oh God. Leave me alone, Michael, I have to study. Go now. Go away from me. Close the bedroom door. Leave me alone. I can't argue and learn at the same time. Go! Go! Go!"

IN THE AIRPORT HOTEL, Ginny stood holding her typewriter in one hand and her stenotype machine in the other. Over her shoulder she carried a case full of supplies; extra ribbons, packages of paper, correction fluid. People streamed through the lobby, more purposeful than she was, more sure of where they were going. She looked longingly at the soft couches on which well-dressed women, elegant and confident, were waiting. She guessed they were probably waiting for friends or for business associates, perhaps for their lovers. They had sweeter business here today than she had. She thought briefly of what must wait upstairs; clean rooms with smooth bedspreads tucked sharply under new pillows. And beyond the hotel windows—the buzzing airport, filled with people beginning or ending their trips.

She would never fly anywhere. She would never have a ticket in her hand to Jamaica or Hawaii or France, or even to New York. The women in the lobby had bigger lives than she would ever have. She felt her life was so little, so circumscribed by fate and by her own limitations. What did she know? What could she *do* that was worth anything at all?

Well, if she passed this test today, she would be able to do one thing well: take down at high speeds the words that other people spoke. Even that would soon be an obsolete skill—it almost was, with all the tape recording machines around. But machines could always mess up, and so far, people were still more reliable than machines. At least the courts considered them to be so.

Feeling the weight of the machines pulling on the muscles of her back, she dragged herself after two women carrying only their stenotype cases. They were doubtless going to rent typewriters—it was highly recommended by her teacher at the College of Court Reporting; if a rented typewriter broke down during the test, it would be replaced with another instantly. All the test-taker had to do was wave a hand, and the exchange would be done. But Ginny didn't have the extra $25 to rent a typewriter. She had had to borrow the $40 from Paula to register to take the test.

Finding a registration table set up in the long corridor, Ginny was given her room assignment. She passed a row of pay phones beside the rest room area and was tempted to call home and see if Adam was awake and well. He had been sleeping when she left at 5:30 this morning to take the long drive to the airport and avoid the early rush hour traffic.

She had given Michael instructions as he made waves in the waterbed by humping his back up and down. "Don't do that for one minute. Listen to me. Adam is invited to a birthday party across the street at Horace's at 2 this afternoon, Michael. Just take him across. The present is on his dresser, all wrapped. It's a Slinky." She had also told Michael about this last night, but he wasn't always able to remember instructions. She thought she should call him now and remind him, again. She hesitated. What if he started some long discussion? She had only twenty minutes before the test and she wanted to warm up first. She decided it was safer not to call, and passed by the phones.

She found her dictation room, opened her machine, and said to no one in particular, "Wish me luck."

On the stage were four speakers: the judge, the witness, and two attorneys. In the back of the room were the timekeepers whose job it was to signal the four speakers to slow down or speed up their speech to maintain the required number of words per minute. The students were given last minute instructions by the teacher playing "judge": "All right now, when you've taken your dictation, go to the banquet room to which you've been assigned and begin transcribing. You will have three hours to do your work. You may make no more than 50 errors in 2000 words. Corrections must be typed, not written, in, and every word must be legible. Good luck."

The students took their positions, hands poised over the keys. The red light flashed on the stage to indicate the start of the test. The first word rang out, and Ginny became a creature with ears and fingers, nothing else.

In the transcription room, sitting at a long table vibrating with the motors of a hundred typewriters, Ginny struggled with deciphering her tape. She had already typed five pages. Her shoulder blades were burning with pain, her neck ached violently, and her head shimmered with the thunder of pounding keys. What if she didn't pass this test? What then? She stared at her symbols and typed:

"Attorney 1: I have only a blurred copy of that contract. Do you have the original, counsel?

Attorney 2: Yes, here it is.

Attorney 1: I'd like this marked as Plaintiff's next in order.

Attorney 2: I have no objection to your using my copy, but I would like it returned to me and photostats used in the transcripts."

She was so bored. The language used in court was often so drawn-out and dead. At school, during dictation she yearned for colorful words, words of excitement, full of imagery and movement. She wished for music, song. She wanted to dance. Suddenly she felt a tremendous throb of sexual desire low in her belly. Anything was better than being trapped here in this over-airconditioned room, with these robotic humans all about her, smashing at the keys. She wished to be seduced by a dark stranger with fiery eyes. Any man on the cover of a paperback romance would do. She wondered if she could ever act on such an impulse—go down into the lobby, to the bar, and pick up a man, any man? Men acted on such impulses. Michael had. His was not a simple impulse, she knew that—he was sick, but still, he had been able to act on it. She had never asked him to describe his crime to her. She had never wanted to know. Now she wondered. What had he been feeling? Was it this kind of animal desire, this overpowering heat?

She turned her attention back to reading her notes.

"Attorney 1: Did you witness the accident?

Witness: Yes, I did.

Attorney 1: Can you tell the court in detail exactly what you saw on the morning of January 10th?"

A key jammed in Ginny's typewriter, and a letter flew off. As she tried to continue typing, she saw that the "h" was gone. Everytime she typed "the" she got the word "t e." God, what was she to do now? She would have to rent a typewriter. She couldn't worry about the cost. She would have to borrow from Paula. Thank God for Paula. She waved her hand in the air. This was punishment for her daydreams. If she'd been concentrating it wouldn't have happened.

Oh hurry, she prayed, as the typewriter-concession man came rushing up the aisle carrying a heavy IBM Selectric in his arms. *Don't let me fail this. Don't let all this work be for nothing.*

GINNY SAT IN THE CAR IN front of their house, exhausted, unable to think of opening the door and carrying her machines inside. She was drained, slightly nauseated. Her left eye was twitching. As she was leaving the hotel after the test was over, she had caught sight of herself in a mirror in the lobby, and had jumped with a little shock at how old she looked. Her hair was much too long and unconfined, too straight and unstylish to be suitable for a working woman. She looked like a stranger to herself, a character in the outside world, a woman wearing a gray suit, carrying heavy, professional equipment. At home, if she saw herself in a mirror at all, the image that she encountered was of a woman carrying a baby, or a woman just out of the shower, thin, vulnerable, shivering, with one shoulder lower than the other, her spine deformed and crippled. There, in the lobby, among the flowered couches and the deep red rugs, she looked to herself like a matron, sinewy and worn, fading, well-past the bloom of youth.

How odd. She so often felt like a baby. When Adam, in some state of frustration, would screw up his face and begin to scream, she sometimes felt tears welling in her own eyes in sympathy. She *was* a baby. *Everyone* was a baby. Michael often spoke of feeling like an infant, tiny, wanting to be cuddled in the huge comforting arms of his father.

But today, in the mirror, Ginny had seen that she was clearly a grown-up woman. She was as old as her mother had been in Ginny's early memories of her. But what did she know of life? When she was eighty, would she know or understand any more than she knew now? Would she even be *alive* at eighty? Only if she was very, very careful with Michael and did not provoke him.

She sighed, and tested her arms to see if she was ready to open the car door and carry the stenotype machine and her damaged typewriter into the house. She wasn't ready yet; she would give herself another minute.

The house, set neatly back on the lot, looked like a doll house, with its pitched roof and neat little doorway and windows. No one looking at it could know that a perfectly regular family didn't live there—a mother, a father, and a child, each doing his job in life, each one having the best intentions toward one another and toward the world. *If only* . . . Ginny thought. *Why couldn't it have been right for us? Why couldn't we be a regular family? Why did I ever marry him? Why did I do it! How could I have agreed to marry a crazy man!*

She didn't understand herself and felt that she never would. What's more, she had seen the very worst of the *worst* that Michael could do, and still her heart was soft for him. She had taken him back, and now was living with her breath held every second of the night and day, praying he would not crack up and explode in the way that Annie had threatened he would.

Seen from the curb, the house resembled a storybook paradise, with its flower beds and its carpet of emerald grass. Why couldn't they have gotten their home in the normal way, by working hard and saving money for a down payment, and then buying it? Their ownership was so bizarre, having come to them through Agnes and her poodles and her lawsuits and her battles with Michael. But at least the house was legally theirs. With help from Paula and her husband, Ginny had been able to keep up the payments. This home was the most precious thing they owned—their shelter, their security, their beautiful storybook house sitting on their land, with its hammock, its chimney, with curls of smoke coming gracefully from its top.

Smoke!! Coming from the chimney! It was May, it was hot! Why was there a fire inside? She dragged herself out of the car, and hurried up the walk with her arms laden.

She kicked at the door with the tip of her shoe. "Michael? Can you open the door?"

When she got no answer, she set down her machines and dug in her purse for her key. She pushed open the door, and found Michael sitting in the lotus position in the middle of the living room, two feet from a blazing fire in the fireplace. He was playing with the Slinky toy.

"Hello," she said cautiously. "What's burning? Isn't it a little hot for a fire?"

Michael's eyes were following the Slinky, as his palms, balancing the column of flexible spring, moved hypnotically up and down.

"Where's Adam? Is he still at the party? How come you didn't send the Slinky over with Adam? I told you it was a present for Horace."

The only sound was the steady clink-clink of the coils of thin steel as they closed tight and sprang open in Michael's palms. She had the sense that Michael had not seen her come in, nor heard her speak.

"What are you burning, Michael?"

She walked to the fireplace and moved the poker around in the flames. She saw notebooks in the fire, as well as papers and magazines and what looked like the contents of a box of Cheerios.

"It's all over," Michael said, in a low monotone. "The jig's up. We've had it." The Slinky flowed back and forth in his hands like a dry waterfall.

She saw the edges of a page begin to burn; before it shot up into light she was able to make out the architect's drawing of a bomb shelter; Michael had sent away $20 in the mail for the plans.

"We don't need that stuff any more. There won't be a future. Social Security has us fingered."

"What happened?"

"Ross called me. The government's cutting down, they want me off their rolls; me and a million other crazies. They wrote him this letter saying they're checking my eligibility, saying that 'the client *alleges* inability to work due to a psychiatric condition!' Ross says once they finger me, I'm in serious trouble. But he told me not to worry; he wrote them that I'm 'anxious and suspicious with ideas of persecution and a seriously impaired ability to relate to other people.' Nice guy, Ross. He told me he would tell them I'm paranoid schizophrenic and that my prognosis is poor and little improvement can be expected."

"How did you remember all that?"

"I'm an *idiot savant*. You know those nuts who are secret geniuses? Ross told me about them. Maybe I'm one of them. We all know I'm a genius, right?"

Michael spoke above the drone of the clinking toy; it rose and fell, rose and fell.

204

"Do you think I'm an idiot, Ginny? Or a genius?"

"You mean they're going to cut our disability payments? We're *living* on those."

"Go tell city hall. Go tell Reagan. Call up President Reagan and say 'Listen, Ronny—my husband Michael is burning up his last hope, his bomb shelter plans, his plans for our retirement home in the country, his designs for a geodesic dome. Don't do a number on him. He's unstable. He's likely to cross over to the promised land.' Ross said he'd tell them I'm too far gone to ever work. What do you think, Ginny? Do you think I can work?"

Secretly, she had always thought he could work. Anyone could work. If a man could walk and talk, he could work. All he had to do was go to the place where there was work and let the people there tell him what to do and how to do it.

"I know you have problems, Michael. You can't even seem to keep your mind on Adam."

"Who's Adam?"

When she stared at his face to see if he was serious, he broke out laughing.

"Adam's still across the street. I think you ought to call Ross and get the dope on this business."

"I took my CSR, Michael," Ginny said. "Aren't you interested to know how I think I did?"

SHE HARDLY HAD THE STRENGTH LEFT to go across the street and pick Adam up at the party. She fell across the waterbed, exhausted. She wanted to sleep for just a few minutes, then get Adam, but Michael came rushing in. "I forgot to tell you, Ross wants you to write a letter to the Social Security Administration telling them what I do from day to day. It's just a precaution," Michael added. " . . . because what they pay us is peanuts, but we might as well cover all our bases. Ross says no one in his right mind would say I was able to work."

He threw a pad and a pen onto the bed. "I have to go back to my Slinky now," Michael said, "because when that kid gets home, he'll have rights to it. Kids always have more rights than me, you know?"

Ginny stared at the paper, sucked on the pen. Words came to her mind.

My husband, Ginny wrote, *has more periods of violent behavior during which he breaks things. He seems more frustrated and seems to feel others are responsible for his problems. He feels there is a need to go to the country for protection. He talks of suicide. He doesn't censor anything he says in front of our son. He will yell and embarrass me in a store, reasons unknown. My husband is unable to be with other people due to his personality. He talks of fantasy situations, greatly exaggerated. He thinks he is an investor and can make millions. It doesn't matter that he has no money to invest. He sounds radical and is unable to keep a job because he does and says the wrong things. He will not do the simplest chores. When he gets into a morose mood he refuses to do anything. He won't do anything himself, but always insists on my help and company. He thinks people do not like him and he has no friends. He has no tact and will ask questions of adults that are embarrassing, causing very uncomfortable moments. Michael screams curse words at motorists driving by too fast. At times he thinks he is worthless and other times thinks he is the best person there is.*

She put down her pen. How could she describe a man, a marriage, a life, in a few words? How could anyone, reading the words, know the pictures in her mind, the feelings in her heart? It was too hard, too impossible. She didn't want to share Michael's problems with the world; she just wanted to think of a way to go on living with him, coping, somehow, with what he had become. What did the government have to do with what was her private life, her private struggle?

She thought of buying a cage and locking Michael in it with a bowl of water, a toy bone, a soft blanket for him to sleep on. She would walk him on a leash, train him to sit and beg, and let him, when he was good, sleep at the foot of her bed. It seemed a solution. She began to imagine herself walking Michael along the street on a choke-leash, stopping to wait while he sniffed bushes and trees, lifted his leg to urinate, squatted and strained while he stared up at her with his liquid eyes.

Even in her reverie he began to pull her hard, against her will, tugging her along with the power of his muscular legs, tearing her arm out of her shoulder socket. "Sit, stop, beg!" But he was more powerful than she could ever be with all her useless, panic-stricken commands. Why not just let him go? Let the collar go slack, let him slip his sly head out of the heavy chain, and run free? Run anywhere, in front of a truck, under it. Let a truck run a track over his belly, squeezing out his guts, holding him down till he was dead. He had killed her dog Whisper, why shouldn't she do the same to him?

She wondered if she had finally crossed the line and was going mad herself. She remembered a crazy man from the neighborhood where she grew up. He shuffled through the streets talking to himself and sucking on rocks. He had no neck and great fat oily lips. His feet turned out and his shoes were covered with dust. He drooled. *That* was crazy. And she wasn't like that. Michael wasn't like that. Michael could understand anything, learn anything. He was always studying new religions, new investment plans. He could fix a car, build a fence, a wall, a spa, a house. He had made crowns and bridges for human teeth, how could he be crazy?

Then again, how could he be sane, and have done what he had done? Too many thoughts were coming into her head; she was too tired to deal with any of them. She set the pen and paper down, and fell back on the pillow. Maybe she could sleep just a little while . . .

"This is it!" Michael yelled into her ear. "Get up. This is the Light and the Way. This is the Kingdom of Heaven."

Ginny could tell it was dark outside. "What time is it? Where is Adam?"

"What's-her-face brought him back from the party, but I told her to go fuck herself."

"What? Did you say that? What did she do?"

"She took off with Adam. I scared her shitless. Maybe she'll keep him. He makes too much noise, it's not good for me. I have to be able to think." He held something over her head and she thought it was the Slinky and he was about to strike her with it.

"Move away. Let me stand up."

"Get ready for a bi-ig trip. I just made you a first-class reservation on the plane tonight to Texas!" He hit her lightly with a cone of paper.

"What are you talking about?"

"There's an investment seminar in Dallas; in three days they teach you the secrets of commodity investing. We have to cover ourselves. If Social Security cuts me off, we have to have an alternate plan. You don't trust my judgement, right, but you trust yourself, *you're* not the crazy one around here, so you're the one going to Texas. I called and reserved a place for you. It's only $3000, chicken-shit money, we can make five million with what you learn there. You don't want *me* to make our fortune, so you just have to be the one who's going to do it! You want authority, you'll have it! I won't say a word. I'll just sell the house and hand the money over to you, and you can invest it. You can take all the credit for getting us rich. Isn't that generous of me?"

"Jesus Christ, Michael, we don't have $3000. We don't have $30. And I'm not going to Texas on any plane."

"Don't contradict me, you bitch!"

Ginny knew this wasn't a time to argue with him. She ducked out of bed and ran to the bathroom.

"Don't you dare push that bolt on me!" Michael yelled. "That's my lock, I'll tear it out of the door with my bare hands if you ever dare to use it, ever! *Never* lock that door again, do you hear? It's not your lock!" He pushed his weight against the door to keep her from shutting it on him.

"Let me just shut the door, Michael," she begged. "Let me go to the bathroom."

"Don't try to trick me. I'm not stupid. I've never been stupid, no matter what else I am." He heaved himself into the bathroom. "Go. Pee. Don't play shy. You have no secrets from me. Then get dressed. You have to make that plane."

"Please, Michael. It's impossible . . . You're not thinking straight."

"Bitch!"

"I can't . . . "

"Cunt!" He lunged forward and tore the toilet seat from its screws with one violent pull. He readied it behind him in the air as she tried to escape from the bathroom. She could sense it balanced over his head as he got ready to fling it at her.

"Don't! You touch me and you're a dead man!" Ginny screamed. "Touch me and it's over forever, Michael."

He held the toilet seat in the air, held it over his head like a halo, stumbling from side to side in the dark hallway. The doorbell rang.

"It's got to be Adam," she whispered.

"Fuck Adam!" Michael said. "You won't go to Texas?"

"No!"

"Then I have an errand to do," Michael said. "An important errand. Don't expect me back tonight. I may be gone for days."

Fine. Don't ever come back, she thought. *Make it a long, long, errand, Michael.*

"I SOLD THE HOUSE to my broker," Michael announced when he appeared a week later. "And the money is all in gold futures."

Ginny had actually begun to think he might not come back. She had gone to Paula's for a few days, and, now that she was back, after a week of calm and peace, she had a strong desire to tune him out, erase him with the stubby end of her mind.

"How could you sell the house without me?" she asked with a tone of almost friendly interest as she sat on the floor with Adam, watching him arrange his circus animals on their wooden ladder. Michael seemed to be standing on the other side of a wall of fog, not entirely real to her.

"I had to. Social Security cut us off. Ross got word from them. It's all in this letter." He waved a crumpled piece of stationery at Ginny. "So I forged your name on the deed transfer. It's all worked out, we don't have to move because as soon as we make some big money, as soon as gold takes another jump, we can buy the house back."

"What do you mean, Social Security 'cut us off'?"

"Read it for yourself," Michael said. He threw her the piece of paper. "Look at that! Look what the fuckers said!"

He danced from one foot to another while Ginny tried to make sense of the report that had come from the office of the disability examiner. She read the words: "a distinct paranoid personality" and a few lines down the page her eyes picked out that *"Michael Fisher is aggressive, intelligent and has a considerable degree of drive. Therefore, his condition is not of such severity so as to restrict simple work involving minimum contact with others, such as button sorter or trimmer, jobs which are available in substantial number within the regional economy."*

"It says you should get a job," Ginny said, " . . . the same thing I've been telling you for months."

"Keep reading—you didn't get to the punchline yet!"

Ginny tried to make sense of the rest:

"*Accordingly, Michael Fisher is denied disability payments, and furthermore, it is seen from examination of his records that he has been capable of working for the last six months. Therefore, he is required to return to the Administration payments in the amount of $6000, which were unlawfully used.*"

"Can you believe it?" Michael yelled. "A button sorter! What the hell is that? And what should we do—puke up all the peanut butter sandwiches they've paid for? Where do we get six thousand bucks?"

"Maybe we could appeal the decision," Ginny said.

"I'm through begging. I'll never get on my knees to anyone again. But don't worry, I told you, I sold the house."

"That's impossible," Ginny told him. "And if you did, if you really did, Michael, you committed a crime. And if you committed that crime, it means we have nowhere to live."

Ginny didn't care what the gold market did and wasn't aware of the moment it went the wrong way and Michael lost the house. She didn't feel a single emotion when Michael, waking her from her nap, told her he had gone to his broker's office and thrown a stink bomb in the mail chute, causing the entire building to be evacuated. Next week he was going to build a real bomb and take care of the fucker for good. That shit, he said. The bastard had made Michael sign a form stating that he was worth over a hundred thousand. Since Michael was only supposed to invest "venture capital" his broker had urged him to lie. In no time, the broker had promised, Michael would be so rich he'd have more venture capital than he'd know what to do with.

"This is very sad," Ginny said.

"Sad! If you'd've let me invest when I wanted to, we would have owned the world. But no, you had to fight me, stand against me till you ruined me." He grabbed her hair and shook her head.

"Don't hurt me, Michael."

"Hurt? You want to know what hurting is? You want to know what really hurts?"

From nowhere he produced a knife. Where had it come from? It was a switchblade. He pulled her by her hair into the bedroom. She was aware of Adam following behind them down the hall.

"You know what hurts?" Michael asked. He pulled the sheet off the waterbed and jammed the knife into the mattress, puncturing the plastic membrane. He stabbed the bed again and again, until water came jetting out in weak little fountains.

"Next I stick it in my heart," he said. "Or yours."

She watched the water seep out and soak the rug. Adam knelt down and dipped his chubby fingers into one of the snaking puddles.

"Die!" Michael yelled, and swooped down on the baby with a roar, digging his front teeth into Adam's tender scalp.

Adam threw his hands up and Michael hung on like a bulldog. What amazed Ginny was that Michael lifted the baby off the floor with the strength of his teeth. He carried the baby in his mouth and walked with him, dangling, screaming, into the living room. He flung Adam from side to side until the baby's face turned purple. Then Adam stopped screaming. His hands fell down and his eyes rolled up into his head.

Michael let the baby fall from his mouth. He lifted a floor lamp and threw it through the window. He ripped the kitchen table from its moorings and tossed it into the backyard. He used his head as a battering ram and banged it against the wall till he made a hole in it. Blood ran down the wallpaper.

Ginny picked up the phone and dialed her sister.

"What is it?" Paula cried. "What is going on there?"

"I think he's getting ready to kill us," Ginny said.

"Then run!" Paula screamed. "Get the baby and run as fast as you can. Call me when you get to a safe place and I'll tell you what to do next. But hurry and get out of there this minute! Oh God! Run for your life!"

GINNY PARKED THE CAR in the bank parking lot on West Richmond and huddled there, pressing Adam against her breasts. He was conscious now, but very pale, and whimpering slightly. The blood on his scalp had clotted into a black zig-zag tear. His lids were half-open; she stroked the curve of nose very gently—a way she had discovered to make him close his eyes and fall asleep. Shivering, she lay Adam on the seat, got on her knees, and bent over into the back seat to rummage for a jacket she always kept in the car; now she was grateful for this precaution. Reaching blindly for whatever lay on the floor, she grasped a corrugated tube, snake-like, which sprung from her hand. It was her vacuum-cleaner hose, rubbery and black, which slithered back under the seat. It was odd that it should be in the car. She wondered if it had broken and Michael had it in the car in order to take it somewhere to be repaired.

Bending further, she pulled up a green quilted jacket she had worn in high school, and slipped her arms into it. Now she had to find a phone from which she could call Paula.

She wondered if she ought to get Adam to a doctor. His scalp might need stitches. Could a human bite be dangerous? What could she tell the doctor? That his father had bitten him?

Just then she saw a man walk out from under the marquee of the old Granada Theater. He was unshaven, wearing a tattered sweater and carrying, slung over his shoulder, a sleeping bag wrapped in a torn blanket. *She knew him!*

He walked slowly to the corner and leaned against the lamp post. He lit half a cigarette. No, she didn't know him. He just looked like the man she had once seen at this same corner, years ago. She remembered the man's eyes, the harmonica he had made out of his hands, wanting to play a song for her. But this was another man. There were probably hundreds, thousands, of them around. She felt saliva fill her mouth. She wanted to spit!

She remembered the sympathy she had felt for him, her jelly-soft heart, her mothering compassion. That man, years ago, had reminded her of what Michael might have become without her. She should have let Michael *become* that; *let* him be roaming the streets, alone now, with a pack on his back, rather than be looking for her, forever, with his crazed, single-minded passion.

She felt nothing for the man standing a few feet from her car. Let him be homeless, let him be hungry. Let him get a job, hitch a ride, sleep in a ditch. Let him die. But don't let some woman destroy herself for him, be taken in by his needy greed, his lazy manipulation, his craziness, his self-love. She got out of the car and stood with her legs apart, brazenly, adjusting Adam on her shoulder. She stared at the man and he stared at her, making a slight move toward her. He was young and his stance was sexual; he was going to ask for—what? Money? A place to stay? What did he see in her? The same thing Michael had seen—a life-support system, a rag to walk upon, a cunt with a soft heart.

He came toward her, his blue eyes alive. He glanced down the street slyly, waiting for a rig to come along. When he stood two feet from her, he stopped, smiled.

"Would you know where a hungry man could get a good cup of coffee in this town?" he asked in a deep, mellifluous voice, smiling, showing surprisingly good, white, strong teeth.

"Fuck off," Ginny snarled. "Just fuck off, Mister, or I swear, I'll break your fucking balls."

"I'm in a phone booth on West Richmond," she told Paula. "We're all right, but I'm afraid Michael will get a car somewhere and come looking for us. He bit Adam on the scalp. I think he's gone over the edge. What should I do?"

"I've been on the phone since you called me. I have the number of a shelter not too far from here for you to go to."

"A shelter?"

"A battered-women's shelter. It's called Safe Harbor. You'll have to call them and give them your story before they'll take you in. They're very selective and also very crowded there."

214

"Can't I stay at your house? I don't think I need a *shelter! Not for battered women!*"

"You need it, Ginny. You *are* a battered woman. It's time to deal with that. And you can't stay here. Michael would be here in five seconds! He's already called me, he's looking for you. He says he's going to check out."

"What does that mean?"

"Your guess is as good as mine. But don't worry about it too much. What does it matter?"

"That's right," Ginny said. "What does it matter what he does?"

"This is it, Ginny," Paula said. "This is the last crisis. You've got to make up your mind now, once and for all."

"It's made up. I don't care if I never see him again."

"Well, good," Paula said, "because if that's true, I'll help you all I can. If it's not true, if you're going to go back with him again, I don't want to waste all my energy."

"I'm finished with him," Ginny said. "You should see Adam's scalp. It's oozing blood."

"Jesus. This is really it, Ginny," Paula warned her. "After this, if you get soft again, you're on your own. If you want to die, it's your business."

"I said I'm through with him. How can I get to talk to someone at Safe Harbor? I'm ready."

"HEY BROTHER," Michael called through the bars to the family of orangutangs. "I'm your pal. How about a little wave?"

The apes, three of them, sat in the shadowed recesses of their cave, staring out with belligerent, orange eyes. He liked the look of the biggest one, the father; his expression was fearless, arrogant, vicious. He was a blood-brother to Michael.

The infant ape entwined its pink fingers in the shag of its mother's fur. It was searching for a teat. The mother threw her head back and gave a grunt of impatience. She pulled the baby away and turned him, with one powerful arm, upsidedown over her shoulder.

Michael and the orangutang exchanged a look of understanding. Females: *they never give teat when you want it.*

He was feeling good. It had taken him hours on buses and the last of his money to get to the zoo, but he needed to be here where the purity of the animals could comfort him. He felt they would give him courage, strength, peace. When he ruled the world, he'd have his own zoo, like the guy at Hearst Castle used to have. Antelopes running past his window. An unobstructed view of the ocean. Great works of art in his bathroom. A man should have no less. *No less!* He was beginning to feel bad now.

He dragged his lame foot along the path, looking for the signs to "Africa." The elephants would be good to him, they were kings of the jungle, and he was visiting royalty. He would leave them an offering, a sacrifice, his gold elephants. Gold had ruined him, it was time to give up the worship of it. He didn't know *what* to worship anymore; he had tried so many things, and not one single God had appeared to him, not one burning bush had spoken. His mother had always promised that Jesus would hold him in the palm of His hand, but all he got was shit.

The elephants were his soul-mates with their wing-like ears and their heavy tusks. Flapping their ears, hoping for miracles,

216

they wanted to fly but were weighed down. They were neither bird nor beast. Their trunks were worm-like, bashful, delicate and slow, but their tusks were sinister, their eyes beady. They were rooted by the trees of their legs, strapped into the earth. Like Michael, who was half-God, half-man, they were an anomaly, a failed but brilliant mixture.

Tears came to his eyes for all creatures like them, misfits, God's mistakes. Even his precious time at the elephant cage was ruined; a throng of kids was hanging over the rail, throwing peanuts and shouting "Hey Dumbo, look over here!"

He blew his nose. He found he was crying and couldn't stop. Three elephants—mother, father, and their baby—walked in circles in the sawdust, flapped their ears, undulated their trunks in the poisoned air, but got nowhere. Everyone but Michael was part of a family. Somehow he had lost his. He had once had a wife and a baby, but they had been sacrificed.

He felt in his pockets till he touched the spiky tusks of his gold elephants. He had made them with love and with all his patient skill. He had carved them like an artist.

The kids threw peanuts in their shells to the elephants, screaming in glee as the elephants snorted them up.

"Just give me two peanuts," Michael begged one of them. "You'll have eternal life if you do."

"Hey man, you crazy," the little kid said, but dumped two peanuts into Michael's begging palm.

Turning his back, Michael squatted, took his knife from his pocket, and made sharp slits in the pocked shells. Removing the peanuts, swallowing them down like pills, with four convulsive tosses of his head, Michael buried a gold elephant in each shell. He sealed the pieces together with a long filament of grass. Then, giving it all up, knowing it was the end, he flung the peanuts into the enclosure, and watched as the kingly creatures devoured themselves till there was nothing left of them.

SHE WAS AT HER THIRD PHONE booth. First she had called Safe
Harbor from the phone booth on West Richmond. The woman at
the shelter had asked her a thousand questions. It was almost as
if she didn't really believe Ginny. It was only when she told her
that Adam's scalp was beginning to bleed again that the woman
said they would take her in. "Call me again when you get inside
the city limits, and I'll give you directions."

"I can't come right away. First I have to get some clothes, I
have only what's on my back. And I have to get my son some
diapers; he still wets at night. We left with nothing. My sister is
going to meet me at the mall with some money. She's going to
lend me a nightgown . . . "

"Well, then, that's okay as long as you get here by seven.
We lock the gates then. Just call me as soon as you get to the
city, and I'll give you further directions. My name is Conchita
and I'll be your counselor."

Paula met her under the Dippy Donuts sign. Her sister
looked the way she had looked in the days she used to wait for
Ginny at school when they were kids—she looked responsible
and extremely serious. She looked like someone Ginny could
count on. Paula held out a paper bag.

"Look, see if this will do. There's a hairbrush and mirror, a
new toothbrush, some blouses of mine, two nightgowns, a porta-
ble radio, some T-shirts of the girls for Adam." She took Adam
out of Ginny's arms and kissed both his cheeks and the tip of his
nose. When she saw the wound on his scalp, her lower lip turned
down involuntarily, as if she had seen something repulsive. "My
God," she said.

"I need some jeans," Ginny said. "Can we just go into Wards and get some, the first pair that fits me?"

"Sure, let's go right now."

The hangers clicked on the racks like skeleton bones. Ginny felt her teeth begin to chatter, a racketing, uncontrollable sound. Paula came to her and hugged her.

"You'll get through this."

"Yes, but how?"

"However it works out."

"But what if . . . ?"

"What if?" Paula echoed her.

"What if he kills himself?"

"Are you willing to do whatever's necessary to prevent that? Go back to him?"

"Not right now," Ginny said.

"But later?" Paula let go of her.

"No, not later either. It's just that I'm so scared, I'm really terrified now, because I actually left. Just my leaving is going to make him more dangerous than he ever would be if I were with him. But you know, I had to leave, Paula. I finally had no choice left because of Adam. I couldn't have him growing up with that."

"But for yourself—you could have taken more?"

"God—I don't know. Maybe. Who knows? I seem to have a very great tolerance for what Michael can do."

"But now that you've made your decision, Ginny, you can't turn back. You mustn't even consider it."

"I'm not, I'm not," Ginny swore, and her guts turned over thinking of what Michael might be doing right then, swinging a rope over a beam in the living room, standing on a ladder, jumping . . .

"It's either you or him now," Paula said. "Don't think I don't feel for him, my heart is torn, believe me, he's a human being, he's tortured, he's sick, but I want *you* to stay alive. And I think it's possible that you won't, and Adam won't, if you let him at you anymore."

"I know, I know all that," Ginny moaned. "I can't think straight. I told Conchita I'd be there before seven; that's when they lock the gates for the night. I have to hurry. Let's not talk anymore. Let's just buy these jeans and get out of here."

When Ginny called from the next phone booth, at a big supermarket, Conchita recognized her voice. "Oh hi, Ginny," she said. "This is Conchita, your counselor. How're you doing?" "Fine," Ginny said. What was she supposed to say? She was feeling so nauseated she thought she would faint at the smell of garlic bread coming from the bakery.

"Okay—so where are you exactly?"

Ginny told her.

"Good. Now drive four blocks south on Orange Hill Drive to Grove and then go two blocks east and you'll see a place called Ernie's Taco Stand. There's a phone booth there. Call me as soon as you get there and I'll tell you how to get here."

"Why can't you tell me now?"

"We have to be very careful," Conchita said. "We never take any chances with security."

When Ginny called her from the taco stand, Conchita said, "Are you certain you're not being followed?"

"How could I be? He doesn't even have the car!"

"There are ways. Just look around. Be certain."

"No one is here."

"Okay then. Look north from where are you right now. See the white fence and the big green mailbox out front? You should be able to see it, there's a streetlamp right at the gate. That's Safe Harbor. I'll have the gate open for you. Drive right up the driveway and park your car way in the back so it can't be seen from the street. See you in a couple of minutes."

Conchita was a pretty Mexican woman with strong shoulders and wide hips. She shook Ginny's hand in the driveway, peered seriously at the cut on Adam's head, then led Ginny up the path to one of the six tiny cottages, and knocked on the door. She pushed it open without waiting for a reply.

"Ola will be your housemate," she said. A tremendously overweight and pregnant black woman was sitting on the orange plastic couch, drinking a Coke. Two little boys were at her feet, eating corn chips from a bag.

"Ola, I would like you to meet Ginny Fisher and her son, Adam. Ginny, this is Ola and her sons, Rafe and Cleance."

"What your man do to you?" Ola asked at once. "Mine—he gave me two black eyes and then cut off his ring finger with a hacksaw."

Conchita said, "Give her a little time, Ola. I'm sure Ginny will want to talk to you eventually. Just let her get settled in first, okay? Why don't you show her around?"

"Yeah—sure. Come this way for the grand tour." Ola struggled to her feet and motioned for Ginny to follow her into the vacant bedroom.

"I'll see you later," Conchita said, "I'm going back to the office right now."

"Here we got two metal bunkbeds," Ola said. "It's the same in the other bedroom, where me and the boys sleep. Now, watch this loose board. There's some kind of hole in the floor and we don't want the rats coming up. Now follow me—this here is the bathroom. See all these Clorox bottles—well, that's a hint. We got to disinfect all the time. To keep diseases down, you know. You don't need to worry about me. I married my man at seventeen, and you can see he kept me busy, so I didn't fool around. I hope you're a clean woman." Ginny just kept nodding. She followed Ola into the kitchen, where a huge red sign over the sink warned: *Do not rip off linens, utensils, pots, or silverware. If you need them when you leave, talk with your counselor about other ways to obtain them!*

Ola invited Ginny back to the living room. "Let's get the kids together to play," she said. "Rafe and Cleance—you be good to little Adam here, you hear?"

Ginny leaned her head back on the couch. She listened to Ola talk. Ola said she'd been here two weeks, and it was the pits because they had so many rules. They wouldn't even let her keep her Valium, which was the only thing that saved her from going nuts. She had to go up to the office every time she wanted one, and they would dole it out to her like she was some kind of baby. Before she could move in, they made her swear not to use alcohol or drugs, to swear *never* to call her husband, and not keep weapons of any kind with her.

"I ain't no gun freak," she said to Ginny. "Do I look like any kind of freak?" She sat there, in a flowered muu-muu, on the tattered plastic couch, her belly hanging between her legs, her shining black face and her little dancing pigtails beseeching Ginny for an answer.

"Do you mind if I talk to you later?" Ginny asked. "My son and I are very tired."

"You get beat up a lot?"

"What?"

"Your old man—he whomp you around all the time?"

"No, no, he wasn't like that."

"Then why you here?"

What could she say? That Michael had bought gold futures? That he dreamed of making her happy? She said, "I'm really feeling strange, Ola, and I have a bad headache. Would you mind very much if I talked to you later?"

She lifted Adam on her hip, carried him into the dim bare bedroom, and laid him down on the lower bunk where he seemed to fall asleep instantly. Ginny sat down on the floorboards beside him and took a pencil and a scrap of paper from her purse. She knew she wouldn't be able to sleep and some words had just come to her mind which she wanted to write down. The only other time she had wanted to put a feeling into words was when she had taken LSD. Michael had done it for her then. She almost felt as if she were on LSD now. Zig-zag flashes of light were shooting up from the edges of her vision. The air all around her shimmered with dancing darts of color. A pressure was building in her head. Her mother had had migraine headaches, but this was Ginny's first. It was a trip—a real trip. She began to write:

Wads of hope stuffed between
the rotting timbers,

> *He begged me to remain upon our ship,*
> *I dared to jump and try uncharted waters,*
> *He begged, Oh please return, I cannot swim.*

She read it over, surprised by the voice she had written in. She was already beginning to think like a different person and she had only been away from Michael for a day. She added, with the stub of her pencil:

> *I never will return, I said.*

She put the poem in her purse, climbed to the upper bunk and pulled the thin blanket over her body. Was he dead yet? She thought the question casually, as if she were inquiring about some stranger in a distant country.

There was a tap on her door. She lifted her head from the pillow.

"I just want to say goodnight," Conchita said, standing in the doorway to the bedroom. "And I want to congratulate you on being here. It's your new start and you're lucky to get it. I just want you to know that more than four hundred women apply for admission each month, and only 8 to 12 of you get in. Also I want to tell you a few important rules."

Ginny understood she was about to hear the standard speech, so she sat up in the bunk and pulled the blanket over her shoulders.

"Okay," Conchita said. "For the first three days that you're here, you can't call anyone at all. When we do allow you to use the phone, you first have to have permission 24 hours in advance, and the call can't last more than five minutes. I know this sounds tough, but we have our reasons. You are not to ask for any news of Michael, nor may you send any messages to him. The point," Conchita added, "the point is to stop *re*-acting to Michael and start acting on your own. While you're here you're supposed to find out what *you* want, what *you* need, the direction *you* need to take. Most battered women are so used to adjusting their lives around their men and their men's moods, outbursts, drunken rages, scenes, that they've never stopped long enough to ask themselves if they deserve a life, or deserve to get their needs fulfilled. The fact is, Ginny, that you're a person too, believe it or not. *You have needs.* It takes some of us years to figure that out. It took me having my husband put a shotgun in his mouth in front of me and my kids and blow his head off. That's what it took for me. That's why I'm working here, to help women like you get the message sooner than I got it. I came within one hair of having him blow off *my* head. The gun was in my mouth first. Apparently he changed his mind and figured it would be better punishment for me to carry the picture of him, bleeding from his ears, the rest of my days. If that was his wish, he got his way."

"My God," Ginny said.

Conchita shrugged. "Don't feel sorry for me. I *let* myself be walked all over. I have only myself to blame. We are each responsible for ourselves. And there's no place for feeling sorry in this shelter, not for poor sweet old sad hubby, and not for yourself. We have to get tough here, Ginny. This is like joining the Marines. It's a hard course, but once you get out you know you can take care of yourself. Are you ready to do all the hard work?"

"I guess," Ginny said. "I'm just a little shaky right now."

"That's natural. You get some sleep and in the morning we'll start putting you together."

IN THE MORNING, Ginny lined up with the other women in front of the supply cottage to get her food. Each woman picked up a small cardboard carton from a pile beside the door. A woman with an acne-scarred face handed out supplies. Ginny was given a small, whole frozen chicken, a package of pork hot dogs, 3 plain-wrap cans of beans, a half-dozen eggs, a pound of margarine, and a white bread. Milk, she had been told by Ola, had to be paid for out of her own money since it was consumed in such large volume by the children who lived in the shelter. As she was given her portion of food, the woman who dispensed it said, "Remember, we don't want you hoarding any food for when you leave! Take only what you will eat till the next food pickup."

Ginny bowed her head. Here she was, where she had always feared to be, on a food line, taking handouts. Adam clung to her hand, his eyes wide. Where did he think they were? What should she tell him? That they were taking a little vacation? In an hour he was required to go to a drawing lesson with the shelter's art therapist, and after that, he was to have a play hour in the playground, while she went to the required therapy sessions. She had to know where he was every second. Conchita had explained the elaborate security system at the shelter. A "No Trespassing" sign on the gate gave the shelter the right to have anyone arrested who came onto the premises without invitation. An alarm bell—a direct line to the police department—would bring officers within minutes. Conchita warned Ginny, "Keep your son with you at all times unless he is at art class or with the playground supervisor or at Child Care while you're at Group. If your husband spots him and takes him away, there is no law that can get him back for you."

Ginny was also warned to keep Adam clean, to keep the cottage clean, and to leave no food around to encourage roaches and rats. There would be frequent spot checks to guarantee this.

Ginny listened, nodding. For the first time in her life she felt like a bad girl, shamed, as if she were essentially evil and would do bad things as soon as she was out of sight of the authorities. She was warned to scour the toilet before she used it; the shelter could not guarantee the health of its tenants. The spread of venereal diseases, though not likely, was always a possibility.

"The main thing, the most important thing," Conchita said, "is that you must absolutely not contact your spouse *in any way*! Not by phone, not by letter, not through a third party. If you do, you will be expelled from Safe Harbor immediately! If your spouse calls here, the staff will deny all knowledge of you. The office phone is identified only as a hotline, not as a shelter, and the pay phone in the office, if it rings, is described to callers as just a public pay phone in a public place. If your husband should, by whatever means, discover our location, you will be asked to leave at once."

"How could he discover this location?" Ginny asked.

"You'd be surprised how it can leak out," Conchita said. "You'd be surprised how many women have a change of heart after a few nights of sleeping alone."

"Not me," Ginny said. "I have no desire to talk to my husband."

"Good," Conchita said flatly. "Let's see if your resolve lasts."

"I wish I could talk to my sister," Ginny said to Ola. "I don't think it's fair to be kept in the dark this way. Don't I have a right to know if my husband is alive or dead?"

"They don't *care*, honey, if the motherfuckers is alive or dead. Soon you won't care neither. They going to get that into our heads one way or another. That, or we'll get our heads bashed in someday." Ola, talking loudly and constantly, followed Ginny around the cottage, her two little boys crawling after her. "Sometimes I pray myself to be a widow. Other times, I just forget everything and only remember those nights when he gets under my skirts and I could just about die. But how come, I always want to know, he can turn into a tornado—he just blows up out of nowhere and knocks me down. He gets to drinking and the devil gets in him." She scratched her head. "Lice in here—did they tell you? You can't help but get 'em if you stays here. They won't kill you or nothing bad, but the medicine in the shampoo stinks to heaven and burns your eyes. You got to use it every week, or the eggs hatch. Then you got to comb out the nits. It's easy for us, you and me, we got black hair, and we can see them white suckers. But there was a blonde lady here last week, she had a breakdown trying to find them things."

"Oh God," Ginny said. "I don't believe this. Lice!"

"Try not to be on any high horse here," Ola said. "We all in this boat together. Rich and white ain't excused from battering. No one is, even the Queen of England. That's what they teach us in Group. We got to go to Group every afternoon for two hours. We get free baby-sitters to go to it. At home I never had no baby-sitters. It was me, me, me, do all the work day and night."

"What time is Group?"

"Right now," Ola said. "We can't be late or they take away visiting privileges."

"When will I have visiting privileges?"

"Second week. Between 8-10 pm, only, and you need to have 24 hours permission. They tell you all about it. If you got a father or brother you still care about, they can visit you in the office, but never in your cottage. Only womenfriends can come into the cottage, and they have to swear never to tell your husband where you at."

"Jesus. Why would I be here if I wanted my husband to know where I was?"

"That's a puzzle," Ola said. "When I think about how my man punched up my eyes so I couldn't see, I could spit. And then, in the black dusty night I can almost taste it, how he loves me up, and croons spidery stuff in my ears, and I want to head out of here so fast, I'd have to leave my big belly behind."

Ola wiped her son's nose and chin with the bottom of her muu-muu.

"Why did you marry your husband?" Ginny asked.

"He full of big dreams, bigger than I could dream."

"That's why I married mine," Ginny confided.

"Paula, it's Michael, I've decided to get myself circumcised and I have to get this information to Ginny right away."

"You sound weird, Michael. Are you all right?"

"Is a leper all right? Is he all right if his fingers are falling off? Is a cripple all right? Is paraplegic all right? Put Ginny on this phone."

"She isn't here, Michael."

"Well, where is she?"

"She's just not here. Listen, Michael, can you let me get this call on another phone? The girls have the TV on and it's too noisy in here. Will you hang on a second?"

"I have all the time in the world . . . " he said, "till the sands of life run out in ten minutes. I can wait."

He held the phone over his head, and let it swing back and forth. He heard clicks. Paula hanging up the phone. Paula picking up another phone. A loud click, and a hum.

"Michael, are you still there?"

"You know, Paula, you sound just like Ginny; you know that? You and my wife have the same voice."

"Where are you, Michael?"

"Home, in my bed, where else would I be?"

"I don't know, Michael. I'm just asking. Your voice sounds strange."

"My bedless bed. My waterless ocean. You heard about the flood?"

"No."

"Oh—I thought Ginny told you everything. She didn't tell you we had a little disaster with the waterbed?"

"No."

"Hey—is Grant on this fucking phone?"

"Grant is at his office, Michael."

"I thought I heard him pick up the receiver. I hear some kind of funny humming."

"It's only me, Michael."

"I tried to patch the bed. I tried. But if sharks tear up an entire marital bed, you can't patch it with a bandaid, you know. But now I have this air mattress to sleep on, double size—I got it at a garage sale down the block—you can blow it up with the wrong end of the vacuum cleaner, but the goddamn hose is in the car and Ginny has the car and I have to get the car back. Shit! That's why I'm calling! That's why I have to talk to her. I have to have the vacuum hose or how the hell else can I blow up my bed when it gets low or clean the house?"

"I'm sure you don't have to worry about vacuuming now, Michael."

"I had to blow up the bed with my own lips! My lungs! You think I'm superhuman or something?"

"No, I don't Michael."

"I'm only partly superhuman, Paula. I don't die. I tried, you know. I tried so hard to die. My voice is weird, isn't it? That's from the heroin. Three packs, I shot up three packs and it was shit, they ruin it out there on the street, you can't even count on checking out with it. They cut it with sugar—I shot up and laid down to die, and nothing happened except I slept for two days and now I'm still here to partake of the joys of life on earth. I can't do anything right, Paula. I'm a tough bird—I couldn't get it done when I jumped, and I can't get it done now. I'm doomed to Eternal Life, like Jesus Himself. So let me talk to Ginny, Paula. I know she's there."

"She isn't, Michael, I swear."

"I've been unconscious for two days," Michael said. "Tell her that. That'll bring her around. I haven't eaten anything for two days."

"You should eat, Michael, or you could die. You don't want to die, Michael."

"Not if I can talk to her."

"She can't be reached. She's in a shelter."

"What kind of shelter? A bomb shelter? I've been talking shelters to her for years."

"Not a bomb-shelter, Michael. A shelter for battered wives."

"You're kidding." He whistled. He held the phone away from him again and let it dangle like a club swinging over his head. "She's not a battered wife. I'm a battered *husband*, you know," he said. "They ought to have a shelter for battered *husbands*. She pounded the hell out of me by running away. She's guilty for what she's done to *me*. I'm the last person in the world she needs protection from. I'm the one who protects her! She knows that! I'm the only one who *can* protect her. She sure as hell doesn't need protection from me."

"She thinks she does, Michael. You scared her badly. She thinks you really want to hurt her."

"Hurt the person I love the most? She's out of her mind."

"Maybe you went too far, Michael."

"Just let me talk to her, to tell her that I appreciate her a lot and want to be with her forever and that's it! So what's going on? I'm back from the dead, and the thing is, by not being here with me she's forcing this to happen. It wasn't happening till she decided to make it happen."

"If you kill yourself, Michael, no one's making it happen but you."

"She had no reason to leave."

"She said you bit Adam."

"*Hey!* I couldn't help it, you know? It was a bad day. Finally a little thing, a hair, snapped inside my head, the hair snapped or something, and I just picked up a lamp and got rid of it, that was all, and then I smashed up the table. And then I dug into Adam, but it wasn't anything to worry about, it was no problem, I don't *think*—it shouldn't be, it was a minor thing, it's just a couple of hundred dollars table, that's all."

"You frightened them very badly."

"But what about me? *I'm* here, *my* fears are real. I'm real. Just let her give me a little slack, let her treat me like I matter and I count, and in no time things could be much better, a hundred percent better. She doesn't stand a chance to lose anything except the ability to be right where she is and so what? What's the difference, she's got me, and if that's not good enough for her, then the hell with her!"

"She got frightened when you lost all that money, Michael."

"Yeah, she thought, 'Hey, I'm going to be poor' but there's no reason to believe we'll ever be poor. She wouldn't try. She gave up and she wouldn't let me try."

"You lost the house, Michael."

"Hey! Now you sound just like her! I don't like that, you sounding just like her. Do you think I need another goddamned wife arguing with me? And that was minor, losing the house was minor! I'm worth as much as the house, maybe more, but she doesn't care, she's willing to lose me just like that."

"You don't have to be lost, Michael."

"That's her decision. If she's not with me, she knows what has to happen. But if she wants that terrible legacy on her, that's her business. Let her go and find some Jewish guy who makes a lot of money. Let her marry a rabbi with pink cheeks and no balls. Hey Paula, you better give me her number, right now, Paula, unless you want the responsibility for sending me off. This time I'll do it right."

"They don't let *anyone* call there, Michael. I swear. The shelter has rules. They want the women to get back on their feet and not be influenced by their men. If you called the shelter they would say they didn't know anyone of Ginny's name even if she's there! It's their policy."

"But I *hate* policies! I *hate* edicts! I *hate* bureaucratic bullshit—you go into a place and you ask them something and bullshit comes out, and you fill out four hundred forms and it's still bullshit that comes out."

"But Michael—"

"That's enough. Okay, she'd rather cash in her chips right now, let her. Let's get it over and done with. If you have anything to say, say it . . . "

"My hands are tied . . . "

"Mine are tied, too."

"Michael, you need help. You need to check yourself into a clinic and let someone help you. You can't handle it yourself anymore. It's gone too far. We're getting nowhere now."

"I need a job, not a clinic with some fucked up shrink telling me what to do. A job is what I need. If I had a job, she'd be right here by my side. That's what she always tells me, to pull myself together, and then she'll respect me. So that's what I have to do now to get her back. I have to read the papers now and find myself a job. Call her and tell her I'll have a job by tomorrow. I'll be circumcised and I'll have a job. What more perfect combination could she want from me?"

"Eventually a job would be wonderful for you, Michael. But first I think you need to cool down, get some food into you, let some people with professional training take care of you for a few days till you get your bearings." ˉ

"If she calls you, Paula, tell her I'm pretty wonderful. I see myself as a pretty wonderful guy."

"Yes, Michael."

"I could have been an Eagle Scout."

"That's very good, Michael."

"I've always trusted you and Grant."

"We know . . . "

"So do you think I could come there to have dinner or something? Couldn't you treat me like just regular old me and let me come and have dinner with you?"

"Oh, I don't think that's possible now, Michael."

"I'm not used to being without Ginny. I've never been so alone before. I want my family back . . . "

"Are you crying, Michael? Look, Michael, go and get yourself something to eat. Then call Mental Health, I'll give you the number if you don't have it, and ask to see someone. Tonight. Tell them it's an emergency."

"Shit!" Michael screamed. He began to sob. "I'm so goddamned scared! Please come and pick me up and let me have dinner with you there, Paula. I'm only human. I'm not a monster."

"I'm sorry, I just can't let you come here now, Michael. And the truth is, if Ginny wants a separation from you, I have to respect that."

"If I killed Ginny it couldn't be worse than what we're going through now."

"That's a threat, Michael. Do you recognize that what you just said is a threat?"

"It's not a threat. It's true."

"Michael, try to listen to reason . . . "

"Don't give me any more fucking crap, I said I don't need another wife! Forget it I'm wasting time. I have to get going now. You women are all the same, so it's time to move on. The sooner the better. I'm through now. You understand me?"

"I don't understand any of this, Michael."

"Soon enough you will. Soon enough you all will, I can promise you that."

"LADIES, LADIES—MAY I HAVE YOUR attention please?" The counselor at the front of the room reminded Ginny of Annie; she had a no-nonsense look, and arms like a wrestler. "Shoes off. Flop out on your mats. Shake down like rag dolls."

All around Ginny, suddenly, as if a flock of birds had been sprung from a cage, came the flapping of loose hands and the tossing of heads. She had a vision of lice leaping like colorless raindrops from each woman's scalp and flying to land on her own. "Now," the counselor said, "*In rain during a black night, enter that blackness.*"

Ginny looked around. The women, ten of them, slumped and inhaled deeply, violently. Her housemate, Ola, had her cheeks puffed out till finally she exhaled a long, shuddery breath. Everyone exhaled forcefully and was silent. They all seemed dead.

"Good. Breathe again. By the way, ladies—before we get into this too intensely, I want you all to meet Ginny; she just moved in with Ola, she has a son named Adam. Ginny—raise your hand please, so everyone can see you. Good. I'm Cara, I lead Group, and we always start with a little relaxation and meditation. It helps a lot to be relaxed before we have to do hard thinking." She clapped her hands. "Okay, another exercise. Here it is. *Simply by looking into the blue sky beyond clouds, feel the serenity.*"

Now everyone was staring out the window. Ginny thought she saw a face looking in. It looked like Michael's face. What if he found them? He would steal Adam from her. How could she be sure Adam would be safe in the play-yard? The knowledge settled on her like a shroud: neither she nor Adam would ever be safe anywhere. As long as Michael was alive, he would hunt for her. Eventually he would find her. There was no doubt in her mind about this.

"Relax, Ginny," Cara said. "Get centered and forget yourself."

Ginny took a deep breath and let it out very slowly.

"Good," said Cara. "Now try this one. *At the edge of a deep well look steadily into its depths until—you feel the wondrousness.*"

When the hour was up, Cara said, "Okay now," and handed each woman a sheet of paper. "I want you to write down a list of specific goals. I'll tell you the first one to write down—the same one we write every day. *I will not spank my kids while at Safe Harbor.*" She stared at the faces of the women. "I can tell from your expressions some of you still think it's okay. Hey! Your kid spilled the milk again, so you think it's okay to slap him? You want me to tell you what kind of little boys turn into battering husbands? Kids whose mothers slapped them to get results. A man is just a grown up kid who wants results. So what does he do? He learned it at his mother's knee. All you have to do is hit—so he beats up his wife. It's simple. His mother did it to him, he'll do it to his wife. So that's number one, ladies. We do not hit to get what we want. It doesn't work, right? Did it work with you? Did your husbands get what they wanted? Maybe for a while they did, but what about now? They're all begging on their knees. They *lost* what they wanted. They don't have you anymore because no woman in her right mind can take abuse forever. Some can take it for a mighty long time, but almost no one with any self-respect at all can take it forever. Right? Am I right?"

The women surrounding Ginny nodded. She felt her head bob up and down. Yes. It was true. No one could take it forever.

"Okay, now let's get to thinking about some more specific goals. Try these headings: *Where will I live when I leave Safe Harbor? Who will I live with? Where will I work? Do I need money to get started in relocating myself, and who can help me till I get on my feet?* You know the general idea. Safe Harbor can't give you money, but we can advise you on sources of money, on budgeting, and on job training. Safe Harbor is *not* a place to stay while your husband calms down. It's a place where you plan to leave him and start living *for yourself!* And you need specific plans! You need to know

235

where you can leave your kids while you work. You need to think about who you can trust! If you have to leave the area, if your spouse is dangerous and won't respect your wishes to have him stay away, we have contacts in other cities who can help you relocate. If your spouse is alcoholic and you think he will accept counseling, we can contact him with information. But *he's* not the issue; he's already had his chance and messed up. We don't *care* about him. We're not here to get the two of you back together. In fact, we are happy to help you get legal advice if you want to dissolve your marriage. We can also help you get restraining orders so your spouses don't harass you or any of your relatives. I know this separation is hard for every single one of you, but remember, you've already taken the hardest step! You're here. You got away, some of you with your *lives*. You saved the most precious thing you could—your future and your kids' futures."

Ginny watched the women as they listened to Cara. She realized she was the only white woman in the room aside from Cara. There were seven black women and three chicanas. She knew that last week a blonde woman had lived there; the one who couldn't find the nits in her hair. Ginny wondered if she were the first Jewish woman ever to be a battered wife in a shelter.

"Okay. So now write your lists. Turn them in to me, and then just get yourselves laid back again and listen to the stereo— I'll put on something real mellow—or do your Yoga, or sack out. Later, in about a half hour, your individual counselors will talk to you about your lists, and give you suggestions if you need alternatives. Right now, you just take advantage of this time without the kids. Think *me, me, me*. It's about time you thought about yourselves. You have to love yourselves, ladies, because that's where it all begins, self-love. *I'm okay, I'm worthy, I'm good, I deserve a goddamn piece of the pie!*"

In the evening, after Ola and Ginny had cooked and shared with their children a small chicken and some beans, Ginny thought about her mother. She felt dispassionate; she wasn't

236

angry at her mother, but neither did she feel any other emotion. She knew Paula conferred with their mother, but she didn't care to know her mother's opinions. Her mother thought in certainties. *He's crazy. He's dangerous. She'll be better off when he's dead.* A woman like her mother understood no shadings, no degrees. All she did was go around with a little rubber stamp to define everything and clear it up forever. *My daughter is happily married. My son-in-law makes a good living.* Luckily, she could do this with Paula and Grant. She never had to worry about them again after she gave them their stamp and settled it all in her mind that the stamp was true and final and permanent.

Ginny's mother was hopeless as someone who could help her. And her father was dead. Adam was too small to understand. There was only Paula, who could help with practical things, and Michael who would never help her again. So there was no one, really, but herself.

She lay in the upper bunk bed, staring at the cracked ceiling, listening to Ola yell at her boys. Yelling seemed her natural mode of talk.

"Adam?" she whispered.

He was asleep. She hung her head down and saw him in peaceful repose, like a child in a painting. His cheeks were rosy, his eyelids long and graceful. What could he possibly make of all this?

"I guess you still awake," Ola said, coming into the room. "I got the creeps, hearing the news of Rosanna, just now. You remember the blonde lady we had here?"

"What news?"

"Morgana from next door, she just come by to tell me. Rosanna, she went home last weekend. She didn't go *home*, she was hiding out, but he found her and he came in, and in the middle of the night, he says, 'I jes wanna talk to you about God.' He says, 'Hey let me just lie behind you on the bed and hold you so we can talk about God.' So, she trusts him and he climbs in the bed with her, and he takes this knife and holds it at her throat. God almighty, that motherfucker slit Rosanna's throat. All the time she thought they was going to have God with them. Her little boy, he tried to pull his father off, and the father dragged him into the bathroom, and then slit his own throat over the toilet while the kid watched."

"Is Rosanna dead?"

"Just as good as," Ola said. "She has no voice if she lives. If she lives, she has no *hope*."

"My God," Ginny said.

"My man would never do that. I know it. Would yours?"

"I don't know."

"You think he would?"

"How can we know anything?" Ginny asked.

Ola reached up and took Ginny's hand. They held onto each other.

"Jesus save us," Ola said. "We sure can't save ourselves."

To My Wife:

You have given me more than I deserved. I should have had the courage to cut you loose and let you find a man you respect and desire to surrender your body to. He should be a cross between Einstein and Beethoven. He and you will someday have a good, trusting relationship. If I never have you again, it will be enough to know you are alive, happy, and growing.

*

Dear Mrs. Fisher—

Though I am angry, there will always be an embrace and total security for you with me. Money is no problem. I have two jobs lined up. One will be the hardest work I have ever done, in the oilfields, doing manual labor, grinding and carrying steel for minimum wage. A welder's helper by day, and at night, companion-nurse to an old man. Because I have reached the lowest point of ultimate pain ever felt by a human, I know I can turn on an old man near death and comfort him.

*

This is an invitation to come to a barbecue and entertainment next Saturday. There will be a perfect environment, just as civilized as you have always dreamed of. Try to arrive hungry at 2 p.m. Don't bring too many friends as the facilities are stretched as it is. I am in no way the monster you have imagined and will never be a threat to anyone.

*

I HAVE TO HAVE THE CAR, *god damn you to hell!* How can I drive up the coast to the oilfields without the car. I want to have it reupholstered in order to be more comfortable. I am expanding, ambitious and hard-working. Even if I get a job it will be too little too late. If I end this letter I feel as though I'll lose you forever.

*

GET THE FUCKING CAR TO ME AT ONCE OR I CAN'T PROMISE YOU RATIONAL ACTIONS ON MY PART. I NEED THE VACUUM HOSE TO BLOW UP MY BED AND TO DIE WITH.

"I FEEL GUILTY," Paula said, "sneaking these letters in to you and breaking the rules." She unwrapped a chopped liver sandwich on dark rye and pushed it toward Ginny across the splintered wooden table top in the cottage. "But I want you to see how he's deteriorating."

"Believe me, the letters have no effect on me," Ginny said, sliding the last letter back in its envelope. "In this one he sends me a hair—from his head. He's going to have his hair analyzed to see what critical minerals are lacking from his diet. It costs $300 for the treatment. He says he's got to find the answer to his problem somewhere: then I can love him fully and completely. Then—listen to this—in the three weeks I've been in the shelter, he's been to the Self-Realization Fellowship, the Church of Scientology, the Swat Shabd Yoga—whatever that is, the Movement of Spiritual Inner Awareness, the Hare Krishnas, and the Nichu Pen Sho Shu Japanese Buddhist meeting house." She took a bite of her sandwich. She called Adam over to have some. "Come on, your Aunt Paula brought us some special Jewish soul food."

"He wants you to know he's getting circumcised," Paula said, talking softly. "Do you think they can hear?" She motioned toward Ola and her boys, who were in the living room, watching television on a little black and white set that Paula had brought for Ginny.

"I don't think so."

"He wants you to know that once he's a Jew you can all go as a family to temple on Friday nights, and church on Sundays."

"I can't wait. My heart is pounding with joy at the thought." She took a sip from the can of Coke Paula had brought. "Paula, I'm a rock," Ginny said. "I can't be moved. I can't remember even his eyes. Not even his brilliant blue eyes. I'm totally brainwashed. Look at my face, it's hardened. If he could see me now, he'd know. I'm finished with him, Paula. You know how he said

241

something snapped the day he cracked and bit Adam? Well, something snapped in me, too. Did you know that in one year 1200 wives in America were murdered by their husbands? And something worse—60% of young boys under 20 jailed for murder killed the person who was battering their mother! Can you imagine? In ten years if I stayed with Michael, Adam would probably kill him."

Ginny looked at Adam chewing his crust of rye bread. "I'm getting hard as steel here, Paula. Conchita says I'm making great progress. Cara said so, too. I have outside privileges now if I want them. I can go down to the little market, or to the taco place, or to the park. In a week, if I have a place to live, I can leave here, and come back for Outreach meetings. So—the thing is, I need a place to live very soon. Will you get the classifieds and start looking for a place for me to live?"

"How will we keep it a secret from Michael?"

"We just will. He must never know where I am from now on."

"Ginny—he'll always know where *I am*."

"Are you afraid?"

"Sure I am. How could I not be?"

"Maybe I'll leave California then. Go somewhere far away."

"He'll always know *I* know where you are."

"But maybe he'll finally give up and won't keep hounding us. Other men leave their wives alone. I mean, if you tell a man you don't want him a thousand times, eventually he gets the message. You can't force love out of a rock."

"Michael thinks he can. He's been calling me every night. Do you want to know what he says?"

"No."

"I've been taping his calls."

"Why! *Why on earth!*"

"We might need them for . . . evidence. Grant thinks it's a good idea. I mean, if he makes threats we might have to call the police . . . "

"If you do it," Ginny said, "just don't tell me about it. What he does is not my responsibility. That's what I'm learning here. I'm only responsible for what I do, for my own actions, not for his. So please, Paula, start looking in the paper for a tiny, cheap apartment for me and Adam. The thing is, I'm desperate to get back into the house to pack some clothes and things. I left with nothing. I'm just terrified that I'll find him there if I go back."

"Look, Ginny," Paula said. "Why don't you let him have the car? Maybe he'll use it to get a job. If he gets a job, he'll be away all day, and you can go to the house. He might even be able to pull himself together, imagine that he can survive without you. Give him your car and you can have my car any time you need it. In fact, Grant has been wanting me to get a new car—so I can probably give you my Honda if you want it. It's old, but it works okay."

"How would we get this car to Michael?"

"We'll work something out. Don't worry."

Suddenly the alarm bell began ringing outside. Ginny went rigid.

"What's that?" Paula asked.

"It means a husband is trying to get in. A man. It means someone is trying to force the gate open." Ginny lunged forward and grabbed Adam up in her arms. She had her eye on the sandwich knife on the table. She was ready if it was Michael coming to get them.

"You're shaking," Paula said.

"Look what he's done to me," Ginny hissed. "Look at me! *This is what that man did to the woman he loves.*"

"*I'M GOING OUT for a green beer to celebrate St. Patrick's Day,*" Michael wrote on a sheet of notebook paper and stuck it to the refrigerator with a furry-bear magnet. Wherever he went now, he left notes for Ginny in case she came back and wondered where he was. He was a very busy man these days, socializing, getting educated, getting analyzed, making his life *big.* He had therapists and hair doctors and athletes and counselors and gurus and elders and priests giving him the cream of their knowledge. He was getting to be a true Renaissance man, competent in all skills, all arts, all areas of knowledge. When Ginny came back, not only would she find the house spotless and everything he had broken replaced or repaired—she would find him leading the big life she had always dreamed of—bigger than the lives of doctors she worked for, bigger than politicians, bigger than millionaires . . . He had his finger on the pulse of the world, on education, religion, on politics, on medicine. And especially on the art of love. He had taken a dozen books out of the library: *Living and Loving with Gusto; Sexual Fulfillment in Marriage; Handbook of Intimacy and Tenderness; How To Give And Get Back Love A Hundredfold, Making Your Old Wife Into A Hot Mistress.* This last he had bought in the drugstore, but it was full of great tips, things Ginny never would have thought of in a hundred years. And he, too, would never have thought of doing certain things. How often had he been careful to see that the sun wasn't in her eyes? How often! Never! That was how often. And he had just read this morning that it was absolutely essential: *When you truly love someone, you must take excruciating care of them—you must see that the sun is never in their eyes.*

That's why his marriage had gone on the rocks. He had never once protected her from the goddamn sun! Or walked on the outside of the street in case a car ran up on the curb. He would gladly have sacrificed himself for her, but he hadn't thought about it. Ignorance! Severe, terminal ignorance! He had to tell her what he had learned. When she heard about his new sensitivity, she'd have to come back, she'd know that no man on earth could do as much for her as he could.

He was groggy. He had Valiums all over the house, and he ate them like candy. But he still couldn't sleep. He slept maybe four hours a night. If he got both jobs, as a male nurse and the one in the oilfields, he would only be able to sleep three. But so what? He could take it, he was strong.

He was glad the heroin hadn't carried him off because what Ross had said was true: suicide was a permanent solution to a temporary problem. Like sugar in a tea pot his problems were dissolving. He had two jobs, and the knowledge to be the world's most tender husband and enlightened lover.

It was true he had to get out of the house soon, the broker was taking legal action to evict him, but where would he go? He had called his mother twice, but she had hung up on him. He didn't know why; maybe their big lawsuit against the county wasn't looking good. She was a bitch anyway. Gooey and sticky with concern one day, a witch the next. She would love to hear that Ginny had run out on him; she had always thought Ginny was nothing, less than shit. And now Ginny was proving her right by abandoning him in his time of need.

Twats and cunts, all of them! Fuck them. He was going out to get a green beer and celebrate.

He opened the front door and two cops stood there.

"Mr. Fisher?"

"Yeah, that's me."

"Please give us your social security number, Mr. Fisher?"

"Why? What's going on?"

"Just checking something out, sir. We need to verify the number on this warrant for your arrest."

"My arrest! You're shitting me."

"No sir. Your social security number, Mr. Fisher."

If Michael knew anything, he knew his social security number. He gave it to them.

"Well, there's no mistake, Mr. Fisher. Same name, same number. You're not carrying a machete under your shirt, are you?"

The cop stepped behind Michael and began patting him down while the other cop looked on.

"Who's got it in for me? Irving Fuckface? Or is it my wife? Did she get me on something?"

"It's an old offense, Mr. Fisher. Malicious mischief and vandalizing public property. Bail at $250."

"Jesus! Have a heart! It's St. Patrick's Day. My wife walked out on me. You can't do this! Was it the time I threw my tray at the TV in the hospital? I have a right to know, don't I?"

"It doesn't say what you did on the warrant, Mr. Fisher. It just gives the Penal Code sections you're charged with. Is there anyone you want to call about bail?"

"Yeah—sure, I can call lots of people. My mother. My wife. My wife's sister."

"One call now, Mr. Fisher. The rest you can do from the station."

"Paula, the men in blue are here."

"What are you talking about, Michael?"

"Did you send them? You wouldn't do that to me, would you?"

"*Me?*"

"Can you bail me out, Paula?"

"How can I, Michael?"

"How can you *not?*"

"I have to go, Michael . . . my kids need me . . . I'm busy today."

"I can't make any promises, then, you know."

"What kind of promises?"

"*You know what I mean! I don't do well in jail. You know whereof I speak.*"

"What did you do that you're being arrested, Michael?"

"What does anyone do? The best they can."

"Is the officer there? Can I speak to him?"

Michael handed the phone to one of the cops. "Mind if I go to the bathroom?" he asked. He walked down the hall and the

246

other cop followed. The cop stuck his head in the door and glanced around the bathroom, then motioned Michael in and stepped out. Michael closed the door and got a handful of Valiums from the false bottom of Ginny's bath powder box. He hid them in his sock. When he came out, checking his fly, the cop on the phone was saying to Paula, "If no one bails him out, he'll probably be kept over the weekend till his arraignment—two or three days."

"Tell her I won't last two or three days," Michael said.

"He says to tell you he'd like to get out," the cop said. "Goodbye, Ma'am."

THE MOVING TRUCK SAT LIKE A monolith in the moonlight as Ginny and Paula pulled in behind it in the driveway.

"We have got to do this very, very fast," Paula said, "on the infinitesimal chance that Michael may somehow get out tonight. I called the jail, and all they could tell me is that the offense is 'malicious mischief'—something Michael did when he was in the hospital, and it just came up on their computers. I don't think it's anything too serious; the bail is only $250—and he may be able to raise it, somehow, so he could possibly get out sooner than tomorrow morning, so we have to count on that. I've told these movers it's a divorce thing going on, and you're only going to take what rightfully belongs to you. One of them asked me if they should 'expect trouble' and I told them I didn't think so. I agreed to pay them more than double their regular fees for coming out at night like this."

"How did you do it, Paula? How did you do all this in *one* afternoon—rent me a house, call the shelter and get Conchita's permission to let me come down here, call the jail to be sure Michael was still locked up?"

"Just good organizational skills. And the house was pure luck—Grant saw the for-rent sign being put up as he was coming home last night, and he realized it would be just right for you—a tiny guest house in the back, off the street, reasonably priced, a fenced yard for Adam, right near us . . ."

"God, I'm so lucky to have you," Ginny said. "Conchita calls you my life-support system. I wish Michael had a support system; Michael has no one who cares."

"We can't get into that," Paula warned. "Michael—as I know you have been told day and night lately—is responsible for his own actions; if he had acted appropriately, if he *could have*, he would have had a support system like anyone else—friends, relatives . . ."

"He would still have me." Ginny shivered. "I have this weird feeling . . . " she said, " . . . that I can't go in the house. As if he's right here, watching me, he has the mind of God and he can see everything and he can't believe I'm doing this, sneaking here in the middle of the night and taking away all the stuff we own together."

"I thought you were hardened."

"But it's different here," Ginny said. "This is where we *lived* together. It's his house, too. I keep thinking of when he gets out—and comes in the front door . . . and finds everything gone."

Paula reached across the front seat and took her hand. "Just put one foot in front of the other, remember? Now we have to do *now* things, later you can worry about later."

"Right," Ginny said. "Right." She opened the car door and walked up the path.

She had the sensation that a tidal wave was about to engulf her. Once she opened the door, the forces over which she had no control would overwhelm her, send her tumbling, powerless and terrified, through their vortex. It wasn't the first time and it wouldn't be the last, although the very last time, when she was about to die and knew it was inevitable, would probably be the worst. If only it were possible to do that thing—*stop the world, I want to get off*—and escape these trials, but this was the price of living, you had to go through every minute of it, good and bad.

Adam's natural mother, swollen at the end of her pregnancy like a punch-ball about to pop, couldn't back out, couldn't change her mind, undo him, absorb his muscle and blood back into her tiny egg, back through her tubes, back into her ovary where he would dissolve, disappear. She had had to brace herself and go through the whole long ordeal, the anticipation, the pain, the real time, the recovery. It was all one way. Once you started, you had no choice but to carry on, hateful as it was.

Ginny had gone through bad times again and again—the years the doctors were making red circles on her back and chest; the weeks when her father had lain dying; her knowledge of what Michael had tried to do to those girls. Hard, hard things to face, deal with, live through. As she stood at the door to her house, she knew she would survive this, too. She would survive every terrible experience of her life unless it actually killed her. But each survival made her a little weaker, a little more bitter, hopeless, resigned. *This* was the fruit of knowledge, not the knowledge of sex, but the knowledge of just having to hang on. Life was always saying *I'll show you. I'll show you who's boss. You can't win this one.*

If only it didn't take so long to feel better after some great catastrophe. She knew that leaving Michael was going to be a big one: weeks, months, years of letting the bad feelings fade away.

Sometimes she felt she was living in the drawer of a file cabinet, and the first file was the terrible event which had just happened, and the second file was the next day, so close to the first, still filled with the horror, the fear, the thud in the chest that knocked the air out of her. And each day another thin little sheet would slide in, hardly anything to reduce the pain and the memory, hardly a space to push it away any useful distance. But then, after a while, the drawer would fill up with thin little sheets of living, and she'd get further and further away from the first sheet, whatever the catastrophe had been, and she'd remember it a little less clearly, and think of the details of it a little less often. And when the drawer was half-filled, she was half-well, and then finally, it was all full, and the drawer was closed and she could shut it away, and think only of the drawer, and vaguely of what was in it, but it was bearable then, it was just part of the baggage she piled behind her, the story of her life.

Yet tonight a new drawer had to be started. Here she was, up against it, ready to go again.

The three movers were young bearded men, sweet-faced and kind. One of them stopped in the hallway to hand Ginny a tissue to wipe her eyes. "My name is Cliff," he said. "You'll be all right. I know this is rough on you."

"It's only all this dust," she explained, trying to smile. "I don't think anyone dusted here for weeks."

"Yeah, well that's how it is," Cliff said very kindly. He was wearing a T-shirt with the words "Orange Bombers Little League Team." He probably had a son a few years older than Adam. He probably had a nice wife.

She began dragging one of the empty cartons down the hall to Adam's room. The Superman poster on the wall over Adam's bed made her jump; the square-jawed beautiful actor smiled at her with his sweet smile, with the curl of hair over his forehead, his triangle chest, his beautiful groin.

If only, she thought. If only there were a Superman who could lift her out of this, fly with her, her hair streaming, her face lifted to the sun, and take her away, enclose her in the wing-soft spread of his powerful arms.

Men and their saving powers—fuck it. Forget it.

She tossed things into the carton: Adam's circus set, his stuffed panda, his shirts and diapers and rubber pants and cowboy hat. His holster and gun she kicked under the bed; Michael had wanted him to have it. She hated the sight of the gun.

She was sweating; she heard Paula in the kitchen, tossing pots and pans into a box. "Do you want me to take everything in these drawers? Do you want to leave him anything?"

"Take everything, I don't care!" Ginny called back. "It doesn't matter to me if you take every toothpick!" She wasn't merely packing, but was throwing things fiercely into the box, pitching her life off the walls, out of the drawers, ripping it off the beds and from the cabinets.

In the bathroom she found Adam's goldfish, a prize won at a carnival in the park, swimming peacefully in immaculately clear water. Under it was a note in Michael's hand: *To whom it may concern: I may not see any of my blood relatives again in this incarnation. If so, I wouldn't realize it, only you would know it. I'd be dead. If such a thing should happen, explain to all that what did or didn't happen is unimportant. Regret is shit. Accept yourselves and others. To love everything: why isn't it easy? I haven't said much, or maybe I have. I love existence but I wasn't meant for it.*

At the bottom of the page was a postscript. *I have the power in me to prevail.*

In their bedroom she found the remains of their waterbed nailed, a crinkled plastic shell, to the wall. It was covered with little black crosses of rubber tape, and looked like a cemetery after a great battle. The air mattress, on which Michael had been sleeping, was deflated to a wafer. On it Ginny saw books Michael was reading, books dealing with how to live and love better. She read a passage underlined in red in a book called *Love Can Happen To Anyone, Anytime.* The underlined words were: *Love is the fruit of dreams. Love gone stale is the smog of despair. As numberless broken hearts will attest, love hurts. Above all, show your love daily, open up the confluence of magnetism.* She tossed the book down in disgust.

Under the blankets she found the precious picture albums— proof that she and Michael had once had a real life, smiling with their baby, blowing birthday candles on a cake. She began to look through them and her heart started to miss beats. She dumped them into the carton. Then she moved on to the other rooms. Over the fireplace in the living room she found another cluster of lists. In Michael's writing she read:

My Irrational Beliefs:

1. *I must be loved or approved by everyone for virtually everything I do.*
2. *I believe that certain acts are sinful, wicked, or villainous and that people who perform such acts should be severely punished.*
3. *I can't stand it when things are not the way I would like them to be.*
4. *I need someone stronger or greater than myself on whom to rely.*
5. *I don't have control over my emotions or thoughts.*

Another list in his hand was titled: *WAYS TO SUCCESS:*
1. *What you give is what you get.*
2. *Nature abhors a vacuum.*

3. *Do it now, get it now.*
4. *Action cures fear.*
5. *Eliminate negative input.*
6. *Stimulate positive input.*
7. *I'll see it when I believe it.*
8. *State the problem.*
9. *State the solution.*
10. *Never talk about the problem again.*

Ginny balled the lists up in her hand. The men were struggling down the hall with the refrigerator. Their faces were red with great effort. They grunted involuntarily She loved them deeply for doing this for her, for using their life's energy to salvage the wreckage of her marriage. She could have kissed each one of them; she could have made love to all of them.

She went outside and sat on the damp grass of the lawn while they tore out the insides of the house. Through the open door she saw her sister in the kitchen, doing this terrible job. Her sister's face was a study in sadness. In the faint moonlight of the yard, the hammock swung, shriveled to a thin line.

She heard the door of the house next door open, and then close quickly. She stood up and walked to the mailbox at the curb. She pulled down the metal door and extracted a handful of letters. Standing under the street lamp, she leafed through them: The Burk Westford Investment Letter; The Inflation Survival Newsletter; The Gold Standard News; The Commodity Trading Bulletin. Everything was addressed to Michael. But at the bottom was a letter addressed to Mrs. Ginny Fisher from the CSR Board. She had almost forgotten that she had taken the test! It had been so long ago—so much had happened since then.

She tore open the envelope, feeling a vein thudding in her temple. This hope would probably go down the drain with everything else. But the letter began with the word *Congratulations!* She moved so the light fell across the page more evenly.

Dear Mrs. Fisher, We are happy to tell you that you have passed the Certified Shorthand Reporters Examination!

"Paula, Paula!" Ginny cried. "Hurry, come out here!" She danced across the lawn, shouting. The light from Adam's empty room fell across the grass.

"What is it? What's wrong?" Paula came rushing out, holding a soup pot in her hand.

"Guess what? I'm a person, finally," Ginny said, her voice rising up to a little ecstatic squeak. "I passed my CSR test. Oh God, Paula, I can do something on my own now!"

The three moving men were just carrying the couch into the truck. "Something good?" Cliff asked.

"Oh yes," Ginny said. "Finally—something good."

"Well, I'm glad for you Ma'am," Cliff said. "Because it's mighty sad breaking up a home like this."

"Paula? This is Michael. I'm out of jail and the picture albums are gone. I could have a lawsuit against her, you know. She can't steal community property. Those pictures are mine, too. I need to look at her face when she was happy. Too bad she isn't happy now."

"No one can be happy all the time, Michael."

"Happy. Shit, Paula! I'm sitting on the *floor* right now. The bitch took my big frying pan! *I have to have it back!* How else can I make goddamn *chili rellenos?* So I'll make it easy for you, there's this guy I met in jail, he's my good buddy now. He's going to drive me to your house to get my frying pan and my car. So just have Ginny bring it over there. My one condition before I get out of her life forever is that she has to be at your house when I get there. I have to see her face one last time. She can't deny me that. I won't touch her. You can have Grant and the whole fucking police department there if you want them. I won't stay more than five minutes. Just tell her I have to look at her face one more time. I want her to realize that Adam will have to grow up without me supervising his homework. I want her to know what she's losing."

" I don't know if that will be possible, Michael."

"Make it possible, Paula. You love your husband? You love your children? I have wherewithal, Paula. I can follow you to the ends of the earth. You'll never be safe."

"I'll hang up if you make threats."

"Just five minutes is all I ask. And then I'm gone. You'll never hear from me again."

"I'll see what I can do, Michael."

This is the maiden all forlorn
That milked the cow with the crumpled horn . . .

Adam sat on Ginny's lap, his hands cupping the sides of her thighs for balance, and she read to him. They now lived in a house that looked just like the picture of "the house that Jack built" in Adam's storybook. It was a house like the houses the children at Safe Harbor had drawn in art-therapy class. Their new house had two little red steps going up to the front door, a little chimney, a little slanted red roof, two little front windows, and a door behind which she and Adam were sheltered from the dangers of the world. Cramped as they were, Ginny felt the house was the perfect size, enclosing them in its miniature fairy-tale embrace. To the side was a tree with green leafy branches. Above was the blue sky, with birds, shaped like V's, flying against the sun.

Inside, all their furniture was piled to the ceiling, deftly fitted in by the movers like pieces in a jigsaw puzzle. Ginny had to walk sideways through the living room, but it was good—she felt as if she were in a fortress, protected and secure. The crowdedness was balanced by the vast comforting emptiness inside her, the space left by the absence of argument, the thing which had filled her for all the years of her marriage to Michael.

. . . that tossed the dog, that worried the cat, that killed the rat, that ate the malt, that lay in the house that jack built!

Adam laughed and slid from her lap. He was wise and beautiful and smart. She adored him every moment of the day. He was her responsibility, and now she felt she was almost equipped to assume the task of raising him. She hummed, setting up her stenotype machine in the little space in front of the couch. She needed to practice, to keep her speed, to hone her skills. She thought of Annie at Mental Health and felt a rush of gratitude. She ought to write her a thank you note and tell her that the story *had* had a happy ending, after all. She *had* left Michael, and she had gotten strong. She hadn't backslid. She hadn't messed it all up. And the thing she feared most, that Michael would pursue her to the ends of the earth, was not going to be a problem. Michael had promised Paula—sworn to her—he was going to get out of their lives. He had a job lined up. All he wanted was the car—and one look at her face, and he'd leave them alone forever.

For some reason, here in this little bright house smelling of spring flowers, with Adam sitting peacefully on the floor, engrossed in balancing the animals of his circus set on their hoops and ladders, she actually believed it.

"We are going to s t limits as soon as he comes to the door," Grant said. "Okay?"

"Okay," she agreed. "Whatever you say." She was grateful because Grant had a PhD and knew all about how to handle psychotics. Paula had sent Adam to a neighbor's house with the girls and warned them not to come home with him until she phoned.

"This visit must last no more than ten minutes," Grant said,

"—which gives you plenty of time to hand him the car keys and have a neutral exchange, nothing more."

"That's fine," Ginny said. "I don't want anything more."

"Keep your physical distance," he said. "You on the couch there, Paula and I will be between the two of you—he can stand in the entryway, or sit in the rocker if he wants to. I just want you to maintain a safe distance. In any case, I have a canister of mace in my pocket if anything goes wrong."

"It won't," Ginny said. "There won't be trouble."

When the doorbell rang, her vagina flooded. When she saw his face, when she received the impact of the tragic glance from his reddened sunken eyes, when she felt the prick in her heart of the sharp angles of his cheekbones, his pointed overgrown beard, she was certain that this was the way Christ would look if he ever returned to earth. He was wearing yellow cotton pants, like the ones he had worn to carry her off to Mexico, and a white embroidered shirt. Where had he got them?

He dipped his head at Ginny; he looked at no one else.

"I've come to study your body language," he said.

Everything on her was crossed; her arms crossed across her chest, and her legs crossed, to keep him from catching her scent. She was quivering in every cell of her body.

"I can see," he said, "that they have won you over to their side. I had to see it for myself that your face was hardened, and now I see it."

No one else spoke. His concentration upon her face was so great that she felt her features melting in the heat of his gaze.

"I won't kill you here and now, though I easily could," he said softly.

"Don't start that!" Grant warned him. "We don't want to hear any of that, Michael."

"There has never been a household in America less violent than ours," he said to Ginny. "You misperceive everything, and because of it, you destroy the world."

"I understand you want the keys to the car, Michael, and here they are," Ginny was able to say. She took the keys from the coffee table and tossed them through the air. They fell, jangling, at his feet.

"I'll never ask anything from you again," he said. "But this one thing . . . I want your wedding ring."

"Why?"

"It's my last request, that's why."

"Well, I don't care, you can have it," Ginny said. She had been planning to take it off, anyway. She twisted it from her finger and threw it after the keys, to the floor.

"That's all," Michael said, falling on it as if it were a crumb of food and he were a starving man. He pressed it to his lips.

"I filled up the car with gas," Grant said. "We're going to let Ginny use Paula's car, so that won't be a problem for her."

Michael seemed not to hear. He was staring at Ginny, imploring her with a look in which she thought she could read a message. He took three steps toward her and bent forward, so that she could almost feel his breath on her face.

"One last hug," he said.

She shook her head.

He shook his head also, not to mean *no*, but meaning something else, something deeper and darker.

"You *know*," he said, his eyes black tunnels coming for her. "You know."

She rose and stepped toward him. He thrust his arms around her and her blood plummeted from her head, leaving her skull white and empty, an eggshell, devoid of its pulsing center. As he held her fiercely against him, the chasm between her legs closed violently, opened, closed, shook her with such violent fibrillations that—when he let her go—she fell back on the couch, faint and gasping.

"You *know*,"Michael said. And he went out the door quickly, pulling all the air in the room with him.

MICHAEL RODE HIS CAR across the desert, digging his heels into the floor, holding Ginny's ring between his teeth like a bullet. The car beneath him was his winged horse, its shanks thumping and quivering through the cosmos toward the place where he was to meet his savior.

All the spiny, hideous, humped and misshapen growths of the desert were blooming in their brief Easter reprieve from terminal ugliness. Out of their thick hides, their pulpy oozing guts, their grotesque limbs, burst yellow blossoms, purple bouquets, orange trumpets. He had one last card to play, and he would play it in the grand empire of gambling, in the glittering, last-chance arena of Las Vegas.

He'd been given a hot-tip. It was amazing how things fell into place when you were at the end of the line—it was exactly as Reverend Hotrock on *Fly With The Lord Show* on TV said: "Sinner, it's always darkest before the dawn, so give your life unto Jesus and he'll take your burdens on his shoulders and bring the sun up like a golden egg before your eyes." Sure enough— when there wasn't an egg left in the house, when there wasn't a shred of toilet paper in the can, a paraplegic he was playing pool with at Griffy's Bar gave him the hot-tip. "I know a man who can undo all the shit that comes down on you," the guy, a Viet Nam basket case, had told him. "He got me back my hard-ons." Michael had the clipping the vet had given him on the car seat beside him, torn out of some newspaper.

Presley the Psychic guaranteed an astounding success rate of 90% in getting movie star plum film roles, getting politicians elected, getting wheeler-dealers the right stock deal at the right time. Right in the newspaper he stated, "All I do is put my whammy on someone, and it's done. I do anything that's legal, and I don't worry about moral or immoral. I had this one famous movie queen come to me and say, 'I need a big powerful guy who will lay down the law for me and make me pray at his knees,' and in a week, I had got her the guy she wanted."

It was fate that Michael had learned about him at the critical moment. He had always believed in luck, in fate. Presley's *specialty* was influencing the thoughts of lovers to make them come back to the ones who had lost them. "I charge high, but then again, talents like mine don't come cheap," the article quoted him. "I make two million a year, but let's face it, I'm worth it."

That was Michael's theory all along; get the best, money was no object and nothing was too good for him. Why should he ever take less than the best? He didn't have a dime on him, it was true, but if he could get in to see Presley, he could convince him of the desperate need of his case, and promise to pay him a thousandfold as soon as the whammies got his life going right. In the article Presley compared himself to Jesus; he said Jesus Himself was a psychic, otherwise how could the star have guided the wise men to the manger? When John the Baptist was baptizing Jesus, he saw a form in the shape of a dove descending from heaven. It *proved* Jesus was a psychic. How else could He have walked on water, turned water into wine, raised Lazarus from the dead? If He wasn't psychic, how could He have predicted His own arrest, the betrayal, His crucifixion and resurrection? Presley declared that anyone with his kind of psychic powers was in command of great dimensions which were waiting in the outer reaches of consciousness to be discovered. He could also free people who had been possessed by demons after playing with a ouija board. A man of many skills!

Michael needed a miracle now if he had ever needed one! If he couldn't get through to Jesus himself, he could at least hire Presley, and get him to stop this tragic, permanent conclusion Ginny was forcing on them.

He spurred the car to its limit, letting it take off, watching the abrasive terrain recede as he ascended, seeing the dry riverbeds below shrink into ant trails. The tumbleweeds and yucca plants flew past him, sand peppering his eyeballs. He would never stop, not to eat, not to pee—his bladder, even without surgery to have it stretched, was bigger than an elephant's, and he had given up eating the moment his eyes had fallen on Ginny's face.

Poor, lost thing. She was doomed, he had seen it at once in her colorless eyes, her locked thighs. They were both doomed if they didn't save each other, join themselves again till the end of time. He knew it, but she didn't; she couldn't forsee the future as well as he, he was blessed with the gifts of a psychic himself. He knew it as well as his heartbeat that they couldn't survive alone, each without the other. Her Jewish glue had dried and crumbled. It was his mission to save them both; he was on his way, flying faster than Superman to avert the catastrophe.

He made his landing in the arena of Las Vegas at night. The stars, beaming from the desert sky, were obliterated by the neon glow that surrounded the city in nuclear phosphorescence. The pounding started in Michael's head at once, brought on by the flashing marquee bulbs, by the blaring horns, by the high beam headlights coming at him from the lines of Cadillacs and Lincolns backed up at traffic lights. He drove to the place the vet had told him about.

He gave the finger to the red-suited monkey at valet parking, and guided his mount to the underground labyrinth where the desert creatures were corralled in their stalls.

Inside, waiting for the elevator in the casino, in the cold rush of hellish smoky-black air, he sensed the sky was finally falling as silver meteors clanged and sparked, hailing down among the screams of the lost, denting their tin souls.

"I must see Presley, the Psychic," Michael said to an oiled, half-naked female who came to the door. "I have the biggest challenge of his life for him."

Presley himself appeared behind her, bald, with a little fringe of hair, like a knot rescued from the shower drain, glued in the center of his forehead.

"If I save your life," Presley said, "what can *you* do for me?"

Room service sent up lobster dinners for the three of them; Michael and Presley were sitting at a glass-topped table under the skylight dome of the penthouse suite, and the girl, named Cherry, had taken her tray to the round bed, where she lounged on satin pillows and watched herself in the overhead mirror as she popped little bites into her mouth. Between the table and the bed was a heart-shaped pink jacuzzi that bubbled and steamed like a subterranean tar pit.

"I can sense special qualities in you," Presley said to Michael, "I get emanations from the bones in your face. I sense you were an Egyptian Pharaoh in another incarnation; someone noble."

"The curse of Tutankhamen," Michael said.

"Certainly a curse," Presley said, sucking on his fingers. "You are certainly under a curse at this time."

Michael chewed the rubbery flesh of the lobster, aware he was breaking his fast, but only temporarily. Lobster didn't come his way very often. Jews were forbidden to eat shellfish, and if he went through with the circumcision, this would be his last chance to have it.

"I sense there *is* definitely a very bad curse on you," Presley said. "Very strong evil spirits are inhabiting your soul at this moment." His mustache matched the patch of clotted hair on his head—it was made of swirls of twisted filaments glued above his lip. "I sense you've had a mysterious run of bad luck, that you can't handle one more fuck-up, and that it's the end of the line for you." When Michael nodded, Presley went on: "Men like you are often the victims of powerful curses. They're getting more and more common; with Haitians coming in with their voodoo, selling their techniques to folks with grudges. The thing is, usually you don't know you've been hexed till the damage is done.

Some people think God is punishing them for their sins, but what's really going on is that a curse is put on them which surrounds them with a field of negative morbid attraction which draws evil and danger like a magnet."

"That's right," Michael agreed. "That's it!"

"So what happens is that the victims are beset by one disaster after another, one tragic loss in a spiralling vortex till finally the curse destroys them."

"Yes," Michael said. "That's where I am—ready to be pushed over the edge."

"Then the thing to do is to hire me to place a psychic shield of protection around you. What happens then is that the spiral of destruction is boomeranged back with equal strength at the evil powers. You know how bullets bounce off Superman? Well, that's what my shield will do for you." Presley held up his fist so that his thick gold ring, with a lion's face on it, glittered with reflected light.

"I brought my wife's wedding ring with me." Michael said. "My wife has hardened her heart. I saw her face this afternoon— it was like a moon gone dark. It's over between us. I took her wedding ring, though . . . "

"Is it gold?"

"Yes."

"Then you're saved, man," Presley said. "If you have her ring, your worries are over forever. Give it to me."

Michael took the ring off the first joint of his little finger and handed it over into the pink greasy palm of Presley's hand.

"Yes, oh yes," Presley said, "If you have a woman's jewelry in your hand, you hold her soul." He closed his eyes. "I can feel your wife's vibrations coming into me right now. Gold has the strongest psychic power. Watch me." He got up and brought a red candle in a holder to the table. He shut off the lights in the room and lit the wick with a match. Holding Ginny's ring above the flame, he chanted, "In this ring I place my spell of love to make you always true to me." He smiled at Michael over the flickering light. "She will never be unfaithful again."

"She never was," Michael said.

"Well, now she won't be. I don't know if you want revenge

or not, but we could also use this ring to put a curse on her," Presley said. "Whatever you want. You know the Hope Diamond? It's been killing its owners since the 17th century."

The girl, Cherry, had taken off her clothes and was coming toward the jacuzzi. Her breasts shimmied as she kicked off her high heels. Michael wondered if he could get in the tub with her; it seemed the perfect opportunity. His luck had already turned around. As soon as he had met the vet in the wheelchair in Griffy's, the wheel had started turning. Money was round, like his mother said, one day you have it, one day I have it. Love too, was round. It rolls away, it comes back.

"What do you charge for all this?" Michael said, unbuckling his belt.

"Everything's free if you do some work for me," Presley said, picking up on Michael's wish like a true prophet. "The hot tub is free, Cherry is free, the blow job is free, the spell on your wife is free, curses on anyone you hate is free. There's just one thing I want you to do for me. I want to bring the clientele out here from Beverly Hills, so when you get back to LA, I want you to place some ads for me in certain publications. The thing is, I want to keep my identity a secret for personal reasons—so I just want my box number in the ad, and my name, of course, but I want you to pay for the ads with your own personal check . . . "

"I don't have much cash in my checking account," Michael said. "Not these days."

"That's no problem. I'll give you a check for a thousand bucks, and you can draw on it as you need it. The thing is, I don't want reporters here bugging me, which is why you have to pay with your check, which has your name on it, not mine. Got it?"

"No problem," Michael said, though he didn't quite understand the reasoning.

"And when I get clients through the ads you place, you get 40% of my take. How does that strike you?"

Michael had his yellow pants off, and his white embroidered shirt. He laid them on the rug, and they took on his shape, looking like the shell of an Indian guru whose soul had flown out of his body.

Presley was writing on a sheet of paper. "These are the newspapers I want you to place my ads in. Make yourself at home with Cherry in the tub. I have some business to attend to downstairs. So take your time, enjoy yourself. If you want to drive around later, visit the casinos, you and Cherry can use my Cadillac. Just tell the bellhop you're doing an errand for Presley. I know it was fate that brought you here; I have a premonition that our meeting foretells the greatest of alliances. And I'm getting vibrations, Fisher. You were definitely royalty in another life," Presley said.

"King of the World," Michael explained.

"Exactly," the psychic agreed.

GINNY LET ADAM KISS the *mazzuzah* every time they came into the house. She didn't even really know what was in it—just a rolled up scroll of paper containing mysterious symbols—but Paula had given it to her for good luck, and it was pretty, a graceful decoration on the doorframe in the shape of a green pitcher with a single Hebrew letter on it.

She sometimes thought of what she had told the social worker, Adele Ginsberg—that she was going to raise Adam as a Jew, but she didn't really know in her heart what that meant. If it meant praying to God on Friday nights, and joining the sisterhood, and selling raffles to raise money for Israel, she wasn't going to do that.

But if being Jewish meant being loving and helpful and kind to Adam, she would do those things. If it meant cherishing him, trusting him, teaching him all she could, and letting him live his life, she would do that. She didn't know what was Jewish and what wasn't—but what seemed to matter was being respectful to the person Adam was, not the one she wanted him to be, giving him a fair chance without clamping down with a thousand tyrannical rules, restrictions, punishments and warnings. Children weren't automatically evil. Pious Christians, the ones she knew and the ones she heard on TV, seemed to think *everyone* was automatically evil, and that, without the threat of hell or the promise of heaven or the aid of Jesus to relieve them of their sins, everyone was doomed.

To her, Adam seemed absolutely good. If he sneaked a cookie, or played with his penis, or broke a dish, she didn't see the need to threaten him with hideous punishments. She wanted him to use his good sense, not frighten him with a hundred rules which he would have to break in one way or another. If he was naturally desirous, or curious, or if he wanted pleasure from his body, why should she stop him? She often thought it was jealousy

268

that made righteous people curse others who were enjoying sexual feelings; as if, if *they* weren't having that kind of joy, no one else should either.

Ginny wasn't having sexual joy these days. In fact, she was sick now, with a raw bronchitis which crept down her chest to the bottom of her lungs and made her sound like a frog. She couldn't get rid of a cough easily because of her crooked spine, which curved so far out of line that it compressed her lung. She'd been in the house all week, taking cough syrup, resting, practicing on her stenotype so she could start looking for a good job as soon as she was well, and thinking about big subjects like whether or not to raise Adam as Jew, and whether or not she missed having sex enough to care, and whether or not Michael was alive.

She believed she could do perfectly well without sex forever if she had to. She was grateful to have had her thrilling times; in her happy moments with Michael she had experienced the most magnificent, electric, wild, out-of-control sensations—probably the best life had to offer. She had felt Michael's tongue on the quick of her; she had been, if only for a short time, right there, at the exact place where all the world's songs and love poems led. Even in Paula's living room last week, just the sight of Michael, the momentary feel of him hard against her, had caused a single, blistering convulsion at her center which had almost blacked her out.

The truth was forever clear to her: Michael had been the great love of her life. He *still* was. She adored his childlike soul, and she would never love anyone in that innocent, hopeful, trusting way again. No man's body could ever again be so delicious to her, so beautiful. She didn't doubt that Michael was her mate till the end of time. If a woman ever loved a man with all her heart, she loved him.

But that didn't mean she needed to put up with everything else to have him; it didn't mean she needed him more than life itself. She had come to this understanding slowly, but she was firmly arrived at her conviction now. She could—and she would—live without him.

She had feared for two days after he took the car that she would learn he was dead; she had seen that look in his eyes when he took her ring, when he drove off like a devil into hell. But as the days passed and she heard nothing, no fearful call in the night, she began to imagine that he would make it. He would take that job in the oilfields, or he would drive a truck cross-country, pounding over the highways of America on long dark nights with his heavy load. Or he would go to India and join an ashram, or go north to Oregon, live in a little cabin, and work with the loggers, felling redwood trees. She began to relax, almost believing that he would really have a life, some life, somewhere, without her. He could even have a woman if he liked, someone who would be good for him and not exacerbate his pathology. Ginny would be happy if he did. She felt she had reached some great maturity, some perfect wisdom, wanting a good life for him, but not wanting him.

She was dozing on the couch with Adam sleeping soundly—his face curved against the warmth of her breasts—when the phone rang. Adam jerked as if the ring had pierced him, his arms flailing out in panic the way they used to when he was an infant and a loud noise startled him. She cupped her palm against his warm, damp cheek and stroked the dip of his nose with her index finger.

"Shh," she whispered.

His eyes flickered open as the phone rang again, and when he saw her leaning over him, he stared at her face with complete comprehension, then peacefully let his lids float down again. His head, resting against her, was heavy with life. She felt blessed by his beauty and his trust. She reached to answer the phone.

"Ginny, it's Paula!"

"What's wrong?"

"Michael has called three times in the last few minutes, demanding to speak to you. He's hysterical. On the last call he said if he didn't hear from you in ten minutes, he was going to kill himself."

Ginny tried to find her bearings, wake up. She felt so warm and content, so sluggish with peace and love. It was difficult for her to revise the picture she had devised of Michael's future, extract him from the high and mighty cab of his rig on that long dark trucker's road, or take him out of the rugged logging camp where she had assigned him a home and a good life with a good woman in a cabin smelling of wood pulp.

"I made a tape of his last call that came just two minutes ago," Paula said. "I'll tell you, he frightened me this time, Ginny, because he's really desperate now. I think this may really be it. I felt I should call you, just in case. Grant thinks I shouldn't be calling you now, that *nothing* Michael does now is your responsibility, but I don't want to be the one to make that decision at this point. Not the way he sounds. I told him I would call you. Hang on—I'm just going to play you this tape whether the shelter would approve of it or not."

Ginny heard the phone receiver clunking into something, heard a buzz, some static, and then Michael's voice coming into her warm cozy mind. The words weren't clear at first, but what was perfectly clear was his panic, his terror, the noise of his ultimate threat, and his hysteria. It was all completely familiar, and it was boring. She didn't want to hear it. She felt no pity, no fear, no confusion. The sound of him, his *music*, was tuneless static, the buzz of an irritating disease-carrying mosquito. She wanted to sleep, to rest, to be at peace. She embraced her child.

His words spun off the tape in a whirlpool of begging, anger, and manipulation. He cried, he pled. Ginny yawned, warm in her little house, past it all. She had a sense of herself as an old beautiful woman rocking before her fireplace, satisfied with a long full life, well-led.

"What should we do?" Paula said, coming back on the phone. "He's at his house. Do you want me to call the police?"

"I'll call him," Ginny said drowsily. "Don't worry. He's mine. I'll take care of it."

MICHAEL HUNG UP AFTER the third call to Paula and threw the phone against the wall where it cracked—just like the lobster shell had cracked off that rubbery white poisoned meat that Presley the Psychic had forced on him. He had had diarrhea all the way home, vomiting and shitting all over the desert. He couldn't believe it! It had gone from bad to worse—not being able to get it up in the hot tub. Even with Cherry there, a top-notch call girl or whatever the fuck she was, with all her tricks, with the bubbles going up her cunt, with her tits floating like strawberry blimps, with her long-nailed fingers raking his limp gray cock, all he could think about was Ginny's skinny back, the frail ridges of her vertebrae, the twisted vessel of her ribs, her flat, sweet, fragrant chest with its innocent tender breasts.

He had ridden through the desert with Presley's thousand dollar check in his pocket and a loan of twenty bucks for gas to get home. Ginny's ring, hot on his finger again, was full of a newly cast spell which was guaranteed to bring her back to him on her knees.

He was hopeful, but how hopeful could he be when he had to stop to puke his guts out among the cactus plants and the rocks all the way home?

And then all week—he had run to the places Presley had listed for him—not Beverly Hills newspapers, but strange weird places, like *The Black Neighborhood Chronicle*, and *The Chicano Newsletter*. As Presley had requested, Michael used his own checks to pay for the ads at the offices of two dozen dinky little papers—church newsletters, ghetto throwaways, crappy little publications no one on earth had ever heard of but Presley and a few pathetic destitute souls. Then, as part of the job he had agreed to do, Michael had had five thousand flyers run off:

I CAN MAKE YOU WEALTHY!
TEACH YOU TO PUT A CURSE ON YOUR ENEMIES!
BRING YOU LOVE! BEAUTY! FAME!
HEAL YOUR FATAL ILLNESS!

Each flyer had Presley's box number to write to on it.
Michael had run his feet off distributing the flyers all over the
beach cities, and in south central LA, where some black fucker
tried to mug him in front of a liquor store. With his bad leg, and
not being able to eat because of the food poisoning, or maybe
Presley had put a whammy on *him* (although he doubted it, what
would be the sense of that?), he barely could drag himself from
place to place, house to house. Still, it was the best deal going.
He would get forty percent of the take—it was worth it. From
the way Presley lived up in that penthouse, it was pretty clear he
charged an arm and a leg for his curses and hexes and whammies.
Having a connection like Presley meant Michael's troubles were
over. With his new fortune, he would win Ginny back, move with
his family to Jamaica, where labor was dirt cheap, and where he
could build a villa for peanuts, exploiting the natives.

But then, each night, Michael would come home to the
house where there was no furniture, no family, no food, and finally, no electricity. Shit! One of these days, when he wasn't so
tired, he would have to take money down to the electric company
in person and pay his bill, and then they'd *have* to turn it back
on. After five terrifying nights, sitting alone in his empty house
in total darkness, he decided not to tough it out anymore, and
went to his bank to get the money. The bitch at the window said
he'd have to wait ten full business days for Presley's check to
clear before he could draw on it, and Michael made so much
noise that the manager offered to call Presley's bank in Las Vegas
to make sure the check was good—and guess what? *The mother-
fucking check was no good!*

Michael nearly broke up the bank! He threw a handful of
ball point pens at the cunt behind the window, tore up a pile of
deposit slips, and ripped a calendar off a table. Then he went
dancing out into the street, foaming at the corners of his lips,

hopping and cursing and pounding the hood of every car he passed. He couldn't believe it! They couldn't do this to him! Not again! He was being fucked over again! Holy Jesus! How much could a man take!

He drove home roaring at the top of his lungs all the way, and crashed up and down the hallway of the house, kicking the walls, crying out to the heavens to give him a break. Superman hung there on the wall of Adam's room with his smug little grin, with his bionic chest, and Michael spat at his face. *Fuck you! Fuck You! Fuck You! Fuck Superman and fuck my mother and fuck Jesus and fuck God.*

He began to cry, because it was getting dark and he had no lights, and his stomach hurt, and he couldn't survive one more night in the empty dark house, and his bed was flat as the boards of a coffin and he couldn't blow it up because Ginny had the goddamned vacuum hose . . .

But no, the vacuum hose was in the car and now he had the car and now he could blow up his bed finally, and at least maybe sleep some of the hours of this terrible long dark night—but then he remembered that Ginny had taken the vacuum when she had cleaned him out, so now he had the *hose* but no vacuum, *so fuck Ginny, too.*

He dove for the phone and it still worked. *That* was the miracle, the only miracle he was ever going to get, and he trembled so hard trying to call Paula's number that he had to start all over three times, and when she got on he shouted as loud as an angel's trumpet that unless he was able to talk to Ginny right away, wherever the hell she was, in the shelter, or in a cave or in hell itself, he would be dead in ten minutes! Paula had started with her full-of-crap calm-down routine, and that's when he had hung up, but was sorry at once, and called her twice more, begging, screaming, shouting, roaring like a tornado, and when he hung up the third time, that was when he flung the phone at the wall and cracked it like a lobster shell.

Now he knelt before it in the dark, praying it would ring, that it *could* ring, that Ginny would take pity on him in his last hour and call him, because that was what his life hung on, this little ring which could come shivering out of the broken phone, or not come out, and that would decide everything for him.

He lay down beside his bed on the floor on his stomach, with both hands on the phone, to be alert for its electric tingle in case it rang, and he clung to it feeling the night heaving under him, pulling him down into its black waves just the way Ginny's dog Whisper had been sucked under—that poor fucking hopeless son-of-bitch animal.

When the phone rang, Michael held it in his arms like a dying baby, kissing it up and down its black dumbell receiver before he answered it.

"Let me come back to you," he prayed to Ginny. "At least listen to my plans. I'll build you a villa in Jamaica, with a terrace over the ocean."

"I don't want to hear your plans," she said.

"I met a man who can make wishes come true," he said, his tears wetting the phone so that it felt slimy to his fingers. "Please, *please,* give me another chance. I can't do it without you, Ginny, I'm too weak."

"Then get strong," she said.

"I have my *rights,*" he sobbed. "My son, my family, you can't take them away."

"I can do what I have to," she said. "I'm sick, I have fever, Michael. Don't bother me. Don't call me. Don't call my sister. Figure out what you have to do and do it."

"I *have* figured it out!" he roared. "*Don't you realize that?*"

"Then do it," she said.

"Just one more question, please, I beg you, just answer this one question."

"All right, what is it?"

"Do you love me?"

"No," she said.

"*Thank you! That's what I need! Thank you for your help! Good-bye forever!*" He smashed the phone against the floor and it broke into pieces. Blind in the dark, he pounded on his chest like a great ape, and ran from the house. The car, his patient winged horse, waited, faithful in the moonlight. He whipped it to the skies, landed it on the top level of the Star Villas parking structure, between two sailboats. Somewhere, maybe right in the building underneath him, was his mother, who had started him in

275

this big mistake, living. He would do a number on her, what a number he would do.

The vacuum hose waited, a coiled black snake, a lethal, obedient helper, in the back of the car. The conclusion was going to be foolproof this time, he knew it. He worked with perfect efficiency and coordination, like the Eagle Scout he was, hooking the hose over the exhaust pipe, pulling it into the back window, stuffing his shirt in the crack.

Michael started the motor. He felt at last he was getting something done. He leaned his head back. His heartbeat slowed. He breathed deeply, passionately, sucking on Ginny's wedding ring. With his tongue in its gold center, he let the sooty fire enter his lungs. The husk of his body would be left below, empty and cracked, and his kingly soul would rise to the place where there was no more suffering.